Acclaim for Mario Escobar

"In *The Librarian of Saint-Malo*, Escobar brings us another poignant tale of sacrifice, love, and loss amidst the pain of war. The seaside town of Saint-Malo comes to life in rich detail and complexity under German occupation, as do the books—full of great ideas and the best of humanity—the young librarian seeks to save. This sweeping story gives us a glimpse into the past with a firm eye towards hope in our future."

—KATHERINE REAY, BESTSELLING AUTHOR
OF *THE PRINTED LETTER BOOKSHOP*

"Escobar's latest (after *Auschwitz Lullaby*, 2018) is a meticulously researched story, recreating actual experiences of the 460 Spanish children who were sent to Morelia, Mexico, in 1937. Devastating, enlightening, and passionately told, Escobar's novel shines a light on the experiences of the victims of war, and makes a case against those who would use violence to gain power. Although painful events in the story make it hard to read at times, the book gives a voice to so many whose stories are often overlooked, while inspiring the reader to never give way to fear or let go of one's humanity."

—*BOOKLIST*, STARRED REVIEW, ON *REMEMBER ME*

"Luminous and beautifully researched, *Remember Me* is a study of displacement, belonging, compassion, and forged family amidst a heart-wrenching escape from the atrocities of the Spanish Civil War. A strong sense of place and the excavation of a little known part of history are reverently handled in a narrative both urgent and romantic. Fans of Arturo Pérez-Reverte, Chanel Cleeton, and Lisa Wingate will be mesmerized."

—RACHEL McMILLAN, AUTHOR OF *THE LONDON RESTORATION*

"An exciting and moving novel."

—*PEOPLE EN ESPAÑOL* ON *RECUÉRDAME*

"Escobar highlights the tempestuous, uplifting story of two Jewish brothers who cross Nazi-occupied France in hope of reuniting with their parents in this excellent tale . . . Among the brutality and despair that follows in the wake of the Nazis' rampage through France, Escobar uncovers hope, heart, and faith in humanity."

—PUBLISHERS WEEKLY ON CHILDREN OF THE STARS

"A poignant telling of the tragedies of war and the sacrificing kindness of others seen through the innocent eyes of children."

—J'NELL CIESIELSKI, BESTSELLING AUTHOR OF BEAUTY AMONG RUINS AND THE SOCIALITE, ON CHILDREN OF THE STARS

"*Auschwitz Lullaby* grabbed my heart and drew me in. A great choice for readers of historical fiction."

—IRMA JOUBERT, AUTHOR OF THE GIRL FROM THE TRAIN

"Based on historical events, *Auschwitz Lullaby* is a deeply moving and harrowing story of love and commitment."

—HISTORICAL NOVELS REVIEW

The
Librarian *of*
Saint-Malo

The Librarian *of* Saint-Malo

a novel

MARIO ESCOBAR

THOMAS NELSON
Since 1798

The Librarian of Saint-Malo

English Translation © 2021 Thomas Nelson

La Bibliotecaria de Saint-Malo

Copyright © 2020 Mario Escobar

First edition published in Spanish by HarperCollins Español

Published in Nashville, Tennessee, by Thomas Nelson. Thomas Nelson is a registered trademark of HarperCollins Christian Publishing, Inc.

Spanish Editor in Chief: Edward Benítez

English Editor: Jocelyn Bailey

Translator: Gretchen Abernathy

Thomas Nelson titles may be purchased in bulk for educational, business, fundraising, or sales promotional use. For information, please email SpecialMarkets@ThomasNelson.com.

ISBN 978-0-7852-3991-8 (hardcover)
ISBN 978-0-7852-3993-2 (downloadable audio)
ISBN 978-0-7852-3992-5 (e-book)
ISBN 978-0-7852-6047-9 (international edition)

Library of Congress Cataloging-in-Publication Data

CIP data is available upon request.

Printed in the United States of America
21 22 23 24 25 LSC 10 9 8 7 6 5 4 3 2 1

To Elisabeth, who walked the walls of Saint-Malo and witnessed this novel come to life from my lips.

To the reader who told me her life story at a book signing in Zaragoza and who inspired this book.

For most men, war is the end of loneliness.
For me, it is infinite solitude.
ALBERT CAMUS (1913–1960), FRENCH AUTHOR

A Note from the Author

The *Librarian of Saint-Malo* speaks to us of love, revenge, conscience, guilt, and the past that traps us and shapes our lives.

The idea behind this novel grew out of a visit I made to Saint-Malo in September 2018. The city, mostly rebuilt, immediately captured me. Its imposing walls, vast beaches with cinnamon-colored sand, bleached-rock fortresses, and tides that batter the small peninsula in the ocean's attempt to reclaim those haughty walls . . . I was a goner. As we walked along on top of the wall that surrounds the old city, I told my wife, Elisabeth, "I've got to write a story about this place."

My earlier books had focused on the devastating fallout of the Holocaust, but I wanted to show the suffering of the common people during the German occupation of France and home in on the terrible persecution that the occupation unleashed on culture and books in particular.

Sitting in front of Duchess Anne's castle, I recalled the thrilling experience a reader had recounted to me the year before in

Zaragoza, Spain. The young woman told me in a few words her incredible story of love, pain, and illness. The two ideas melded and became this novel, inspired by real facts.

After France's surrender on June 22, 1940, the Nazis occupied the area of Saint-Malo and turned it into the stronghold of its famous Atlantic fortress to control the northern area of French Brittany. The inhabitants tried to passively resist their occupiers; they came from a long line of pirates and fearless men. But Andreas von Aulock, the colonel in charge, was ruthless and stamped out even the subtlest attempt at opposition. The German commander ordered the purge of the city's bookstores and libraries to get rid of subversive writings as outlined in the famous Liste Otto.

The Librarian of Saint-Malo tells the story of Jocelyn and Antoine Ferrec, a life full of love and literature. Pure hearts will shine out even in history's darkest moments.

MARIO ESCOBAR

MADRID, OCTOBER 2019

The
Librarian *of*
Saint-Malo

Prologue

Dear Marcel Zola:

Time takes care with no one. It weighs us down, bowing our backs to humiliate us; it slows our stride into insecure, hesitating steps. We start out running but gradually get to the point where we can't even walk without holding on to something. After health and beauty have left us, little by little it steals away everything we care about, all that really matters: the people we love—first our grandparents and parents, then friends, and lastly, if we manage to live long enough, our own children.

No one can beat the god Chronos. There are no winners. As we grow up, we lose our life moment by moment until everything's taken away from us the day we die. Existence orbits around the certainty of loss. Old age is not the passing of years but the destruction of all we hold dear. That is what I observe in your writings: your ability to detain the inevitable passage of time. That's why I love literature: Chronos

1

is powerless over it. The words of Plato, Aristotle, Seneca, Balzac, Tolstoy, and all the authors the world has given us are the only things that can hold back the monster that devours everything and leaves it a pile of dust.

I am an ardent fan of your books. There are only three things I love in this world: my beloved husband, Antoine, the beautiful village of Saint-Malo, and the historic library I manage. The Hotel Désilles, where the library is located, was built in 1628 by Jean Grave, Sieur de Launay, and his wife, Bernardine Sere, shortly after they were married. André Désilles, the hero of Nancy, was born there, and now it houses the oldest and most beautiful books in the town. You may ask why I'm telling you all this. Who am I, a provincial librarian, who knows so little of the world and has only an old building for her kingdom? I ask myself the same. Perhaps because I fell in love with your novel, *The Blight*, and with that simple yet gut-wrenching description of the destruction of a city. Yes, Mr. Zola: I wept at the misfortune of your characters and Gabrielle's terrible illness, but now I'm living my version of it, France's very own plague.

You might not believe the things I'm about to tell you or, what's worse, you may not even care. I'm not just doing this to write a book about my love story and the horrible occupation of France by the Germans. Rather, my hope is that someday, when humanity regains its sanity, people will know that the only way to be saved from barbarianism is by love: loving books, loving people, and, though you may call me crazy, loving our enemies. There's no doubt that love is the most revolutionary choice and, therefore, the most persecuted and reviled. Augustine of Hippo's thrilling phrase still reverberates in my ears: "Love, and do what you will."

Prologue

My grief began the same day as my happiness. It's always hard for humans to accept misfortune, as if bad things only happen to other people and we ourselves are out of harm's reach. The same day the Germans attacked Poland and plunged the world into a merciless war, Antoine and I were married in the Cathedral of Saint-Vincent in our lovely town of Saint-Malo. This is our story.

Jocelyn Ferrec

Part One

One Summer Day

1

The Honeymoon

Saint-Malo
September 1, 1939

Our good friend Denis Villeneuve, Brittany's most well-known bookseller, walked me down the aisle. Antoine and I had met in his bookstore two years prior. While I was flipping through a first edition of *Les Misérables*, the handsome young man behind me tripped, and a huge pile of books cascaded across the scuffed hardwood floor. I started to smile, then noticed his haste, so I bent down to help him collect the books. The young man looked up, and our eyes locked, just a few inches from each other. His blue irises were the intensity of the turquoise sea that bathes the city's beaches on sunny days. I had only been back in Saint-Malo for a few months. I had studied at a school run by nuns in Bordeaux and later in Rennes, then gotten a degree in

philology. Nearly a decade had passed since I was last in town—
after the car wreck that took my parents, nothing anchored me
to Saint-Malo. But one of my professors in Rennes told me that
the librarian's assistant position was open, so I applied, though
without much hope.

As I walked down the long aisle of the cathedral, I could not
hold back my tears. Antoine's family filled the front rows, but I
had no one else in the world. Yet the sadness dissipated when I
looked into the face of the man I loved. His dark red curly hair
flopped over his forehead, and his features were soft. His thin
lips were spread wide in an intoxicating smile.

The ceremony was simple and unadorned beyond the beauty
of the cathedral itself, and the priest performed his duties effi-
ciently that Friday afternoon. Our train would leave for Paris in
about an hour, and if we did not arrive in time, we would lose
our reservation for the sleeper car and for the Hotel Ritz the following day. That was no small matter for my librarian's salary
and Antoine's modest earnings as a police sergeant.

As we walked back up the aisle, I greeted the guests while
Denis fetched the car to take us to the station.

We hurried down the cathedral stairs, but before we reached
the sidewalk, the bottom fell out of the dark clouds that had
been threatening rain since the morning. The heavy curtain of
rainwater soaked us to the bone before we even reached the convertible car. Denis raced to put up the car roof, then jumped back
into the old Renault, and we bumped and jolted our way down
the cobblestone roads of the walled city. Leaving the port behind,
we headed inland as fast as possible toward the station.

Denis stopped at the entrance and got our suitcases out.
Antoine picked me up and carried me so I would not have to step
in the huge puddles in the cobblestone street, and thus we crossed

the threshold into the train station like newlyweds entering their honeymoon suite. We dashed toward the platform. The train was revving up, blowing out steam as the passengers lingered over their goodbyes, as if fearing to never return. Summer's end left Saint-Malo rather empty and sad. The thousands of summertime visitors who soaked up its beaches and ancient fortresses disappeared every year at the coming of autumn.

"I'm green with envy! Paris is the most beautiful city in Europe!"

"Don't exaggerate, Denis. You know very well we won't be strolling down the Seine or the Champs-Élysées, not even touring Notre Dame," Antoine quipped.

"Ah, the Champs-Élysées . . . You know, in the Greek world, the Elysian Fields were reserved for virtuous souls." Denis winked after helping us hoist our luggage onto the wagon. He was always making such highbrow statements, seeing the inseparable connections between life and literature like sky and ocean at the horizon.

"Then come with us," I said.

"It's your lovers' journey. The City of Lights will have to wait."

We hugged our friend and, just as he hopped down to the platform, the train started to move. We leaned over the railing and waved at him with our gloved hands until he was no more than a speck.

As soon as the train left the station, the fat, cold drops of the rainstorm drenched our faces again. We locked eyes like that first time in the bookstore and walked smiling to our compartment. It was a sleeping car, but before turning in for the night we wanted to eat dinner and to toast with champagne. A wedding just isn't a real wedding without the clink of glasses filled with bubbly wine.

We took a seat at the last available table. Beside us, an elderly military man smiled. He must have noticed I was still in my wedding dress, though it was admittedly so simple it could have been mistaken for a white silk evening gown.

"Good evening," we greeted him.

"So, life goes on," he answered. Antoine raised his eyebrows, not following.

"I'm sorry, what do you mean?"

"You haven't heard the news?" We turned our full attention to the officer, the waiter not having come yet.

"No, we got married less than an hour ago and came straight to the train," I explained, wondering what the man meant.

"Germany just invaded Poland, apparently over a skirmish at the border. If the Germans don't pull back, France and Great Britain will declare war on Germany, and we'll be in another armed conflict," the officer explained.

I was so shocked that Antoine put his arms around me and kissed my cheek.

The elderly man continued. "The president of the Republic and England's prime minister have given Hitler three days to put down his weapons, but that Austrian corporal will never surrender. In short time he's managed to grab up the Saar, Austria, a good bit of Czechoslovakia . . . and he won't stop."

"Well," Antoine offered, "we all learned from what happened during the Great War. Nobody wants another conflict."

The officer shrugged. "You didn't fight in that war, young man. We won in the end, but the price was too high—such carnage, an entire generation gone. Things have changed, and the next war will be even worse. I'm a military man, but I swear I hate nothing more than fighting. It pains me for the younger men. We old men always start the wars, but the young men are the ones who die in them."

The waiter arrived, recommended a dish, and then brought a bottle of champagne. The dark news had dampened the mood, though. We hardly tasted the food and sipped the champagne without toasting, just to refresh the fear that had started to dry our throats.

An hour later, we undressed silently in our compartment. Every now and then the moonlight broke through the clouds and rain and shone through the window as the train sped to Paris. We kissed, and Antoine's tender arms made me feel more alive than I had ever been before.

"They'll call you to enlist. Surely there will be a draft," I said.

"Let's not think about it now. We just got married, we're going to Paris, and all we have is this moment," Antoine said, trying to calm my fears with his kisses.

We had no idea that dark years were piling up like storm clouds above. The strangest part was that everything seemed the same as it had been just a few hours before: the raindrops drumming against the train car roof, the rhythmic sound of the metal wheels on the rails, the fields and forests flying by in the grip of darkness.

———— •◆• ————

The next morning, the train arrived in Paris. We had slept in, had a late breakfast of fruit, and watched the passing of the endless landscapes, rushing rivers, and towns that grew steadily larger closer to the capital. We passed through the city's outskirts, the dingy gray working-class neighborhoods, and middle-class neighborhoods with nice flowery yards until the great scenery of Balzac's *The Human Comedy* dazzled us. And that was the point, the reason the beautiful city of love was built: the dazzle.

A porter helped us carry our luggage to an old, run-down taxi. A few minutes later the doors to the famous Hotel Ritz opened to receive us. The luxurious entryway was like a palace, with the spotless white awning, the concierge in jacket and top hat, the bellhops shuttling the suitcases of the nobility in golden luggage carts, and the middle class from the provinces come to the city for the adventure of a lifetime.

We walked along the blue embroidered rugs and by the cloud-soft velvet curtains with bright gold tassels. The receptionist assigned us a small room on the second floor. When the bellhop opened the door, Antoine once again picked me up in his arms, carried me over the threshold, and placed me gently on the bed.

"It's so nice," I said when we were alone. "Do you really think we can afford this?"

"No, darling, but we'll only get married once. Today we're alive and healthy, and that's all that matters."

After sinking into the ocean of linen sheets together, we showered and got dressed. We wanted to explore the bouquin-istes before they closed. The riverside book stalls had flanked the Seine since the sixteenth century, withstanding church censorship, religious warfare, the French Revolution, Napoleon's empire, and the Great War.

It was a pleasant, almost cool afternoon as we walked toward the river. Some of the wooden crates were already shut up, but we managed to flip through several books and bought a few volumes of François Villon, Charles Perrault, and George Sand. We found a nearby café and sat, reading snippets of the books and watching the Parisian foot traffic in the light of the sun that had finally managed to break through the clouds.

"I can't believe how well preserved these are!" I said.

"They're dead people's books," Antoine said to egg me on.

"Books don't have owners; they're free agents we just happen to hold for a brief time. Look at this one, inscribed with a woman's name and dated to 1874. But now I'm carrying it around, and maybe in another hundred years, another woman will be reading it. Every time someone opens a book, it comes alive once more. Its characters wake up from their nap and start acting all over again."

"You're always going on about *The Human Comedy* . . . I don't know what you see in Balzac. He was a cheat, a word peddler."

"But aren't all authors?" I asked, my eyebrows raised. I did not like the way Antoine and the world of critics classified literature, relegating some as first-rate and the rest as second-class.

"Cheats or word peddlers?"

"Both."

"Life itself is a scam, my dear. We're born, we think we're eternal, and then we disappear forever . . ."

My face grew stormy. I did not like talking about death. For Antoine, death was just an abstract idea, but for me, it was the dull reminder of my parents. My chest ached all of a sudden. I had been plagued by a cough for weeks, and sometimes I could not get enough air.

"Are you okay?" Antoine asked when my repeated throat clearing did not seem to help matters. He handed me a pristine white handkerchief, and I coughed into it. The fabric was spotted with red, but I shoved it into my pocket before he could notice. I did not want Antoine to worry. Death and illness nip at our heels from birth. To escape, we have to run faster and faster— and at the time, on that day in Paris, books were the only escape valve that could anesthetize my soul.

2

Death's Embrace

Saint-Malo
January 2, 1940

Winter seemed set on destroying Saint-Malo at all costs. Every morning, despite my illness, I bundled up as best I could, went up on the wall, and watched the waves pounding the ancient stone barrier between sea and city. The ocean refused to give up its centuries-long mission to flood the streets of the old fishing town founded by the Gauls. The doctor had suggested exposure to cold, clean air to improve my symptoms, but I was growing steadily weaker and often could not catch my breath between coughing fits. Then I would pull out Marie de France's medieval poem "Laüstic" and read while the chilled northern air and salty ocean spray freshened up my face. That story about two knights who love the same woman is heart-wrenching: the

15

beautiful wife whose love toward her spiteful husband has grown cold, and her chaste lover who is content to talk with her through the window on warm summer nights. At the time it was a metaphor for my own illness. When the woman's husband suspects something, she says she is spending nights in the garden listening to a nightingale. So he orders the bird to be captured and shut up in a cage. When the woman begs him to free it, the man kills the bird and hurls it at her, staining her dress with blood—blood just as red as that which flowed out of my nose and mouth.

That morning, the roaring of the ocean distracted me from reading. I pulled my coat tighter around me and walked with the little book in my pocket toward the library. Our apartment was a few hundred yards from the Hotel Désilles. I opened the door and went in. I knew few would come by in that weather, but I preferred the company of books over the solitude of our apartment.

I hung my coat on the wooden hook. The light was on, and Céline Beauvoir was already sitting at her desk. She had retired the year before and left the management of the library to me, but she could not keep herself from spending the mornings in the building, helping me with the card catalogue or repairing damaged volumes.

"Why are you out on a day like this?" she asked. "You've got to take care of yourself. Health is a treasure we really can't afford to waste."

"And it's precisely one I don't have," I answered, slumping into my desk with a hard-won breath.

"At least you've got your youth. This tuberculosis won't take you down. Have faith."

"I wonder about faith," I said, putting on my glasses and

revising the list of overdue books. Céline was a very devout woman, something beyond my comprehension. Faith had always been at odd with books, in my view.

"Was your family not Christian?" she said.

Her question was so direct that I glanced away. I didn't want her to see my confusion. "Yes, both sides were from a long Huguenot saga. I went to church all the time when I was little, but I left the faith after my parents died. My aunt sent me to a school run by nuns, but their rigor convinced me that truth was in books."

The older woman smiled, her deep inner peace radiating out. "Books certainly help us ask the right questions, but they rarely give us the answers, my friend."

I lowered my head and immersed myself in the tomes piled high on my desk. Now that Antoine would certainly be drafted, with my illness growing worse and war in the air all around, I did not want to think about death or what it might mean.

The door chimed and a boy no more than thirteen years old entered. He was wearing school uniform shorts despite the cold that was blowing all outside the library walls.

"Mrs. Ferrec, Denis the bookseller has sent me."

I smiled at the young man, who just looked at me, uncertain, for a few moments.

"Yes, go on," I encouraged him.

"The bookseller, Mr. . . ."

"Yes, I know him."

"He told me that libraries are the poor man's bookstore. I like to draw, and maybe you have some books about sketching and painting."

I pointed to some shelves. For the uninitiated, the library can be an undecipherable labyrinth, but ours actually followed an orderly circular design: the oldest books were in the center, and the most valuable were locked away.

"Thank you," he said.

"After you choose one or two, you'll give me your name and address so I can make a card for you."

The boy walked gingerly to one of the shelves and stared with his mouth open at a volume. He took it to one of the study tables and spent the rest of the morning poring over it, oblivious to everything around him.

Céline came up to me and smiled. "I hope I haven't offended you. I didn't mean anything with my questions. I just wanted to cheer you up, and sometimes hope is the only thing preventing us from going crazy. Life is so full of trials, and I can assure you I haven't found any anchors that reach to the bottom of the depths."

"Thank you, Céline. You aren't a bother in the least. It's just that whenever I talk about religion, I remember my unfortunate parents. They left for vacation and never came back. When we lose someone in such a way, we're stuck with the feeling that they'll come home at any moment."

"Being an orphan is one of the hardest things in the world to get over, especially if it happens when you're young enough for the whole universe to revolve around your parents. We live through the deaths of others more by fear than sadness. It makes us feel insecure, knowing the past doesn't exist anymore and at the core it's just a story we tell ourselves."

"I'm scared." The words escaped in a whisper as I started to cry.

"We're all going to die, dear. No one escapes it." Céline patted my shoulder with her chilled, bony hand.

"That's easy to say when you aren't in the middle of dying.

Do you have any idea what it feels like? Every night I close my eyes scared I'll never open them again. Death is the end; I won't feel anything else after that, never get to see the ocean and the big gray clouds and this wonderful room full of books."

"You're right. I hadn't considered that. And yet I think we avoid thinking about death too much. Doing so scares us. But getting old is a way of dying little by little until you let your spirit abandon your weak, sickly body in one final breath."

"I'm not ready for that," I said, my voice choked with tears. "These books and Antoine's love are the only things keeping me on my feet. We spend every afternoon in the sunroom drinking tea and reading together. Sometimes he stops and looks up, stretches out his hand and takes mine, like he's trying to make sure I'm still here. Then we go on reading, each of us in our own book, holding hands. Mine are always cold and his nice and warm, 'til the sun goes down and I have to face the night alone."

"Child, don't live in the past or fear the future. Just stay right here in the present, where the sun is always shining."

The boy crept up to us. The book he carried seemed to make him float through the air, and the ancient hardwood floor did not even creak to give him away. His unvarnished face shone with life and future, and I envied him for a breath. Then he smiled. His youthfulness returned me to the immediacy of a day's work.

"May I take this one? My name is Pierre . . ."

I smiled and filled out a card for him, and he went on his way. The rest of the morning went by quickly, which is what I liked most about going to work. Staying home tended to make me feel useless and invalid.

———— ◆ ————

Back at home, I stopped in front of a pastry shop and admired the delicacies in the window. I bought a few, and on my way home devoured one. The taste delighted and distracted me for a passing moment. Then I dragged myself up the stairs, fighting for every breath and hoping Antoine was already home so we could sit by the window and read. Books lightened the pain in my soul and stood guard before the advancing embrace of death. The cloth-bound cardboard covers made me invulnerable and immortal, like the characters on the pages within.

3

The Draft

M any people called the conflict a "phony war," but I could tell they were wrong. The Soviets had taken over half of Poland while the Germans occupied the other half. Rumors swirled about prisoners being treated terribly and Germans forcing Poles out of their homes. The Soviet Union, encouraged by the impunity of their actions, had invaded Finland, and people feared the Germans would do something similar in Denmark and Norway. And we started to wonder what would happen when the Nazis turned their cannons toward us. Yet in those days, what I worried about most was my declining health.

One morning, after an exhausting and interminable coughing

spell, Antoine decided to call for Dr. Paul Aubry, one of the best doctors in town.

As soon as the bell rang, Antoine rushed to answer the door and speak with the doctor. I knew he was deeply worried and wanted the doctor to know all about the progression of my disease. They thought I was resting in bed, but I was awake and heard the whole exchange.

"Dr. Aubry, Jocelyn is worse. She can't stop coughing, and I can tell she's losing her strength every day. I'm really worried about her."

"I understand. Tuberculosis is a dangerous disease, but in young, healthy individuals like your wife, with the right care . . . The vaccine is effective in children but not in adults who have already contracted the disease. Research for a cure is ongoing."

"Do you think it would be better for her to visit a recovery home? She doesn't get any rest here. She wants to return to work and pushes herself to keep the house in order."

"Your wife is very strong, and maintaining her activities will help her. Most illnesses are fought more with the will than with medicines. As long as she's stable, it's best not to remove her from the environment she's accustomed to. The air of our city is pure and fresh. I'm confident she'll begin improving soon. Within a few months she may very well return to life as normal. In the meantime, though, find someone to help with the housework so she won't worry herself with it." The doctor spoke in such a peaceful, soothing tone that the comfort reached even me.

Over the months, I had thought a lot about my death. I felt my life was slipping away from me with each cough and each drop of blood that came from my throat. I had hardly touched Antoine for months, much less kissed him. My skin was so pale it had taken on grayish hues, and my bones were beginning to show. I looked like my flesh was eating itself and my body was wasting away.

I had not been able to work at the library for over a month, and in my long mornings in bed I read *A Confession* by Leo Tolstoy. His life and mine could not have been more different. The Russian author was an overcomer—hot-blooded and irascible—while I tended toward melancholy and introspection; but his words were good for me. It is not normal for a person so young to think about death so much, but I was obsessed with the idea. Sometimes everything has to come crashing down for us to understand what we have built our lives upon. Mine was set on a foundation of my love for Antoine, my passion for books, and my dedication to the townspeople of Saint-Malo. I longed to be a mother and dreamed of becoming a writer, but none of that mattered at the moment.

Socrates's words grew clearer and clearer in my day-in, day-out existence: we get closer to the truth the more we are freed from the "folly of body."

Antoine came into our bedroom, followed by Dr. Aubry, whose pleasant smile brought me out of my reverie and back into the world of flesh and blood.

"You seem to be looking better, your face more full of life," he lied to encourage me, but I chose to believe him. Invalids do not care if people lie to us so long as they make us feel better.

"Thank you, though I know I look terrible," I said, smoothing down my hair.

"You're the prettiest starfish in the ocean," Antoine said, caressing my forehead. I drew back, fearful of infecting him.

"I hope you'll be able to get out of bed in a few weeks. Keep the window open as much as possible. The pure ocean air is the very best medicine."

I curled up between the blankets, but I could never get warm enough. The air cut through the fabric like wind filling sails on a boat adrift.

"How is the war going?" I asked the doctor impatiently. Antoine tried not to speak of it around me. I knew he would be called to serve any day now, and I had no idea what would become of me when he left. His family did not hold me in overly high regard. At least I still had Denis, who would come by after shutting up the bookstore and read poetry aloud while I stared at the patch of sky I could see from the bed.

"Some think the Germans will try to reach an agreement. The British are none too eager to start a full-scale war, and our government—well, you know, it's a mess of pacifists, communists, and social climbers who haven't yet come up with a response. Just look at how they handled the Spanish refugee crisis. Totally overwhelmed and always making things up as they go."

"The situation isn't easy for anyone," Antoine said. He was less conservative than the good doctor. These two visions of France—and so many more—that had always been at odds now flared up as danger closed in. "The world has gone mad."

The doctor nodded once. "I must get to the hospital, so I'll be going. They're drafting all the younger doctors, and we're doubling up on shifts. If not for that change, I would hardly be able to tell we are at war."

Dr. Aubry headed for the hallway, and Antoine walked him to the door. Moments later he was standing by the bed again.

"How are you?" he asked, hoping I would answer in the positive.

"It's natural to want to live . . ."

"You've been reading a lot of philosophy lately. Schopenhauer is not necessarily a great pick-me-up. Surely things will get better once winter is over."

"Sometimes I think my life is a cruel joke. An orphan all alone in the world with nothing to my name, and the very day my happiness returns, I get sick and now am on the brink of death." My tears fell as I spoke.

"Jocelyn, we're going to get through this. By the time I'm back all of this will be over."

My eyes darted to meet his own. "When you get back?" Then I saw the envelope sticking out of his jacket pocket. All day I had sensed he was a bit off, but I assumed he was just worried about me.

"I've been called up. Yesterday I went before the draft board and explained our situation, but the infantry is short on non-commissioned officers, and I've got a policeman's experience with weapons. There's nothing else I can do."

"Nothing? You can disobey. The state can't take you away from your dying wife. It's immoral!"

"If we lose this war, who's going to protect you when the Germans come? This is my duty." Antoine's voice was charged with grief. Though he'd been a policeman his whole career, my husband despised violence.

I closed my eyes and turned away from him. He remained standing by the bed for a while but eventually heaved a sigh and left me. I heard him shut the door and go out to the street, probably going to a café or to see a friend and have a glass of wine and forget everything happening in his world.

I struggled to sit up and dress myself, and my weakness became abundantly clear as soon as I was on my feet. I was in a cold sweat, hands trembling, and I hardly had the strength to stay upright. I took my coat from the rack by the door, my hat, and a new scarf Antoine had given me for Christmas. I had not yet been able to wear it, but I draped it around my neck and stepped out onto the landing. When I got to the door, I wondered how I would ever get back up the stairs again—then pressed forward and out to the street. The rain fell, and the waves slapped the wall in the ocean's eternal attempt to scale it and invade the cobblestone streets. After walking for a quarter of an hour, I had to stop and lean against a wall to keep from fainting. I made it to the building I sought and went to the office of the draft board. Two or three young men waited there, their young faces reflecting the innocence that believed a war was one of life's most heroic options. I knew, however, the only ones to ever stand out during war were the murderers and the sadists.

I knocked at the door and went in without waiting for an answer.

"Madame, do you have a number? We're about to close. If it's about an urgent . . ." The desk worker trailed off when he saw me slouch into the chair. "Are you all right? Aren't you Antoine Ferrec's wife?"

I took as deep a breath as I could and gathered my strength. "Yes, I'm Mrs. Ferrec. You've called my husband to enlist, but we had sent in an exemption request. I'm very ill and have no one to care for me."

"I'm sorry, Mrs. Ferrec. We're at war, and we need every last man. Besides, your husband is experienced."

"And are *you* going off to the war?"

"No, madame, but my post is vital here. I have a wife and four children, I'm over forty, and the younger reserves are called up first."

"So why don't you enlist as a volunteer? Antoine can't go to war. His duty is to care for his wife. Will you be the one to send him news of my death while he's at the front?" I asked, frowning. An energy I had not felt for weeks had taken possession of me.

"There's nothing I can do; it's not up to me. I'm so sorry. I'll call a taxi to take you home."

I started to cry, which only made me madder. I hated breaking open inside and showing my emotions to that stupid paper pusher, as cold and impersonal as the state he represented.

"There's no need," I said, rising to my feet. But my head started to spin and then everything went dark.

———— •◆• ————

I have no idea how long I was in that office or how I made it home. I was sweating and shaking with fever, and I could feel my life slipping out of every pore in my skin. The only thing tethering me to life was Antoine's hand tightly holding mine. I knew it was he even with my eyes closed. One flesh that desires and responds to another has no need of vision to recognize the beloved.

"Don't leave me, Jocelyn. I couldn't bear it," Antoine said through a sob. His tears on my cheek were like holy water to bring back the dead. I opened my eyes halfway. How I longed to drink in that salty water! The taste made me recall going to the beach with my parents in the summer. They would sit in the sand while I built castles with my bucket. Their eyes spoke so much love to each other. I could feel them calling me to their side, but I knew they were so far away now. The chasm of death separated us. I wanted to hold them then, as I had sometimes done in dreams, only to wake up crying with my arms wrapped around nothing.

"Jocelyn, don't leave me!" Antoine begged again.

It took all my strength to squeeze his hand. I knew he was beside me, but in my hallucinations I was still on the beach with my plaid dress, a bucket, and my hands covered in sand. I thought fleetingly of what sweet rest death would offer and how it would stave off the pain and the suffering; but I chose to live, because living meant loving.

4

Bombs

Saint-Malo
May 17, 1940

A week after my resurrection, Antoine went to the front, and
I somehow started to improve. I again thought of the iro-
nies of fate. Céline and Denis took care of me in those early days
of my husband's absence. Céline came at night and slept in the
room beside mine, and Denis helped me eat and pass the afternoon hours until dinner. Antoine's almost daily letters were the
highlight of the day. I always wrote him back right away, though
my responses were short at first given my weakness. By the time
I could send longer letters, he was only sending one per week.

Denis read the newspaper to me, and together we listened
to the radio to learn what was occurring at the front. Antoine

gave very little news about the war, and I was anxious to know, though information changed by the minute and everything seemed to be a mess.

"Is it true that the Germans are heading to Paris?" I asked Denis with dismay.

"That's what I heard this morning, and I've had the radio on all day. The Germans have occupied nearly all of the Netherlands, and the Dutch have surrendered. Now they're tearing through Belgium, have taken over Luxembourg, and are rapidly penetrating French territory."

I covered my face with my hands. The blanket over my lap slipped to the floor. I no longer had to stay in bed, but I wasn't able to go outside much yet. I had challenged myself to return to work the next week, as Céline had been forced to fill in for me during my long absence.

"The Germans destroyed Rotterdam with their bombs and have threatened to do the same with Amsterdam and Utrecht. The Dutch couldn't stop them. The Allied troops managed to evacuate most of the army and are holding out in Belgium, though the German advance has hardly even slowed down enough to stake out new positions and soon will attack again."

"Antoine was in Belgium," I said, my chest tight with worry. "He's part of the Ninth Army under General André Georges Corap."

Denis nodded. "His troops are fighting hard in Sedan, though the Germans are slaughtering them. The government wants to flee Paris, which means the front is about to crack."

I looked at him aghast. "But we've only been fighting a few days. Wars aren't won so quickly."

"The German tanks are steamrollers, and German aviators destroy entire cities without mercy. You remember what happened at Guernica? In Spain? The Germans and Italians bombed the place to death, heedless of the suffering inflicted on civilians."

The idea of death started spreading back over my mind, and I succumbed again to the grip of fear. "Well, surely they won't bomb France. Our air force would stop them," I said.

Denis shook his head, unconvinced. "They're attacking Calais and other cities."

"But Saint-Malo isn't a military target." I was grasping at straws.

"Destroying the ports is strategic. British supplies come through the Atlantic ports, so if they destroy Dunkirk or Calais, they'll shuttle the materials through Saint-Malo or one of the others."

———— • ◆ • ————

An hour later we were having supper. Denis, an excellent cook, had prepared a delicious dish of chicken in a beer sauce. My mouth watered as I set the table, then I heard an unfamiliar humming sound. It was far off, like a buzzing bee, but then the noise got louder. Things in the room started to vibrate. Fearful, I ran to the kitchen. Denis stared at me with his blue eyes jumping out of his head.

"What in heaven's name is that?" I asked, steadying myself against the countertop.

"Airplanes. We need to find a shelter. Where is the nearest one?" he asked in bewilderment.

"At the church, I think, though we could go down to the basement here. Surely they'll just keep flying by and pass us over." I worked to steady my nerves though chills were running up my spine.

As we hurried out, I glanced at the big picture window where Antoine and I would sit and read together. That spot threw his absence into painful relief. Yet my attention this time was drawn to the column of airplanes approaching, flying very low. The antiaircraft battery started going off, including the guns at the port. Explosions filled the sky, and it sounded like a fireworks show. Denis grabbed my arm, but we were both frozen in place by the spectacle. It was beautiful in a way, horror choreographed against a cloudy, dusky sky.

"There are dozens of them," I said, coming back to myself a bit.

The antiaircraft defense only hit one or two of the planes. Their wings flamed up and left grotesquely lovely contrails in the sky. Within seconds the bomber planes were above us, unleashing their vomit of smoke and fire.

The whistling of the falling bombs drowned out the explosions of the antiaircraft artillery. Then came the sonic impact of the bombs once they hit the ground. The glass in the windows shook uncontrollably, and the building trembled with each explosion as if it were an earthquake.

We dashed down the stairs, steadying ourselves against the walls to keep from tumbling. When we reached the bottom floor, all of the building's inhabitants were huddled at the basement door, but no one had the key to open it.

Mrs. Fave skewered us with her haughty gaze and demanded of the custodian, "Who locked the door?" The man just shrugged his shoulders.

A bomb that sounded very close went off, and plaster from the ceiling rained down and covered our clothing. The Remarque children were screaming and crying. Their father was in the army, and their mother, Marie, was trying to shelter them under her arms as if her embrace could deflect the weapons of war.

"Let's calm down now," I said, leaning down to comfort the youngest ones.

"This is unbelievable," Mrs. Fave continued. "If my husband were alive this would never have happened." The wrinkles on her face hardened as one of the windows on the stairwell shattered. She pushed and shoved the rest of us on her way out of the building, sacrificing courtesy in her panicked state.

Denis gripped my hand as we made our way toward the church. The crypt seemed like it would be safe. Plus, rumor had it that the Nazis would not bomb the churches—not out of respect for religion but because Hitler did not want the art inside to be destroyed.

Father Roth was at the door ushering people inside. He patted their backs and smiled, just like a shepherd comforting sheep frightened by wolves.

"Step forward, come along now, down to the crypt. Don't worry, Saint Damian and the Virgin will protect you."

In the enormous nave, the building's acoustics intensified the noise of the bombing. I looked up at the dome and wondered if the nearly eight-hundred-year-old building could withstand a bomb. The gleaming stones had witnessed countless battles and endured the weight of the centuries, but modern warfare was more deadly than all the previous wars combined.

We crammed into the crypt. A long stone bench and a few chairs from the chapel were all we had to get us through the interminable night.

Isabelle, one of the girls from the church choir, started singing. Her angelic voice could hardly be heard above the racket of the bombs, but little by little more girls and women joined her. There were very few men with us, just a few who were elderly.

One of the older boys had brought his accordion and started playing along with the impromptu chorus. The music provided a calm that helped us endure nearly three hours of constant bombing. When the night had grown quiet again, Father Roth said, "It's over. Let's say the Lord's Prayer and you can all return home in the morning."

I joined in the prayer without much thought. The bombs had forced a sense of community unlike anything we had experienced even in a town so unified by its history.

Silence gradually spread among our group. I had never appreciated the peace of the crypt before. I lay my head against Denis's legs and fell asleep in a moment. When I woke, there were tears in my eyes. I had dreamed first about my parents and when we buried them: the words the pastor had said at the grave, how no one had cried and I had forced back my own tears, and how my aunt had held my hand so tightly. Then in my dream I saw Antoine's body in the middle of a battlefield, unresponsive to my screaming because I knew he was dead.

"Are you all right?" Father Roth asked when he saw me weeping.

I wiped my face. The tears had mixed with the dust and plaster in my hair and on my face. "It was just a nightmare," I said.

Many of the neighbors had already gone. Denis and I were among the last. It was already morning, and the day played the cruel joke of being so bright it blinded us as we walked out of the church. Nature was indifferent to our suffering, and as we picked our way along the street, we saw the bombs had not hit many buildings. The damage was worst at the port, but the stench of burning filled the air and black clouds of smoke swirled from beyond the rooftops.

On our way back to my apartment, we passed Denis's bookshop. He let out a great sigh that it seemed to have suffered no more damage than a shattered door window. He opened the door to find fallen stacks of books, the volumes splayed open in piles as if trying to protect each other from the Nazi brutality. We set to work dusting them off and shelving them, and then Denis walked me home.

"Let's go up on the wall," I said before we turned onto my street. We climbed the steep stairs. There were soldiers smoking nervously and keeping watch, their eyes trained on the immense ocean blue. We walked around the city to the port where we saw buildings still burning and some sunken ships sending up foul-smelling black smoke.

"A city is like a woman," I mused.

Denis cocked an eye at me. "What do you mean?"

"Everyone wants to conquer her, but she resists. They may occupy her streets but never her soul. Saint-Malo will be free so long as we keep tending her fire in our hearts."

5

Letters and the Road

Saint-Malo
June 9, 1940

I had never stopped to imagine the chaos of a world without authorities. While our armies were trying to buy time and the British were warm in their beds on the other side of the Strait after fleeing Dunkirk, the poor French recruits labored to hold back the Germans. The government had fled to Bordeaux, and the streets were flooded with refugees. It had been weeks since I had received a letter from Antoine, even though I went to the post office every day or by the draft board office to ask for news about the Ninth Army. But nothing was working like it had in the past, and although we all tried to pretend things were normal, the reality was that the Republic was sinking like a ship. Rumors flew through the city about the Germans being bloodthirsty blond barbarians who went around raping, looting, attacking, and shooting anything and anyone.

I tried to keep my head clear. Every morning I opened the library even though very few patrons came to read or borrow books. My only companions were Céline, who seemed calm despite the reigning confusion, and Denis, who was scared stiff.

"Reynaud and Lebrun won't hold out long. I'm afraid there won't be anyone for the Germans to negotiate an armistice with. The president and prime minister just run away with their tails between their legs. The Nazis will march into Paris any moment now, and our brave soldiers are the only ones still fighting. How I wish God had given me a son to defend France," Céline said, tossing down a newspaper.

"I heard the streets are packed with people trying to escape to the south."

"It's pointless. Where do they think they're going? To Spain, to fall into the hands of that dictator Franco? The Germans will do whatever they want with us. There's nothing to do but pray."

The sound of the phone suddenly ringing made us both jump. I picked up the receiver, took a breath, and tried to focus on the call. "Saint-Malo library. How may I help you?"

I was surprised to hear the confused, nervous voice of a woman. "This is Mrs. Vien. My husband was serving with your husband, Antoine Ferrec."

My heart jumped. I had been tormented for weeks without news.

"This is Jocelyn Ferrec. Do you know something about my husband?"

"I have some letters for you. We left Paris four days ago, but we had to abandon our car. There was no gas to be had, and the streets were crowded with people fleeing. We're near Fougères;

that's as close as we can get to Saint-Malo. We are headed toward Bordeaux. My father is a field marshal and tells me there are boats leaving from there to Africa. Tomorrow some military trucks will be rescuing us from this death trap. The mail service isn't running, so what do you want me to do with your letters?"

Her rambling account confused me, and I did not know how to respond. Céline gave me a puzzled look.

"Please give me your address. I'm a few hours away by car, but I can leave right away. Thank you very much."

I jotted down the woman's instructions. They were staying at an old mansion on the outskirts of the city, so I grabbed my purse and moved toward the door.

"Where are you off to, Jocelyn?"

"There's news about Antoine, and I've got to go. Can you close up for me?"

"Off with you, don't waste time here! Love is the only medicine to heal the soul. Your body is well now, but you've yet to recover your sweet smile," Céline said, ushering me off.

I had not noticed that I hadn't smiled in months. I had forgotten the dimples that were only visible when I smiled. I never put on lipstick or makeup anymore, and there was no spark in my dark eyes or shine in my brown hair, which was always pulled back in a tight bun.

I headed for the bookstore, where Denis was listening to the radio. He had very few shoppers as well.

"Can you come with me?" I asked by way of greeting.

His eyebrows shot up. "Where?"

"To Fougéres. There's a woman who has letters from Antoine, but tomorrow she's going to Bordeaux."

"Let's go!" he said, grabbing his jacket. He shooed off his customers, and we hopped into his car and sped away. The first surprising thing was that in the Saint-Servan area of town, a huge column of people carrying all sorts of wares were filing into Saint-Malo. Thankfully the lane going in the opposite direction was clear. But many people waved at us and tried to get us to stop, and a few men even tried to get into the car.

"What's going on?" I asked Denis nervously.

"They're refugees. Lots of them are escaping the battlefield and others, the steady German advance. No one knows what's going to happen when our government surrenders." He kept his eyes fixed on the road as he spoke. When we got to La Boussac, he decided to get off the main roads because they were too crowded with foot traffic. We could see people for miles around.

"Do you see these children? They look so hungry and afraid. I wish we could do something for them."

He shrugged. He understood that what was happening was much bigger than us. Where would all these people go? Who could receive them and give them food? We had put a good number of miles behind us and passed Saint-Brice-en-Coglès when we heard airplanes coming: two fighter planes. The people on the street ran for their lives, diving down on both sides of the road. Denis turned the steering wheel hard and guided the car into the woods by the road. Bullets started raining down, people screamed all around, and I glanced up and saw shrapnel hit a wagon pulled by two horses. The animals reared and neighed with terror before falling to the ground in their own blood.

"Dear God!" I screamed and covered my eyes. Denis lost control of the car and crashed it against a tree. His head rammed into the steering wheel.

I got out and ran around to his side of the car. "Are you okay?"

"It hurts," he said, his hand moving toward a gash in his forehead. I pressed a clean handkerchief to the wound and secured it with his hat, then helped him out of the smoking car. The planes continued flying low and shooting at the crowd, who ran for their lives.

I made to leave the woods, but Denis held me back. "What's wrong with you? You'll be killed."

A woman with two children was running through the wheat field nearby. The plane hovered right behind her and started to fire.

"Over here!" I yelled and waved for her. She looked up and saw me, picked up her smaller child, and made her way toward us. She had only taken a few steps when the bullets reached them. Despite Denis's warnings, I ran out toward them. I could feel the bullets pulverizing the wheat all around me as I ran toward her and her little ones. When I got to them, I turned the woman over. Her face was bloody, and a young child in her arms looked up at me in terror, also completely covered in blood. I picked him up and he cried, then he closed his eyes. I stayed on my knees in the middle of the unripe wheat, weeping and holding that little boy. His sister, who must have been around four, clung in silence to the skirts of her lifeless mother.

"Leave him, he's gone!" Denis said. Amid the horror, he had run up behind me. He reached for the girl and ran with her to the trees. One of the fighter planes turned to make a final round, but for some reason it did not return. It disappeared as we reached the car. Denis tried to start the engine, but it would not turn over.

We saw a house some distance away and walked toward it with the girl. A fence surrounded the farm. We opened the gate and went up the drive until we stood in front of the main building. A middle-aged man came out holding a gun and kept it trained on us as he waved for us to go away.

"Sir, this child is scared. Her mother was just . . ." Denis could not finish the phrase.

"She's not my problem. Vagabonds have been swarming around here since yesterday, stealing my eggs and chickens. They even killed one of my cows. You'd best be moving along," he warned.

"They aren't vagabonds, they're refugees. The Germans are advancing, and the people are trying to escape. The Germans will be here sooner rather than later," I said, annoyed at this man.

"That's not my problem. I already faced the Boche in the Great War and beat them, but I'm not going to stand here and let a band of thieves steal my family's food."

A woman came up behind him, and her disheveled appearance indicated to me that the farm had been none too prosperous. Then three barefoot boys looked out from behind her skirts. The woman touched the farmer's shoulder, and his eyes flicked to her while he kept the gun pointed at us.

"Please," she said.

He lowered the gun. The woman came out of the house and approached us. She opened her arms and picked up the girl. "We'll take care of her and bury her family. Don't worry about her, and may God bless you." Two tears made their way down her pink cheeks as she spoke. Her green eyes shone with effort as she held the girl close. "Maybe you're the daughter I've always wanted."

"Please, we've got to get to Fougères. Could we—"

"There's an old bicycle in the barn. It's the only thing I can offer you. We need the horses for the land, and besides, they're too old to ride."

"Thank you," I said to the woman. The girl sucked on her thumb and watched me with her wide eyes, but at least she had stopped crying. I stroked her blond hair once, then Denis and I turned and walked away.

6

People on the Run

Fougères
June 9, 1940

The medieval city, surrounded by green pastures and forest, was besieged by the multitude of refugees and military vehicles. People had thrown together makeshift dwellings or were stretched out on blankets, as if spending a pleasant day at a picnic. Yet their dirty, exhausted faces reflected the fatigue and fear of their state. We went through the main gate and down a street with half-timbered medieval houses toward a seventeenth-century mansion beside a lake. Soldiers had taken it over for the residence of those in high command. We parked the bicycle and walked up the stairs.

"Where do you think you're going?" a potbellied corporal with a thick black mustache asked us.

"We've come to see Mrs. Vien, she has some letters—"

"The marshal's daughter is in that smaller house out front," he said, pointing.

We crossed the lawn, and the decorative flower beds and fruit trees throughout the yard lent the air an undeniable sense of peace. Ivy climbed up the walls of the house and fell luxuriously back down. We knocked at the door.

A fortysomething-year-old woman, with an elegant hairstyle and dress, opened the door. She seemed more ready to host a formal dinner than to flee to southern France.

"Are you Sgt. Ferrec's wife?" she asked me after staring a moment at Denis.

I said I was, and she led us inside. The home was decorated in a distinctively English style, with armchairs upholstered in yellow plaid fabric, dark wooden furniture, and matching curtains. The woman had been enjoying tea and invited us to join her.

"I'm so sorry I couldn't get you the letters before," she began, "but getting out of Paris was a nightmare. If you think what you've seen around here is bad, it's a living hell around the capital. There's simply no national government anymore, and chaos has taken hold. People say they want to rebuild the government from Africa in order to take the country back, but that's really just their excuse to get out and save themselves."

"They're cowards," Denis huffed.

"Much worse, sir: they're traitors. The army wants to keep fighting, but the politicians don't have the guts. Wait just a moment," she said, standing. Her satin dress outlined her svelte figure, far from the frumpy, blond housewife I had envisioned when we talked on the phone.

From a secretary desk she pulled a bundle of letters wrapped with twine and handed it to me. "My husband managed to mail them from Sedan before they were completely surrounded. It seems your husband was wounded, and my husband took him by car as far as Sedan hoping they would send him to the rearguard, but then they were captured. They've been taken to Germany. We can only hope they'll be sent back if this war ever ends."

"Thank you," I managed to say, blinded by worry. The woman took my hand in an unexpected gesture of tenderness.

"They're strong; they know how to take care of themselves. They'll be back with us very soon. Men go off to war, and our job is to wait for them with cowering hearts. Then they receive the medals and honors while we put up with their bad moods and war stories. Surely everything will be all right. They'll come home in a few months."

I took a deep breath and thanked her again for her kindness. Then, getting to my feet, I said, "We don't want to impose. I'm sure you've so much to do."

"How will you get back to Saint-Malo? The buses aren't running, you'll never get a taxi, and it's nearly night. Why don't you stay here? I'll ask my father to get you on a transport headed for Saint-Malo tomorrow."

"Thank you, but we don't want to overstay our welcome."

"Mrs. Ferrec—Jocelyn—we women must help each other. You two can get washed up; I think I have clothes that will fit you. We'll eat at the main house in an hour. Most of them are boring old military men, so your company would be a treat to me."

In the end, we accepted her invitation. Denis put on an old tuxedo of our host's father, and I donned an evening gown. Mrs. Vien walked into my room as I was studying myself in the mirror.

"Jocelyn, you're a lovely woman, but you haven't put on any

makeup. Here, let me," she said, lining my lips and eyes and applying blush. When I looked back at the mirror, I hardly recognized myself. There was the bright, happy, young woman from a year ago.

"Beautiful!" Mrs. Vien pronounced. "Just for tonight, if the damned Nazis let us, let's forget about the war and enjoy this fleeting moment. Those monsters have imprisoned our husbands, but they can't be masters of our goodwill, don't you agree?"

The Vien children were already asleep in one of the rooms. She went in to kiss them and leave some last instructions for the caretaker. Then we walked through the dimly lit yard toward the big house that shone like a gem in the darkness.

A band played in the main hall, and officers spoke in friendly tones near the dining room. The war seemed like an ephemeral dream, as did the hundreds of thousands of refugees traveling the streets of France trying to flee their own fears. I thought about how the rich and powerful never lose a war; they can adapt to any circumstance, as if pain and suffering were never meant for them.

Half an hour later, after champagne, we sat down to eat. At least fifty guests, most of them high-ranking military officers, were seated around the massive table.

One official stood and commanded attention. "Gentlemen, I admonish you not to talk about the war tonight. First, out of respect for these ladies, and second, because it's pointless to keep pressing the government to fulfill their responsibilities. The only one with any balls in the whole cabinet is Marshal Pétain. Let's toast to him and to a France free of communists and traitors!"

All the men stood to toast. Denis hesitated; he did not want to stand out, but he raised his glass without enthusiasm. Mrs. Vien and I stayed seated. "Don't let them bother you," she whispered. "These old military geezers still fantasize about a government run by knights and gentlemen. The old Napoleonic spirit runs strong here."

I tried to stay unnoticed throughout dinner, but our hostess's father eventually turned to me and said, "You must be the wife of Sgt. Ferrec. It seems he was wounded during a heroic act. We need more men like your husband in France."

"Heroism is just selfishness," I said before I could stop myself.

The marshal opened his eyes wide, trying to take in my meaning.

Denis jumped in. "Heroism, as most men understand it, is risking one's life with courage and sacrifice to gain a position, trap enemies, or save a wounded companion. Heroes seek glory, but just a few hours ago I saw this woman here run out between the German bullets to save a woman and her two young children. She couldn't save the mother, and one of the children died in her arms. She wasn't playing at war. Women aspire to something higher, Marshal; they aspire to bring men into the world, educate them, and set them free."

Denis's words touched me. A long, uncomfortable silence overtook the table until the marshal stood and bowed in salute. "I congratulate you, madame. You deserve a medal as well."

"Jocelyn, you've won my deepest admiration. Wise men seek death their whole lives and therefore are unafraid of it. This librarian has given us all a lesson, gentlemen. While we're toasting an old regime, the people are suffering," Mrs. Vien said, her voice wavering with restrained tears.

That night I came to understand how blind and deaf the ones who were supposed to guard France were, and I was afraid for Denis and myself and for our whole country.

Within weeks, as the elderly died in their beds with their shiny medals and the next generation reaped what the old guard had sown, the children cheered the Nazi soldiers who marched down the streets of French towns and cities to become our new masters.

7

Burning the Past

Saint-Malo
June 17, 1940

The rumor that the Germans had already entered Fougères and that Rennes was next on their list sent panic running like wildfire through Saint-Malo. To avoid destruction, Paris had been declared an open city, and our army withdrew from all its defense positions. We knew it was only a matter of time before Saint-Malo would be taken; its fortresses and strategic location were well-known.

Everyday staples grew hard to find. Besides the lack of basic supplies, the number of refugees staying in schools, monasteries, public buildings, and private homes continued to increase. Many of my neighbors were uncomfortable, if not altogether indignant, with the presence of outsiders. Though she lived alone and had plenty of room to spare, Mrs. Fave did nothing but complain; meanwhile, Mrs. Remarque welcomed a woman with a baby into her apartment at no charge.

Since our return from Fougères, Denis had found a way to get his car back. Meanwhile I had thrown myself into the work of helping as many as possible. Céline and I had outfitted the library to house about a dozen people; a family of four was living in my apartment; and every day at noon I helped at the church's soup kitchen.

That morning I was trying to buy food at our dwindling market, but most of the farmers no longer tried their luck on the roads. The Germans would shoot at any moving vehicle, which had the effect of clearing the roads for the first time in many days. One of the few farmers at the market, a stout man over seventy, was selling his last few potatoes.

"Could you lower the price any?" I asked. "I have a family of refugees living with me, and their two children are very thin."

"Madame, I can't give this food away. I'm just a poor farmer myself," he said, taking his black beret off and wiping his brow.

"Please, for charity's sake," I begged. The man shrugged, and I ended up paying four times more for the potatoes than I had a few days ago. I lugged the bag back home, but before I got to my door, I ran into Mrs. Fave in the stairwell.

"Good day," she nearly spat from beneath her furrowed brow.

"Good day," I replied pleasantly.

"Are you taking those loafers more food? They'd better head back to where they came from. They're certainly no worse for the wear here in Brittany. How I wish this war would end—it's anarchy! And the last thing we need is for the communists to take over."

"The Germans are just a few miles away from Saint-Malo," I said.

"And what else would you expect? Our soldiers are a bunch of cowards, the whole lot of them giving up."

"Mrs. Fave, my husband—"

"I'm not talking about your husband, Mrs. Ferrec," she interrupted. "Antoine is a good man, though I don't know why he married a Huguenot like you. One could tell from a mile away that you're one of those independent modern women, a freethinker always surrounded by books."

I blushed but could not think of a response. I simply nodded and passed by, carrying my sack of potatoes. I knocked at the door, and Jean, the father of the family, opened it. The Prousts had come from Paris. Jean was a shoemaker with his own shop, and his wife took care of the children.

"Let me help you," he said, taking the sack from me.

We went to the kitchen where Susan, his wife, was making soup. She was delighted to see the potatoes and started washing and peeling them right away. She got out a little oil to add. After several days of only bread, the children would have a feast tonight.

"Where are the Germans heading?" Jean asked.

"They're very close. Sounds like they're headed for Rennes tomorrow, then they'll surely be here the next day."

Jean massaged his temples. "What a nightmare. We got out of Paris, but I don't know what else to do. I was active in the Communist Party when I was younger, so I know the police will still have my file. When the Germans take over, they'll lock me up. Plus, my mother was a Jew, and we all know what the Nazis do with Jews."

"Please don't worry, Jean. Nothing will happen to you. The police would never collaborate with the Nazis," I said firmly.

"Why do you say that? How can you know?" he asked, sinking into a kitchen chair.

"My husband is a police officer. He's a patriot, and he would resist."

Susan looked up. "You'd be wise to destroy anything that could compromise your position. We burned the pictures of my grandparents and a copy of the Torah. They were Jews, and from what we've heard, the Nazis hate the Jews."

"I don't have anything to hide," I said, though I was not actually so sure. We had heard on the radio how the Nazis censored everything and controlled the media.

Eventually I went to my room and looked through my papers. Most of what I had were report cards, academic diplomas, my qualification exams for library work, and other innocuous things of that nature. I had never joined a political party, and I was not officially part of any church or union. My husband and I had voted for progressive parties, but we were not registered with any. Then my eyes landed on my letters from Antoine.

Since Mrs. Vien had given them to me, I had read the letters dozens of times. After going so long without news from him, I had finally learned how he had been doing—though the letters were only dated up to May 16, merely a month ago, when they were transferring him because of a serious injury. Then a new fear gripped me: What if the Nazis did not give medical care to wounded enemy soldiers? Would they have left him to die? If he were dead, I would not know until the war was over. Germans did not give out information about their prisoners, the French government was in shambles, and rumors were running rampant that Marshal Pétain would take the reins and sign an armistice.

I opened the first letter and began to read again:

Dear Jocelyn,

I've been trying to write you for days now, but things are getting increasingly difficult here on the front. Chaos abounds. Soldiers and officers are deserting, and there's hardly ever a break from German offense. It's as though they're possessed with the spirit of attacking, which we certainly do not have.

Civilians are trying to escape the crossfire. I've had chances to speak with refugees from Holland and Luxembourg, and their stories would turn your stomach. Their cities have been bombed, and tanks are destroying farmland, villages, and everything in their way. If the war lasts much longer, there won't be anything, *anything*, still standing with which to rebuild the world.

We've only been in combat for a few days, but morale is already low. The British are falling back, equally as uninterested in fighting as we are; the Belgians are still trying to wrap their heads around how their country was reduced to nothing in a matter of days; there are very few Dutch soldiers, and most have surrendered to the Germans.

It won't be long 'til the Boche reach Paris and then all of France. Please be careful. Don't try to resist. I know your temperament and how you don't tolerate injustice.

My love for you is eternal. I'm trying my best to survive so I can see you again and return to your side.

Yours forever,

Antoine

The other five letters were even sadder. His injury and the hopelessness of being trapped on the front surely made him fear for his life and assume we would never see each other again.

Dear Jocelyn,

I've been sick for several days. They got me in the shoulder; it didn't seem serious at first, but it has become infected. I've had a high fever for several nights running, and antibiotics are hard to come by. Captain Vien is trying to help me. He's heading back to Paris, as his family is moving south; and thanks to his father-in-law, they've changed his position with the government.

I haven't been sleeping. Bombs are going off close to the hospital, and there are cadavers everywhere I turn. I hope I survive, though that thought feels selfish with so many dying around me. Why should I live when they can't?

I miss you. When the pain lets me, I think about our window looking out to the sea where we would sit and read together.

I hope you're all right. I beg God for your recovery and for a day when we may see each other again.

Forever yours,
Antoine

His last letter mentioned securing a vehicle, but I already knew they had not made it out of Sedan.

I quit the room with the letters in my skirt pocket. The Prousts were seated and waiting for me to eat, but I had lost my appetite. I excused myself and went to see Denis. I knew I would find him at the bookstore at that hour. And, if not, he would be in the apartment above, where he lived his hermit life.

I walked through the deserted streets, puzzled at not meeting anyone. Of late the town had bustled with life and activity. Refugees of several nationalities, most of them middle-class, were everywhere. The hotels were full, as were the rental properties along the beach. Most private homes were housing some of the poorer evacuees in a demonstration of generosity that both shocked me and aroused my admiration. War brought out both the best and the worst in us.

I went in the bookstore and found Denis in his seat behind the counter, as usual, with the radio on and a book in his hand.

"How can you read and listen at the same time?" My question came out more like an accusation.

"Practice," he said with a wry smile.

"Any news?" I asked.

"Yes, I'm afraid the Boche will douse Saint-Malo in a bloodbath. They've just bombed Rennes and hit the train station. It's all death and chaos. They even hit a convoy of ammunition and a passenger train. They're bloody animals!"

"Are you sure? I thought the city would surrender without resisting. Why bother fighting? The government's in Bordeaux about to escape by ship!" I was furious.

Denis shrugged. Nothing made sense in war.

I went on. "The family staying with me said I should destroy any compromising documents."

He cocked his eyebrows at me. "Why?"

"They say the Nazis are chasing down anyone who's belonged to the Communist or Socialist Parties, or who's a Jew, or been in a union . . ."

"Well then, I'm a goner. I'm a socialist Jew who's part of the French booksellers' union."

"Give me your papers. We'll burn them in the courtyard."

"But they'll have my card at the union office and the party office, not to mention the fact that being a Hebrew can't exactly be erased."

"Don't be stupid. We need to keep a low profile. They'll probably only be here a few months, then they'll move on after a peace agreement is signed."

"You think so? They haven't 'moved on' from Poland, Norway, Denmark, or Czechoslovakia. The Germans are an occupying army, and now we're their slaves."

His words shook me to the core. Could that be true? Would the Germans stay in France indefinitely? Nothing like this had ever happened before. We had a long tradition of war with the Prussians, but they had never invaded us for very long.

"Well, we should burn all of it anyway. To keep us safe."

We went upstairs for Denis to get his documents and papers, then carried them to the interior courtyard of his building and placed everything in a pile.

"The Nazis have forbidden so many of the books I have in the store. Should we burn all of them too?"

"No, let's hope they don't enforce their laws here. This is still France, the land of the free."

Denis doused the papers with gasoline and then threw a match onto the pile, which licked eagerly into flame. My hand grasped the letters in my pocket, but I did not want to add them. It was just correspondence between a soldier and his wife.

"You don't have anything to burn?" Denis asked.

I shook my head and then looked up at the windows. Smoke was filtering out of many of them. The chimneys were busy that June afternoon, and not because of a cold snap. The lives of thousands of people were burning up in that instant: family photos, papers, diplomas, memories, and incriminating documents. France was trying to erase its past, hoping the Germans would be content to steal our memories, yet fearing they would rip out our hearts as well.

8

The Speech

T he war was lost, or at least that is how we all felt. The government was paralyzed, and the previous day Marshal Pétain
had requested the cessation of hostility on all fronts. For many,
the marshal was a war hero and a prudent sage, but Denis and I
thought he was the very worst of France. The previous government
had been forced to resign, and the more conservative and re-
actionary strains of the nation seemed to be the only ones capable
of assuming control. They all thought the Third Republic was
a failure, especially with the leftward swing of the final stage.
Since the French Revolution we had been two nations at odds:
the agrarian and the urban, the conservative and the revolutionary, the one that defended human rights and the one that sought

to restore the values of the old regime. Throughout the Third Republic, which followed the Second Empire, the positions had only grown more distanced.

Walking to the library, I passed by a window and caught snatches of what seemed to be the inflamed speech of some politician. When I made it to my building, Céline was paying close attention to the radio.

"Another speech? Don't tell me it's the old marshal again."

"No, it's General de Gaulle."

That caught my attention. It was a name I did not recognize. Céline motioned for me to sit beside her.

France is not alone! She is not alone! She is not alone! She has a vast Empire behind her. She can align with the British Empire that holds the sea and continues the fight. She can, like England, use without limit the immense industry of United States . . .

I, General de Gaulle, currently in London, invite the officers and the French soldiers who are located in British territory or who would come there, with their weapons or without their weapons, I invite the engineers and the special workers of armament industries who are located in British territory or who would come there, to put themselves in contact with me.

Whatever happens, the flame of the French resistance must not be extinguished and will not be extinguished.

"Did you hear what he said?" Céline was indignant.

"Yes, he's calling on us to resist, to not give in to the Germans," I answered.

"Well, that's easy to say from London, don't you think? Why did he run away?"

"Who is General de Gaulle?"

She stared at me in disbelief. "Where have you been the past year?"

Her question took me aback. She knew perfectly well that all autumn and winter I had been at death's door because she herself had spent many nights at my side taking care of me. "Well, to be frank, when you're on the brink of death you don't have the luxury of paying attention to what's going on around you," I huffed. Sometimes Céline could be so insensitive.

"General de Gaulle is accusing the government of treason and of selling our nation, insinuating this whole thing is a coup d'état. No ordinary military man does that. He was the undersecretary of war and led an armored division, but he went to London and now wants to raise an army against the Germans."

"Well, I don't hate the sound of that. We've hardly fought at all, and our leaders have betrayed us." I knew I was not alone in thinking this way.

"But the people don't want more war. The Germans will demand reparations and then let us get on with our lives. It's the politicians, not the military, who've gotten us to this point," Céline said.

I didn't want to argue, so I quietly slipped my jacket back on and went out for a walk. At the Bastion de la Hollande I stopped to watch the ocean. The day was so indifferent to the matters of humanity that I wondered why we thought we were so important. We must have seemed like a species of ants to the immense universe we inhabit.

"Where are you, my love?" I shouted into the wind, knowing there would be no reply. I was sorry I had gotten all muddled with Céline. Politics was a horrible subject that could stir up all sorts of strife and do away with a good friendship or even a nation. Then I headed back home. A cold wind had blown in, and the dark clouds that had gathered at the horizon felt like the dark years that were looming over France.

"Resist," I told myself. But how could someone like me stand up to the Germans? I was just a simple, small-town librarian who loved books and wanted more than anything to be back with her husband again.

9

German Boots

Saint-Malo
June 23, 1940

My father always said we should make our lives something to be proud of, and I had always wondered what he meant. I knew he was not talking about being famous or always winning. What he wanted to impress upon me was how important it was for our lives to matter, for life to be worth the effort. But what was life? Sometimes it seemed to me like an absurdity. Yet, contrary to what I had thought, the arrival of the Nazis filled my life with meaning. We all need purpose, to know that we are in this world to fulfill a mission. Very soon I would learn mine, what fate had been preparing me for all this time.

The day the Germans entered Saint-Malo, I was in the library. Most of the French refugees had voluntarily returned to their homes, including the Prousts and the families that were staying in the library. The peace accords signed by the new president Pétain meant there was no reason not to return to their cities.

Céline and I were busy cleaning and trying to restore order among the stacks. Though I often felt weak, especially during physical exertion like exercise or climbing stairs, my illness had nearly gone away. I was dusting shelves when we heard a commotion, so we ran to the windows that faced the street and saw a column of German soldiers marching by. The echoing of their boots on the cobblestone street dominated the air. The ground shook as they lifted and dropped their legs, and their heels clacked against the stones, declaring their intention to stay. Two luxuriously uniformed officers led the formation, oozing martial virility in their gait. They halted in front of our city hall, and one officer gave the order for the soldiers to fall out. The Germans then spread out all over town. They seemed relaxed and upbeat, like a group of students on an end-of-term trip who want to enjoy themselves and tell their friends all about it when they get home.

People watched them in fear, looked away, walked to the other side of the sidewalk, or shut up their homes and locked the doors and windows. I grabbed my purse and headed for Denis's bookstore. I was afraid the Boche would enter the bookstore and do something to him.

On my way, two German soldiers whistled at me. In time we women grew used to this kind of behavior. They would catcall anything in a skirt that was older than twelve and younger than fifty. So few young men remained in our town. Most had gone off to fight, and a few were hiding out waiting to see how events unfolded.

I found the bookstore locked when I arrived. I rang the bell to Denis's apartment, but there was no answer. I began to worry, but I figured he had gone to a friend's house or perhaps to see his parents, who lived just outside of town. Passing through an alley on my way home, I saw three soldiers bothering a schoolgirl.

"What are you doing to her?" I asked in French. Though they would not understand my words, my tone was clear. Instead of stopping, they turned their attention to me and grabbed my arms.

One of the soldiers said something I could not understand, but as they dragged me to the back of the alley, I understood I had now become their target. "Let go of me, you pigs!" I screamed, lashing out with my fists and kicking as hard as I could. Yet they seemed to enjoy my screams, knowing no one would come to my aid.

One of the soldiers started kissing my neck and pulling up my skirt. I wept at my powerlessness and rage. I could not believe what was happening.

Suddenly a loud voice barked a command in German, then shouted in French: "Let those women go!"

The soldiers released me and jumped to attention. As I rushed away, I met the eyes of the officer who had reprimanded his men. He was tall with black hair and brown eyes and very white skin.

"I'm so sorry, mademoiselles. These soldiers will be disciplined, and this will not happen again."

Hearing him speak in French, I frowned and said, "They're barbarians. This is unacceptable among civilized people." I had not yet come to comprehend what this war was. Despite the existence of certain norms, at the core, barbarianism and cruelty were the only language of the conquerors.

"My apologies. Do not worry, these men will be punished."

The schoolgirl took off running without glancing back, and

my body trembled as I walked away. I fought to swallow back the knot in my throat and hold on to my tears. Once in my apartment, I threw myself on the bed and thought of Antoine. If he had been with me, those men would never have dared touch me. Yet then I realized even his presence would have been pointless: If Antoine had tried to defend me, they would have killed him easily.

I picked up a book to help me calm down. Night had still not fallen completely, and through the picture window I could see the ocean changing hues. Like the city, it was cloaked in a darkness much more sinister than a mere lack of sunlight.

Right then I decided to start writing the story of my life, starting with my wedding day. I filled up page after page that night. But the fact that most people are capable of writing things down does not make them writers. That is when I realized that you, Mr. Zola, are the one who should edit this story. I would never be able to. The power of words does not lie in the stories we tell but in our ability to connect with the hearts of those who read them.

10

Vichy

I had never considered myself patriotic, perhaps because if you really love your country there's no need to surround yourself with its symbols or brag about your origins. For me, France was the interminable forests, the towns bursting with flowers, the great cities with their beautiful cathedrals, the magisterial eighteenth-century palaces, wine, bread, Paris, good food, and—most of all—the people: the baker who rose at dawn to bake his delicious bread and fill our streets with tempting aromas; the fisherman who got his nets ready at the dock, spent the night at sea, and hurried to the harbor market in the morning to sell his catch to a housewife or a chef; the seamstress who designed her patterns from Parisian magazines and dreamed of becoming the next Coco Chanel; the rural teacher who helped children dream by reading aloud Dumas's books or mesmerized them with stories of the scientist Marie Curie or the Sun King, Louis XIV.

Thus, what pained me most during the early days of the occupation were not the ration cards—many people thought these would help keep the cost of basic supplies from skyrocketing—nor the detestable Boche everywhere one turned. What pained me most was their attempt to squash the French soul.

As I walked down the Rue de la Fosse, I came to the small plaza and saw two Germans on tall ladders. I stood watching them, and a woman passing by stopped and huffed to me, "Can you believe this? They're changing the clock to Berlin time. Unbelievable. Where will we end up? I, for one, have no intention of heeding these monsters. Unthinkable!"

Two schoolboys stopped to watch for a moment but then continued on to school.

I caught the words of a passerby who muttered, "This is insanity."

I was headed to city hall since we had all been ordered to appear and be issued identification and ration coupons. Also, they would assign us a German to house.

A long line snaked around the building by the time I arrived. People were huffing and puffing, some even complaining aloud, yet most just waited stoically.

"Are you the end of the line?" I asked an elderly man who was waiting with a shotgun slung over his shoulder.

"Yes, madame. I've been here half an hour and have hardly moved an inch. I've come from Saint-Père to turn in my gun. Did you hear the Germans won't allow us to have guns anymore? So no more duck hunting."

This was news to me. The man noted my surprise and pointed

to a sign attached to the front of city hall. "There's a list of new German rules." It was long—surrendering radio receptors and firearms; restrictions on food, clothing, and shoes; requirements for housing German officers . . .

A woman got in line behind me. Her head hung low, and dark circles dampened the intense green of her eyes. She was so thin and sickly that I, who had only started to regain the weight I had lost from tuberculosis, seemed hefty beside her. "Are you all right?" I asked her.

"Yes, just tired." Her accent was different. "I'm not from here. I've come from Lorraine. The Germans are deporting people and have annexed the province."

"I'm so sorry," I said.

"We have nothing left," the woman said, forcing her tears back. "A family outside Saint-Malo took us in on their farm, but we had to leave and make room for a noncommissioned officer. I don't know what we're going to do or where we'll go." She was wringing her hands in desperation.

Two soldiers came up from one end of the street leading their German shepherds on short leashes. The dogs were almost uncontrollable, jumping and biting at the air in every direction. Everyone moved to give them a wide berth as they passed.

The soldiers stopped in front of one man who was particularly cowed in fear. "Documentation!" one of the soldiers barked. The man put a trembling hand to his jacket and brought out his passport.

"Polish! A dirty Jew. You can't be here," the soldier said.

"I have refugee status," the man answered shakily. His dark, limp hair hung around his face, and he was disturbingly thin. His clothes must have grown two sizes too large in his attempt to escape the Nazis.

"Non-French have lost any and all status. Come with us."

Instead, the man took off running. The soldiers released the hounds, who set to the chase. The man had barely reached the end of the block when the first dog knocked the man to the ground and the other sank its teeth into his leg. The poor man called in pain, but none of us made a move. We barely breathed or blinked, knowing the Germans might sic their dogs on any one of us next.

"God save me!" the man cried as the dogs tore at him and his clothes turned red with blood. I took a step forward just as the two soldiers reached the poor man.

"What do you think you are doing?" they asked in French. "Now you've become a problem."

Just then Dr. Aubry approached the soldiers and spoke in their language. The authority with which he spoke to them confused and silenced them, at least for a moment.

"Please," Dr. Aubry said to a man who was passing by with a cart. The man emptied the cart and helped the doctor lift the bleeding Pole into it.

One of the soldiers said, "We have to take this man to the citadel."

"He's injured. Come for him in a few days," the doctor said in a voice that allowed no questions. Together with the cart owner, they rolled the poor man away.

A smile spread over the faces of us who waited in line. Dr. Aubry had done what none of us dared.

The line started moving faster, and an hour later I had made it inside city hall. A young woman was seated at a desk behind a stack of papers so high I could hardly see her eyes.

"Mrs. Ferrec, you're currently living alone in your home, correct?"

"Yes, my husband is a prisoner of war."

"You'll have to house a German officer. His name is Adolf Bauman."

"But I'm a woman living alone. The neighbors, what will people—"

"These are orders. He will move into your house tomorrow. You must provide him with a room, food, and shelter. Understood?"

"But . . ."

The woman handed me a bundle of papers and hurried me along. The woman from Lorraine looked at me with anger burning in her eyes. She had no idea what would happen to her and her family.

The Vichy regime had handed France over to her enemies. Though they supposedly governed "Free France," the reality was we no longer had a country. We were slaves in our own homes, ruled by our new masters, with no right to protest or resist.

11

Officers in Black

Saint-Malo
June 26, 1940

Little is worse than feeling unsafe in your own home. That morning I got up very early, cleaned up the house, prepared the guest room for the German officer, and made breakfast. It was only eight o'clock when I looked at the clock, so I made some coffee and sat down by the big window to read. I did not want to think about what it would be like to have a complete stranger living with me, an enemy who could do whatever he wanted to me and be held to no account. I took a deep breath and tried to concentrate on my book. Reading had always been my escape, even when I had been close to death. When I had finally calmed down enough to concentrate on the story, the doorbell rang. I sprang up and ran to the entryway. Straightening my hair and clothes, I opened the door. The lighting on the landing was always poor, but I could tell the German was dressed in all black. He wore a leather coat and tall leather boots. A suitcase stood beside him, and he held a black leather briefcase.

"Is this the Ferrec home?" he asked in French with a thick German accent.

I nodded. The pressure building up in my chest had stopped my speech.

"May I come in, or will you leave me standing here all morning?" Before I could answer, he picked up his suitcase and brushed by me.

I did not know if he could see how I trembled, but I tried to calm myself. Nazis, like dogs, could smell fear.

"This is your house? Which room will be mine?" His tone was as arrogant as his questions. I led him to the room I had so carefully prepared for him. With a quick glance at it, he spat out, "Do I look like some kind of beggar?" Then he strode down the hall to the room I shared with Antoine, which was larger and looked out to the sea. He dropped his suitcase on the bed, opened the window, and took a deep breath.

"I'll stay here," he announced. "I take my breakfast at six a.m., lunch at noon on the dot, and supper at six p.m. I despise tardiness, noise, and the smallest hint of disrespect. Do you have a record player?"

I was stunned by his words but managed to say, "Yes, sir."

"When I return for lunch, I will expect to find the record player here in this room. What do you have in your hand?" He was looking at me with such disgust that I wanted to drop the book like a burning coal.

"A novel," I answered.

"I can see that."

"It's *The Magic Mountain* by Thomas Mann."

He frowned and crossed his arms, then grabbed the book from me and flipped through it cursorily.

"Don't you know that this degenerate author is forbidden in Germany?"

"No, I had no idea," I said honestly. I had heard about the Nazi book purges and how they burned thousands of books when Hitler came to power, but I did not know which authors had been outlawed by the regime.

"You'll need to remove these books from your home."

I thought for a moment about all the books we had in the library. How many of those would this officer find unworthy of being read? How many would he force me to destroy?

"I've read your file," he continued. "Your husband is a police officer and you're a librarian. You're not associated with any political party, and you seem like decent enough folk, but that isn't enough. France belongs to us now, and certain things we will not tolerate. This will not happen again." Without a word he threw the book out the window toward the ocean. Then he dismissed me from the room.

I trembled all the way to the kitchen, where I sat on a stool and tried to calm down. I had to warn Denis as soon as possible. They would find his bookstore sooner rather than later.

Adolf Bauman, my new housemate, walked out of the room and left the house without saying goodbye. I sighed with relief. It was time for work, but first I had to stop by the bookstore and see Denis.

———— ◆ ————

The morning was warm, but that was not why I was sweating under my heavy winter coat; it was for the shame I had just endured in my own home.

I knocked loudly at the bookstore. The light was on, but the door was not yet unlocked for the public.

"What's going on? Why so early?" Denis asked. I went in and slouched against the counter, crying like a nervous child while my friend tried to comfort me. "Has something happened with Antoine?" he asked.

Denis and Antoine had been inseparable friends since they were boys, even getting crushes on the same girls, though their mutual loyalty stopped them from betraying each other for romance. I was like a sister Denis needed to take care of until Antoine returned.

"The German I have to house came today, and he's worse than I imagined. He's arrogant and has horrible manners and took possession of the house like it belonged to him . . ." I lapsed into tears again.

"What's going on?"

"He saw the book I was reading and threw it out the window. *The Magic Mountain* by Thomas Mann."

Denis rolled his eyes. "Mann is condemned in Germany. He was one of the first intellectuals to go into exile, and with good reason. Those barbarians are out to destroy Western civilization. The only thing they understand is brute force. Social Darwinism has taken up residence in their obtuse, backward brains."

I did not care right then about the diatribes of Nazi propaganda. I was scared—for Antoine and now for myself and my loved ones. The occupation had seemed annoying, an irritation, at first; yet I was starting to feel a noose around my country's neck. Every time a French citizen stood up to the system, the Nazi regime would not think twice about destroying us. The noose would squeeze tighter and tighter.

"What are we going to do? It's not a problem to take some of the more dangerous books up to the attic of my building, but will they come for the books in the library?"

"Of course they will," Denis said matter-of-factly. "And we can respond in one of two ways: disobeying or accepting their orders. The truth is, Jocelyn, I don't have martyr's blood in me. This won't last forever, and we have to look at it like a parenthesis in our lives. I'm hoping the United States will wake up and see how the Nazis aren't just some exotic European problem. They'll have the whole world up in flames unless somebody stops them."

"Do you know which books have been forbidden in Germany?" I asked.

"Anything written by Jews, communists, socialists, and any leftist union leader. Novels that exalt peace, equality between people, or humane values. You start pulling those books, and I'll try to get the exact list from a German colleague."

This plan calmed me down a bit. But I started shaking when I thought about going back to my apartment.

"Don't worry. Antoine will be back. I've heard that the Germans might liberate prisoners of war as an act of goodwill."

My face lit up. Could that be true? I could not wait for the day.

"It won't be long now," Denis said. "In the meantime, try to get used to this Adolf fellow who's living with you. Maybe he won't turn out to be that bad. He just wants to mark his territory. Don't forget they're like wild animals."

"He dresses in all black, his face all eaten up by smallpox . . . He has cold gray eyes, and even his smile is scary."

"He's got a black uniform?"

"Yes—what about it? I don't know much about the military ranks. Maybe he's a lieutenant. He had a skull emblem on his peaked cap."

Denis sucked in his breath and seemed to turn a shade paler. "He's an SS official. I think you won the lottery. The SS is a special Nazi force; you could say the elite of the fanatics. And they're apparently the most dangerous. Try not to make him nervous or give him any reason to arrest you. Members of the SS aren't soldiers; they're heartless murderers."

Denis's words froze my heart. The Germans had put a wolf in my house. How could I keep from provoking him?

Minutes later I headed for the library, praying for Antoine as I went. The mere thought of being in the house with that officer turned my blood cold. I burst through the library door and started prattling loudly to Céline. "So I've got a German in my house, and he's apparently an SS officer! I couldn't have asked for anything worse! Now we have to use their money, their time, their rules, and—"

Céline was gesturing for me to be quiet. I cocked my head at her and then heard a throat being cleared behind me. I turned to see a German officer holding a book. In a hoarse voice, he asked in French, "May I check out this book?"

12

The ERR

Saint-Malo
July 17, 1940

The news spread through the wind that the National Assembly had given President Pétain nearly absolute power, which made him a de facto dictator. His minister of state, Pierre Laval, was not much better than his master. Both had plowed right through constitutional rights and stripped some fifteen thousand people of their nationality, more than a third of which were of Jewish descent.

I tried to carry on with life as usual. We had hidden and locked up the most dangerous books—by authors like Karl Marx, Sigmund Freud, Franz Kafka, or Jack London—on an upper floor, and we loaned them out under strict secrecy.

Every week the officer Hermann von Choltiz checked two

books out of the library and with a nearly Swiss punctuality returned them in perfect condition. Céline and I hardly exchanged a word with him, but then one day he came in while I was alone in the library.

"I don't think you remember me," he said.

"I'm sorry, I . . ." His directness flustered me.

"You suffered a disgraceful incident with two soldiers in an alleyway."

I had tried to block the episode from my mind. I had barely glanced at the German officer who had come to my defense, but as soon as he mentioned it, I recognized him.

"Oh, that's right. I was so grateful for your help. I don't know what those brutes would've done if you hadn't intervened."

"You've no need to thank me. I hope you see that we are not all brutes, as you say—though I cannot blame your compatriots for presuming as much. We are occupying your country militarily and are, therefore, the enemy, but many of us admire French culture."

I just stood there staring. I had no idea what to say. I could tell his uniform was from the regular army, not the SS, but I trusted no German.

"I doubt you have seen me there, but I'm lodged in your building, in the home of an elderly woman, Mrs. Fave."

I was again taken by surprise. I tried to stay out of Mrs. Fave's way. She was a mean-spirited, critical busybody. She was close with my mother-in-law, and I always imagined Mrs. Fave had turned her against me.

"Oh, I didn't know," I managed to stutter.

"We keep different hours, but Lt. Bauman mentioned it to me."

This made me nervous. "Do you know each other?"

"Yes, we work together. He's in the SS. In the Battle of France he fought with the Third SS Panzer Division Totenkopf before he was transferred to the ERR, the Einsatzstab Reichsleiter Rosenberg. I was recruited by the ERR. I'm a specialist in medieval French literature."

The man kept the shocks coming, one right after the other. My face must have registered this.

"Does that surprise you?"

"Yes, absolutely. What does the ERR do?"

"We protect the cultural heritage of the occupied countries. We don't want anything to be ransacked, destroyed, or stolen. We must protect Europe's legacy."

"So you're not part of the SS?" I asked, confused.

The man smiled, and his whole face lit up. His big dark eyes slanted up a bit with the smile, and he sat down in front of my desk. "No, I'm with the Geheime Feldpolizei, the military police of the Wermacht."

For some reason I felt better knowing he was a policeman like Antoine.

"Your husband and I are in the same trade. Before the war, I worked as a policeman in Berlin. I was assigned mainly to crimes around artwork—theft, falsifications, and scams. You wouldn't believe how much fake artwork is sold and circulating."

"Why did they send you to Saint-Malo?"

Von Choltiz paused for a moment before answering. "They've sent me to protect France's cultural heritage, as I said. We must value, analyze, and care for it. Soon it will be your beautiful library's turn; we can't let a single important work get lost," he said with a smile.

"I won't allow you to touch a thing inside this library without authorization from the ministry." The firmness of my voice could only have come from my deep love for the books we housed.

The officer patted my hand as if to calm and reassure me, but his gesture only put me on greater alert. "We aren't going to steal anything, just classify it."

"And what will you do with the banned books?"

"For now, I can assure you that our orders are simply to classify. We'll start with the library in September. We'll be respectful, and I'll bring two of my best men for the job."

Von Choltiz moved his hand from where he had rested it on mine and picked up one of the books I was restoring. "A first-edition Jack London in English, *The Cruise of the Dazzler*. There aren't many of these around. It was published in 1902, and, since it was his first, they didn't print many. It's a lovely book. I read it when I was a boy in Munich."

His manner incensed me. "Isn't he one of your banned authors?" I said.

"To tell the truth, I'm not sure. I heard that Goebbels didn't like *White Fang*. You probably know that our minister of propaganda was a journalist and always dreamed of a literary career. Perhaps he's jealous of Jack London's prolific output," he said with a whimsical smile.

"Do you think it's funny? To censure and burn books? Is that what you do for a living? Your party has banned the works of Walt Whitman, Emilio Salgari, Aldous Huxley, and Ernest Hemingway. Most of those books are harmless, some even childish, and no one should be afraid of them."

Von Choltiz shifted in his seat. My comments had clearly crossed the line, and I had annoyed him. I gently took the book out of his hands and placed it on my stack, and he cleared his throat to speak. "The French are always thinking everyone is the same! How does it go? Liberty, equality, fraternity. And where has this slogan gotten us? It has nearly destroyed the world.

Riffraff thinks it has the same rights as cultured people, but the truth is, we aren't all the same. Since birth each of us has our own unique qualities and gifts."

"We may not all be the same, but we all ought to have the same rights and opportunities," I said without mincing words. I knew full well that the Nazis were unpredictable and deeply chauvinistic.

He hopped up and slapped the table in one swift motion. "If your values are so powerful, tell me why it is we're your masters now. What good have those ideas done for you? Isn't it true that the strongest and most capable always win over the weak?"

My voice shook but I did not back down. "Do you really think you and your people are the stronger ones? There's no greater act of weakness than using violence to win instead of reason, Lieutenant."

Von Choltiz shook his finger at me but reined himself in. The anger in his face calmed a bit, and he left me with a warning. "In September we will begin recording all the works held here. Please cooperate because I do not want you to suffer any harm. I am much more reasonable than Lt. Bauman. I assure you, he will not be courteous."

With that, he turned, walked out, and let the door slam behind him. I was trembling in my confusion. What had just happened? Had I really just argued with a Nazi? I had known people to disappear in the past few months for much less than that. The Germans did away with anyone whom they found problematic. Plus, also at stake was Antoine's return to me. I looked up and studied the library. The city had been collecting books for centuries. We were the soul and memory of Saint-Malo. I had to protect the library's holdings before the barbarians destroyed every last thing they could.

13

Books against Bullets

Paris
August 27, 1940

Travel during the first few months of occupation was challenging. You had to fill out pages of paperwork and have a strong, specific reason for the trip. The trains ran nowhere near their normal schedules, as the railway system's priority was now to transport agricultural and industrial products to Germany. Private vehicles were not allowed for unauthorized trips, and most gasoline was sent to fuel the Third Reich's war machines. I was lucky enough to get a permit to travel to Paris under the guise of procuring more books.

In the weeks that followed the arrival of my undesirable tenant, Lt. Bauman, I tried to be home as little as possible. The woman who helped me keep house served him his meals.

I preferred to eat in my room and avoided running into him in the hallway. The talk with Hermann von Choltiz had made me very nervous.

We had received a directive from the minister of culture informing us that all public libraries would soon be visited by the Germans and the police, at which point we were to turn over all banned books. The Nazis had created a list of prohibited works, which included dissenting Germans like Otto Strasser and Thomas Mann but also many French authors like André Malraux, Louis Aragon, Georges Duhamel, and André Chevrillon. The list included 143 titles that were not to be printed, sold, distributed, or read. All bookstores and libraries of Occupied France had to be purged, as did publishing houses and newspaper offices.

That morning I went to the capital to meet with Yvonne Oddon, one of France's leading librarians. I knew she was creating a resistance network to protect the books, but this was not my only reason for going to Paris. I was also seeking information about Antoine and searching for any way possible to bring him back home.

I went to the Musée de l'Homme, located in one of the most beautiful areas of the city. One side of it offered a breathtaking view of the Eiffel Tower, and both wings of the semicircular buildings embraced the Trocadéro Gardens. I walked by the sitting statue of Benjamin Franklin, another great lover of books and culture. The concierge at the front door hardly glanced at me when I entered, but I knew the way to Yvonne Oddon's office. I knocked, heard a key turn, and was let in.

"Wonderful, Jocelyn, we were waiting for you."

Yvonne's comment took me by surprise. What could she mean? I saw two others in the office, a man and a woman.

"Meet Boris Vildé and Agnès Humbert. You can trust them."

"But I came to—"

"Don't worry, I know what you came for. Just have a seat." Yvonne's short black hair was rather disheveled, she was dressed casually, and she seemed nervous. She continued, "We can't consent to let them despoil our heritage nor let them lock up everyone they consider a dissident. Pétain's puppet government doesn't represent us. Jocelyn, we've learned today is the day of the big book raid in France. In a few hours the Nazis and the gendarmes will seize thousands of banned books. They'll start with the bookstores and publishing houses, but within weeks they'll also have plundered the public libraries and cultural institutions."

Yvonne's face flamed with emotion as she spoke. The man, Boris, nodded, while the woman, Agnès, clenched her knuckles.

"Where will they take the confiscated books?" Boris asked.

"A police contact has told us they'll be kept in a garage on the Avenue de la Grande Armée."

I could not believe what I was hearing.

Yvonne turned to me. "What's happening in Brittany?"

"The same thing. They've started asking for the banned books. In September they'll come by the library and cart off everything on their list. It's terrible!" Eloquence failed me at the overwhelming impossibility before us. There was no foreseeable way to halt the plundering.

"Our only choice is to join forces. I fear that, under the guise of censorship and destroying the books, they will try to get their hands on really important works, the incunabulum we'll never recover if lost. Our duty is to protect them until the war is over."

We all nodded. She continued, "We'll keep in touch with you, Jocelyn. We're going to publish a clandestine newspaper we're calling *La Résistance*."

Something in what she said made me remember right then

that Yvonne came from a Huguenot family just like I did. The name of the paper, *La Résistance*, reminded me of the slogan of the Huguenot women locked up in the famous Tower of Constance at Aigues-Mortes.

A sudden knock at the door froze us. It was Paul Rivet, the museum director. "Don't fret," he reassured us while taking a seat beside me. "There's no one else in the building."

"Have you seen the group of writers?" Yvonne asked.

"Yes, they're willing and ready. There aren't many of them, just about ten, but they will create a network of smugglers to protect intellectuals and authors. For the time being, anyone under suspicion should get to the unoccupied zone. We hope the Nazi influence will be less rigorous there."

"That's a lot to hope. Pétain is a fascist no better than Hitler or Franco," Boris said.

"I've no doubt about that," Rivet explained, "but there are many French loyal to liberty who can help us. There are very few German troops in the south, and the Gestapo and the SS aren't operating there, at least not officially."

When the meeting came to an end, Yvonne walked me to the museum door, lit a cigarette, and offered me one. I politely declined, given my recent history of illness.

"I hope you find your husband," she said, blowing out a slow stream of smoke. "Now all the government offices are taken over by Nazis. We think there are around a million and a half prisoners, and they're only letting the sick ones and the youngest ones go."

———— ◆ ————

I walked away from the beautiful building with my heart heavier than it had been on my way in. I had the feeling that all was lost and questioned the point of resisting. We were a small handful of intellectuals armed only with books, which did little against bullets. I had promised Yvonne to stay in touch and that, if needed, some of us in Brittany could help smuggle out British pilots who were shot down or refugees trying to reach Portugal or England.

Paris seemed frozen in time, though much sadder than when Antoine and I had come on our honeymoon a year ago. There few people were out and about, and café patios were either empty or filled with Germans. What surprised me most was the number of women hanging around the soldiers. In the absence of young French men, the victorious Germans must have seemed irresistible to some.

I made my way to the ministry of war building. German soldiers guarded the door, and a swastika billowed over the main balcony. As I approached the information office, I could see I was not the only woman trying to discover her husband's whereabouts.

One of the women in line gave me a wry smile and said, "I can't believe we're here looking for our men. I'm not sure they would do the same for us."

"I can't say for your husband, but I know mine would."

"So then why did he go off to this damned war?"

"They made him; it was his duty; who knows? I can't begin to fathom, but if you're here it's because you want to see your husband again too," I said as gently as I could. The wryness in her smile faded, replaced by sadness.

After waiting for hours in a room crammed with women, an employee called my name. I went to an office overwhelmed with stacks of papers, and a thin man with sallow skin and round glasses told me to state my case.

When I finished, he said, "Things aren't simple. This isn't the Netherlands. French are considered inferior, if you see what I mean. Germany has taken nearly two million of our men prisoner. That's ten percent of the men in the whole country."

"I see," I managed to respond, my heart sinking.

"According to our records, your husband is in a camp called Stalag II-D northeast of Berlin. If it's true that he's injured, we'll request repatriation from the German authorities, but please hear me when I say this process can take months, and the German administration has the final word. Do you understand?"

"Yes, sir." It came out as a near-whisper.

"I've got your phone number and address. We'll be in contact when we know something. I'm sorry, Mrs. Ferrec. One of my sons is in a camp like this. We're all anxious for them to come home." His voice faltered as he spoke. I thanked him and made way for the next woman in line.

I walked through the city aimlessly until I returned to the hotel for my suitcase. The city reminded me too much of Antoine. I missed him and was scared, awash in loneliness so deep that only those who have been wholly united to another can imagine.

14

J'accuse!

Saint-Malo
August 28, 1940

I was exhausted after traveling nearly all night, but I did not want to leave Céline alone at the library anymore. The deadline was approaching, and we had to hide the banned books as soon as possible. I knocked at the door, and she opened with a cautious start.

"What's going on?" I asked, trying to shake off the stress from my trip to Paris.

"Come in. We should only talk behind closed doors. There are eyes and ears everywhere."

Her answer put me on guard, but sometimes Céline could be overly dramatic. I followed her to her desk, and she handed me a handwritten note.

"What's this?" I said, reading it quickly. The note was an accusation against me for being a communist, against Denis for belonging to the Masons and having Jewish heritage, and against Antoine for betraying the police. "Who wrote these lies?"

"There are hundreds, if not thousands, of these notes. The German authorities have asked for collaboration to help capture supposed terrorists and fugitives from the law. The employees at town hall have been overwhelmed by scads of accusations like these. People are pointing to anyone and everyone, knowing they can do so anonymously. It's a spiteful shame. These notes show the true heart of France."

I was dumbfounded. I sat down and read the note again. It was certainly a woman's handwriting, in nice cursive, though in a somewhat outdated style.

"Do you know who wrote it?" I asked, though I almost preferred not to know.

"Yes. I've been here for decades and have seen the handwriting of everyone who's filled out a library card and written a request for a book. Plus, this handwriting is unique. It's your widow neighbor, Mrs. Fave."

"Unbelievable, the old witch. We've never done anything to her."

"Happiness itself is the worst insult to vile people. Your face glowing with love, your desire to help people, your beauty—it's a terrible mess for jealousy. She's a bitter old woman. Her husband probably died because he couldn't bear to stay by her side any longer."

A rush of rage and hatred flooded through me. I had never experienced anything like this. The whole world had gone mad, and nothing would ever be the same, even if we managed to boot the Nazis out of France. We would not be able to undo how the evil had infected everything and turned our souls into a terrible poison.

Céline put her arm around my shoulder. "I'm so sorry, my dear. I've said many times how humans are evil by nature. Our beloved Enlightenment philosophers were profoundly mistaken. They thought the myth of the noble savage explained the evolution of humans, that people were essentially good until nature corrupted them. The truth is that society only pulls out of us what's really there deep in our hearts."

"But if the Nazis hadn't invaded France . . ." I tried to tease out the reasoning.

"We've never needed a foreign power to find reasons to kill our own. Think about the Hundred Years' War, the Wars of Religion . . . Louis XIV's despotic absolutism that wiped out all religious and provincial minorities, not to mention the Reign of Terror, the Napoleonic Wars, the Franco-Prussian War, the Great War, and now this. I could go on—all the massacres in Africa and Asia . . . Humanity is hell-bent upon self-destruction."

I refused to embrace such a pessimistic view of humanity. "But we've also made democracy, liberty, progress, modernity, cars, airplanes, vaccines, and other great and wonderful things," I retorted.

Céline gave me the smile one gives a child too young to understand things. Yet I did comprehend what she was saying to me; I just did not want to admit it. "I agree that we are capable of acts of goodness. But there is evil inside each one of us, which can destroy everything. Imagine the hatred you feel right now toward this wretched Mrs. Fave. If you don't channel it elsewhere, it could destroy you and compel you to do terrible things."

I grew even more serious. I did not want to admit that I was capable of abhorrent actions or recognize that the only thing separating me from the Nazis I despised was that I had been born somewhere else. I easily could have been cowardly enough to not think for myself and to let hatred, which is always the bastard child of fear, totally control me.

"Why don't you come with me to church?" Céline asked.

"You know I don't practice the faith. It's not that I don't believe in God, but, since my parents died, he and I aren't on good terms, you could say."

"I know, but in times like these we need some faith. Today Father Roth wants to share some encouraging words for Saint-Malo's residents."

In the end, after the day's work, I followed her to church. It was getting late, and I figured I might as well go with Céline instead of stewing alone at home.

The streets were nearly empty, and it did not take us long to walk to the church, where we slid into one of the back pews. Evening mass had been pushed up due to the curfew.

A few minutes later, the priest came in a side door escorted by two altar boys. Religious services had always seemed too cold and solemn for me. Even more, I was unfamiliar with the Catholic litanies. I did not know how to cross myself or when to stand or kneel. Most of the service was in Latin, and though I could read and write some Latin, my mind wandered. About twenty minutes later, after communion, the priest stood at the pulpit and began to speak.

"My dear brothers and sisters, one of the most beautiful things our Savior Jesus Christ ever said was about love for our enemies. When the Pharisees asked him which was the most important of Moses's laws, he answered that the whole law could be summed up in two commandments, which were really just one: Love God above all things and love your neighbor as yourself. But who is our neighbor? It's easy to love the people who love us, but God wants us to love even those who hate us and persecute us."

Right then a door opened, and I heard, without turning to look, the slap of German boots on the stone floor. Whoever had entered sat down in the pew right behind me and Céline.

Knowing that anything he said could get him sent before a shooting squad or to a death camp, Father Roth cleared his throat and then continued. "Classic philosophers always advised us to stay as far away from our enemies as possible. In *Works and Days*, the Greek poet Hesiod encourages inviting good friends but not enemies to a meal. Plato encourages us to do good to our friends and evil to our enemies. Jesus goes much further by telling us to *love* them. Jesus himself withstood his enemies' attacks, insults, and criticism. He knew they were chasing him down to kill him, and even from the cross he asked God to forgive his enemies because they did not know what they were doing."

A murmur ran through the crowd. The priest's words did not sit well with the people. Even those who had begun to collaborate with the Nazis found the priest's talk about loving them to be excessive.

"Vengeance had always been the method of returning evil to those who had done wrong. The lex talionis restricted vengeance to an eye for an eye, a tooth for a tooth. In the book of Tobit in our Bible, Tobit pronounces what we call the silver law, that we should not do to others what we don't want done to ourselves. Then Jesus made the golden rule of doing to others the *good* we want done to us. The most outstanding point of his message is loving our enemies, which is doubtless an invitation to heroism. No one can reject an act of love. St. Augustine said that whoever 'loves men, ought to love them either because they are righteous, or that they may become righteous.' The only way to overcome evil is with good. Such love is indeed a mystery, but Jesus is not asking us to collaborate with the evil in our neighbors, to join it, or to approve of it. Love encompasses people yet refuses to join the wicked in their wickedness—yet this is the only limit."

The priest asked us to stand for his blessing. As we turned to leave, I met the eyes of Lt. von Choltiz. He made his way toward us, and Céline stayed protectively by my side.

"Mrs. Ferrec, the last time we met, we argued. I wanted to beg your pardon."

"I didn't know you were a believer," I said with coldness.

"There's a lot you don't know about me. On September 1, my men will search the library. I've asked them to be respectful. I assure you they will cause as little nuisance as possible."

The frown on my face did not change. I could not imagine why or how he would show up and speak to me like this. "You'll do your duty, and I'll do mine," I said curtly.

"I don't want you to see me as an enemy—"

"And after Father Roth's words, that shouldn't be cause for concern."

I nodded in farewell, and Céline and I left. The congregation moved around the German officer as they exited. Only Father Roth went to greet him. I hurried home, anxious thoughts of Antoine whirling through my mind. I did not know how I was going to bear the wait for news about him.

15

Books and Stables

Saint-Malo
September 1, 1940

I could not sleep at all the last night of August. In the morning, the thing I loved most in the world after Antoine would be ripped away from me: my library. Céline had suggested we start a row among the neighbors to help protect the books, but I questioned whether human life should be put on the line for our cause. A line from Sébastian Castellio's *Contra libellum Calvini* had always stuck with me: "To kill a man is not to protect a doctrine, but it is to kill a man." Castellio had been one of the first to defend freedom of conscience and religious tolerance. The Nazis were destroying France's heart and soul, but not even a drop of blood should be shed to defend a book.

I headed for the kitchen for some coffee. My stomach was knotted tight with tension, and I could not eat. I waited for the coffeepot to finish and poured in a bit of milk. I had just taken my first sip when Lt. Bauman walked in.

"Mrs. Ferrec, I've sometimes wondered if you still live here. I hardly see you."

"Have your needs been tended to? I'm quite overwhelmed at work and go straight to bed when I get home."

He smiled with malice. "I'm sure your hard work is all for naught. Today is the big day. My men will be at your library, and I hope you cooperate with us. I would hate to have to send you to the fort with the rest of the terrorists and rebels."

"You've no need to be concerned. We'll cooperate with your men." I tried not to let my anxiety come through my voice. I had thought von Choltiz's men would be in charge of going through our books.

"Have I taken you by surprise? My man Hermann von Choltiz has visited your library assiduously and is familiar with it. He will be efficient and thorough."

A chill ran up my spine. For some foolish reason I had thought von Choltiz was Lt. Bauman's superior.

"I will not hinder his work," I said nervously. I made for the door, but Bauman stood in my way and placed his hand on my shoulder.

"Things could be much simpler for a woman like yourself. I know you're trying to find your husband. I've looked into the matter, and he is quite ill. I could have him sent home right away. If he doesn't get out of the camp soon, he's not likely to last through winter."

My heart raced. How did this man know all this? Nausea washed over me, but I tried to breathe through it.

"Thank you," I said, "but I hope that things will be resolved before long."

"This is one of the things I hate most about the French: your irrational optimism. Most of you think the British are coming to save you or that the Americans will join the war. Stupidity! No one is going to take what's ours." As he spoke, his hand passed down my back.

The doorbell rang and I jumped. I seized the moment to get out as quickly as I could. The housekeeper was at the door. I let her in, threw my jacket around me, and tore off to the library.

Céline and Denis were already there when I arrived. They smiled to try to cheer me up, then we went inside and discussed our plan.

"These are the books we'll hand over. Most of them are duplicates, and they aren't valuable editions. It pains me to sacrifice them, but it's the only way to keep the Germans happy," I told my friends.

Denis caressed the covers and spines, then left them in the pile.

"Did you do the same thing in your bookstore?" I asked.

He agreed bluntly. Since the Nazis had come, hardly anyone had darkened Denis's door to buy a book. He was barely even able to sell magazines and newspapers. His only income had come from postcards, maps, and tourist guides. Unbelievably, tourism had returned to the city in mid-August, and the beaches were packed despite the war.

We heard loud knocking at the door. Céline opened it, and a half-dozen German soldiers dressed in black entered alongside two policemen. I recognized both of them as Antoine's colleagues. They avoided my gaze. One of them said, "Mrs. Ferrec, we're to search the library and confiscate the banned books. This is the list." He handed me a piece of paper.

I was surprised to find many more titles than expected, including more French authors to be banned. "But this isn't the list," I stammered.

"This is the Liste Otto. It hasn't been publicized yet, but it applies to public libraries. The Propagandastaffel compiled over a thousand works to be confiscated."

His words petrified me. We were not prepared for this. The new list had works by Hermann Rauschning, Carl Jung, and Léon Blum.

"We can't turn these titles over to—" But before I finished my thought, the soldiers split up and spread throughout the library, pulling books off the shelves and dividing them into two big piles. The policemen stayed by us to prevent us from interfering.

I plugged up my ears to stop the sound of books hitting the wooden floor. Denis tried to reason with one of the policemen, but the gendarme pushed him away and ordered him to sit down. Céline knelt to pick up a book that had fallen nearby, and a soldier kicked her away, barking, "Stay where you are!" in poor French.

An hour later, the shelves were empty. The books had all been divided into two enormous piles: those to be destroyed and those to be spared. The noncommissioned officer came up to us, smiling in apparent enjoyment of his work. "We'll go to the second floor now," he announced.

"That's where we keep the most valuable books, and none of those are on the list."

He shoved his face into mine and growled, "I said we'll go to the second floor now!"

Denis tried to jump between us, but a soldier punched him and sent him sprawling. I knelt down to help him up, then Céline pulled out a handkerchief and tried to stop the blood gushing from his nose.

"Savages!" Denis spat out.

"Please, stay calm," I begged him. I worried we would all three be killed right then and there.

Then I heard boots coming toward us and looked up to see Lt. Bauman.

"You promised to cooperate," he said.

"We are cooperating. All the banned books are in that pile, but no one had said anything about the incunabula and the rare books."

Bauman knelt down and grabbed Denis's hair, jerking his head back. "Then I don't think you've understood me well. Give me the key and come upstairs."

Trembling, I went to the desk and fetched the keys for the closet and the security room. Then I started up the spiral staircase. As I turned, I saw my friends terrified on the floor, the two undaunted French policemen, and the soldiers starting to pile the books outside in the courtyard.

The lieutenant pushed me to go faster. I tripped and nearly tumbled down the stairs but managed to steady myself. When I opened the door, the room smelled of being long shut up. Before I could unlock the first glass case, Bauman was already peering through the glass. Then we heard a voice behind us.

"What happened downstairs?" It was von Choltiz.

Bauman turned in a rage and was facing von Choltiz in two strides. "The Jewish bookseller got in the way of my men."

"What are your men doing here? My men were to come first and register the rare books."

"I'm tired of doing the dirty work. I clean up the trash, and you keep the treasure. No doubt you've pinched a few off the top for your private collection. When the war is over, you'll be sitting pretty. So I want a piece of the wealth for myself."

Von Choltiz met the SS officer's rabid gaze evenly and with total calmness asked, "Should we speak with Rosenberg? He has direct orders from Hitler to preserve the cultural assets of the occupied territories."

"I obey Himmler." Spittle peppered the air as Bauman spoke.

"Get your gorillas out of here. You've got what you want, now leave with your trash."

Bauman clenched his fists but turned and pounded down the stairs in fury.

Von Choltiz turned to me. "I'm so sorry. I knew nothing about this."

I was in such shock I could not respond. Then I caught sight of a column of smoke and ran to the window. The Nazis had mounded the banned books into a pile and soaked it with gas. Bauman himself lit a match, looked up, and pierced me with his murderous gaze.

"I'll turn this building into a stable for my horses!" he yelled even as smoke hid his face. My books were quick to burn. The whole event, the memory of dozens of generations, went up in smoke against the blue September sky as the world shifted closer to complete insanity, on the verge of total destruction.

16

The Bookseller

I could not bring myself to go to the library for a full week, though everything was worsened by having Adolf Bauman in my own home. I was terrified of running into him at any moment, but to my great relief he had been sent to Nantes along with some of the Germans stationed in our town in order to put down riots.

The day before, I had gone to see Josua Goll, a high school teacher who often checked books out of the library and was deeply concerned by everything happening around us. He told me that, after a German cadet had been killed, the Nazis had retaliated by killing three prisoners and were registering all the Jews in the country. He believed they planned to deport them to

Germany. For the moment, French Jews were still protected by law, but the Vichy government was starting to limit the jobs and careers open to them.

That morning, when I dropped the books Josua had requested off at his school, I was shocked by what I witnessed. Most of his students seemed quite taken with the Nazi fanfare and ideology despite how Josua had tried to help them see what the racist, populist ideas actually meant.

As I approached Josua's door, I stopped when I heard shouting.

"Silence, please!" I heard him call. Most students ignored him, but one stood up and started telling him off.

"Shut up, Jew! My dad says that what's happening in France right now is the fault of your kind. They invented communism and capitalism, and they want to take over the world."

"That's absurd," the teacher answered calmly.

A student with glasses piped up, "That's what *The Protocols of the Elders of Zion* says!"

Copies of that defamatory text had been in circulation in France for some time.

"That book was a fabrication used by the Russian secret police to blame Jews for the revolutions, but it's nothing but lies. It's already been proven to be a complete forgery," Josua said.

"I don't believe that. Trotsky and the other communist leaders are all Jews," the first boy said.

I heard footsteps behind me and turned to see Philiph Darnad, the school principal. He raised his eyebrows at me and, hearing the voices from the classroom, peered in through the window in the door.

Josua was speaking again, trying to convince his students.. "France is a state that defends liberty, equality, and fraternity. These are the Republic's values and the basis of our society."

Three of the boys stood and ran up to him, and amid the scuffle, one of the boys landed a punch to Josua's face. "Jewish swine! We won't have you around here anymore!" he yelled as the professor's nose bled onto his shirt and suit jacket.

I panicked when another boy punched Josua in the stomach, and he doubled over. The third rammed his elbow down onto the teacher's back, sending him to his knees. I stared at the principal in disbelief. How could he stand there and allow the students to attack a teacher?

"Aren't you going to do something?" I asked indignantly.

He finally barged into the classroom, and the students all stood up at the ready. "What's going on here?" the principal demanded. "I am shocked to see such things happening in a classroom."

"The teacher is a Jew, so it's his fault," one of the students said. Josua was still on his knees on the floor, holding a hand-kerchief to his nose.

I walked into the room and pointed to the students since I had witnessed the incident from the beginning. "That's not true. These boys began insulting the teacher," I explained.

The principal silenced me with a severe look.

"Mr. Goll, you're relieved of your duties today. There will be a file opened, and don't be surprised if we no longer need your services. You know you're not allowed to speak about Jews in class or mention the old Republican ideas. We're under a new regime now. And you can thank your communist friends for getting us to this point."

Josua did not defend himself. He got up and headed for the door, but I blocked his way.

"This is unbelievable! The ones who should be punished and expelled are those rabble-rousers," I said, pointing to the guilty students who were now gloating before me.

"You're a communist just like him. Everyone knows what took place in the library the other day. We'll take care of you next—you and your socialist, Jewish books," the first boy snarled. When I looked closely at him, I recognized he was the pork butcher's son. I also knew half the girls of Saint-Malo were in love with him.

"Young man, I will not allow you to—"

"Out of here, both of you!" the principal interrupted. "This is my school, and I'm the one who imposes discipline here."

I helped Josua pick up his damaged glasses, and we left the building. When we got outside, he broke down in tears. "Dear God, I can't even recognize my country anymore. What are these Nazis doing to us?" Tears and blood mingled on his cheeks.

"I'm so sorry," I said, grasping at comfort.

"My sister said starting this month she has to put up a sign in the window of her sewing machine shop saying it's a Jewish store. They're branding us like cattle before taking us to the butcher. And no one's doing anything about it. Most people just look the other way, and then others seize the occasion to resurrect old feuds."

We walked along the street, and Josua gingerly tested whether he could pull the handkerchief off his nose. The bleeding had stopped, but his face was red from the blood and being hit.

"Are you all right? Can I walk you home?"

"No, but thank you, and be careful. You know the Nazis and French Fascists won't stop until they've done away with every type of resistance. Teachers, writers, booksellers, and librarians— we're in their way. Deep down they're afraid of us. They know we can dismantle their lies in the blink of an eye."

"Surely this nightmare will be over soon." I did not believe my own words, but I tried to encourage him.

"I'm afraid it won't."

We turned onto the street where Denis's bookshop was, and I stopped short at the sight of shattered glass. I ran to the door and saw a mess of books and glass plastering the shop floor.

"Denis!" I shouted. "Denis, are you okay?" Josua and I ran to the back of the store but saw no trace of him. Then we went back out to the street, but Denis was nowhere to be seen. I started to sob. The Nazis had taken him, and I knew it had been that vile felon Bauman. Even from another city his tentacles reached far.

Josua left me at the door to my building. We were like two wretches shipwrecked by the terrible storm of intolerance that was pummeling our beloved country.

I ran into von Choltiz on the stairway. He stood before me and took off his peaked hat, then cleared his throat. "I see you've found out. The SS ordered the detention of your friend this morning for selling forbidden literature. It seems that a mole requested some books by Marx, and he provided them. It's a serious offense, and they've taken him to Nantes. Anything could happen."

I looked at him in horror. "Is there anything I can do for him?"

"If you'd like, we can go there and try to resolve it. But I can't promise you anything. Your friend has committed a serious crime, and I'm not part of the SS. Bauman complained to my superiors because I interrupted the destruction of the library."

"Please," I begged, choking on my tears.

Von Choltiz put his hand on my shoulder. "I'll try to get them to transfer him to a prison run by the army, and in a few days we'll try to go get him. I'll have to make contact with Berlin."

"Thank you," I said, shocked to find myself resting my head on the man's shoulder and letting the tears fall. They had just taken the only person who was keeping me afloat. I had no news of my husband, and I could not imagine a lower blow. Von Choltiz remained inflexibly rigid. When I recovered myself, I raised my head and ran upstairs.

I do not know if we all have a predetermined fate or if we simply float on a nebula of uncertainty. Some days I wonder if both are true at the same time. I went inside my apartment and fell to my knees by my bed, begging God to protect my friend. I could not handle another injury without splitting into a thousand pieces.

17

Denis

Sometimes I wonder why I send you these letters chronicling my life. The detonator was surely that trip with von Choltiz to Nantes. I wanted you, dear Marcel Zola, to make an immortal experience of this miniscule and insignificant thing we call life. It is not that I want my dull existence to pierce the thick shroud of the centuries but rather that no one should forget what these terrible gray years are like. I know that, once I hand over to you the repository of what happened, I relinquish control of what you write, though you, too, will relinquish that control if this story gets published and the readers make it their own. I do not know how those readers will judge me. Surely they will understand that love is the only thing that can turn the prosaic into the epic.

Von Choltiz was waiting for me first thing in the morning at the library entrance. I did not want him to pick me up in front of my apartment building lest the neighbors think there was anything between us. I was nervous knowing that things would need to go well in order for him to help me with Denis. Furthermore, I knew my friend would not be able to hold out long in a German prison.

When I got to the corner, he was waiting for me in a Mercedes convertible. His peaked cap was on the back seat beside a small, worn, brown leather suitcase.

"Good morning. I hope I'm not very late."

"I've only been waiting a few minutes." He smiled, and the dimples in his cheeks deepened. "I've told my commander that you're a librarian and that I need your help locating some rare books in the Nantes library—seventeenth-century Huguenot works of theology and philosophy. We will go to the library before returning tomorrow."

"Is it necessary to spend the night in the city?" I asked hesitantly. He had mentioned it the day before, but the idea unsettled me.

"It's a three-hour drive, though the roads are still somewhat clogged up, and the several checkpoints will slow us down."

He took my suitcase and opened the door for me before settling behind the wheel. He turned the car on, and the vehicle moved along the narrow roads. Few people dotted the sidewalks that early but enough to see me riding beside the Nazi officer in his roofless car. Though most of the city's inhabitants were collaborating in one way or another with the Germans, everyone looked down on women who had romantic relationships with the enemy. If nothing else, many women did it in order to survive. With no work, parents, or husbands, friendship with a German at least guaranteed them food to take home. None of those women could watch their children or younger siblings die of hunger without doing something about it.

We headed out in the direction of Rennes. Besides my quick and sad trip to Paris, it had been months since I had left Saint-Malo. For a moment I allowed myself to feel as though the trip were a spontaneous getaway with a friend, leaving behind the months of fear and anxiety.

We traveled in silence for about half an hour, observing the countryside and the blue sky decorated with strangely shaped white clouds. But the roadway loosened von Choltiz's tongue. "I miss Germany," he said, his eyes on the road. "I don't think it will be long before I head back. Once we reach an agreement with England, all of this will be over."

"You mean the Germans will leave France soon?" I asked, an excited lilt to my question.

"Perhaps not imminently, but we didn't come to stay. As long as France complies with our conditions, we have no reason to occupy the country. All the Führer wants is the return of the lands inhabited by the Aryans for centuries and a region to repopulate in Poland, an unnatural country that has always belonged to Prussia. We'll stay in Luxembourg, the Netherlands, and a few more places, but the rest of the countries don't matter to us. We didn't start this war," he said with pride.

His statement surprised me. The whole world knew Germany had attacked Poland the year before, despite the warnings of France and Great Britain. I struggled for something to say. "I'm not so sure the worst is over. I've heard of confrontations in Egypt between Italians and the British."

"Nah, mere trifles. The important thing is that now that the bombings in England have begun, the prime minister won't delay in begging for an armistice."

I frowned. All of that Teutonic hot air was nothing more than what came out every day in the propaganda news films and the official radio station.

"When will our men return?" I asked. Despite the promises the employee in Paris had made, I still had no news of my husband.

"That might take a while, at least until peace has been signed on all fronts. I'm sorry about your husband."

His comment made me bristle. Who was von Choltiz to speak of Antoine?

"And what about Denis?" I asked.

"They've probably knocked him around a bit in the interrogation, as selling illegal books is a serious offense. At the very least he'll lose his license and will have to close the bookstore."

"Why are the Nazis so afraid of books?"

Von Choltiz threw me a glance, his face a mixture of frustration and perplexity. "I've told you several times already that not all Germans are the same. I studied literature and worked in several libraries and book archives. I've been educated in French and adore your country, but some things need to be set right. France and Western civilization were on the point of self-destruction. Our desire is to rebuild the world purely, without the contaminated atmosphere that arose after the Great War and the crisis of 1929."

"I don't see how the world you're building is any better than the old one. Democracy certainly has its shortcomings, but a one-party dictatorship leads the masses to thinking only one way. Without freedom, the world becomes a nightmare."

"Freedom? What is freedom? No one is free. We're all prisoners, prisoners of the people around us and even of ourselves. Society imposes its rules. We have to study, get married, have children, then retire to spend time with our grandchildren. The only true freedom would be in the middle of a forest, far from society—but who can sustain a life of isolation?"

I took a deep breath to control my tongue. It was a beautiful morning, and the summer heat had given way to a pleasant autumn. The farther we got from Saint-Malo, the more I felt like the war did not exist and that my own life had just been a bad dream. Yet I was not chatting with a good friend. Nothing could have been further from reality. This man was my enemy, no matter how hard he tried to win my favor.

"You're a bunch of barbarians," I muttered.

"That may be, but warriors are the only ones capable of building a new world. All empires have been built on death and destruction, but later they grow more sophisticated. It happened with the Persian Empire, the Macedonians, the Romans, the Spaniards who conquered half the world, and even the British . . . They may seem so civilized to you now, but they've enslaved half the globe. Now people like me have something to say. Adolf Hitler is an idealist who wants to remake the world. How can you not see it?"

"For that goal you have to persecute the Jews and anyone who's different? How many more lives must be sacrificed for the Germans to build their new empire?"

"Of all people, the French should know how to appreciate defeat. We learned from our losses. The failures help us enjoy the victories."

———— • ◆ • ————

After breezing through all the checkpoints, we arrived in Nantes around noon and parked in front of the hotel. We left the suitcases in our separate rooms, then went to the jail. Von Choltiz asked me to wait at the door, but I went and sat at a café across the street. I did not want to rouse suspicion. I was on my second cup of coffee when he stormed out of the building right to my table. I could read his body language to know it was not good news.

"I'm afraid Bauman is one step ahead of us. Denis was transferred to the camp at Dachau yesterday."

"To a concentration camp? Dear God!" I buried my face in my hands. We had all heard about the camps opened up throughout Germany after the victory of the Nazi party. "And they didn't take him there to sell books," I hissed, incensed.

"No. Bauman accused him of belonging to the Resistance. He also gave them your name, but I deescalated the case. That's what took me so long. I had to give my word that you're in no way associated with any rebel group. That is true, yes?"

"You're just like them. You're no different at all. You might think you're better, less savage than the Nazi hordes, but all that does is make you much, much worse." In my fury, I jumped up and pummeled his chest with my fists. He grabbed my hands and held my gaze, the light draining out of his eyes. Emotions played across his face, and he seemed to see the world as it really was for once. I hoped my words had gotten through to him, that he could no longer deceive himself.

I walked back to the hotel, went up to my room, and threw myself on the bed. I knew I would never see Denis again. The war had taken Antoine from me, then my beloved books, and now the most faithful friend I had ever had. That very afternoon I adapted my writing into letters for you. I had no idea how I would get them to you, but I knew you could transform them into something I could not. At the core, being a writer means feeling things at a deeper level than everyone else and knowing how to communicate those depths, helping readers to see reality in a way they never have before.

18

Parisian Friends

Saint-Malo
October 2, 1940

For two weeks I could hardly separate myself from my writing pages. I woke early to write and hardly ate meals, my tears often mingling with my hurried pen strokes. I had gone through some tough times in my life, and it seemed like life refused to call a truce with me. I had always thought that people were good at heart and that the world was slowly improving. Yet when Denis was sent away, I knew I could trust no one. All hope was gone, and existence was absolutely meaningless. Little by little my words on the smudged paper stopped being just words— mere signs and symbols—and became voices from the past that wanted to wake the whole world up from its slumber.

Bauman returned in early October and resumed his place in my old bedroom. Try as I could to avoid him, he seemed to wait and purposely cross paths before I left for work.

"Mrs. Ferrec, what a pleasure to see you again. Your face looks a bit sadder than the last time I saw it. You no longer have the look of a defiant woman willing to die for her ideas," he said, blocking my way out of the kitchen.

"You fail to understand women, Lt. Bauman. We are not moved by ideals—that is a banal game ever played by men. We're driven by something much deeper that really makes the world turn: affections. This is something you'll never understand. We endure pain better than men can, we sacrifice ourselves for the ones we love, we give our lives for our children—but none of that is driven by our ideals. We are driven by love."

He burst out laughing. "Is there anything weaker or more futile than love? After just one torture session I got a man to murder his own mother. Where was his love?" His words nauseated me. "And your dear sweet friend screamed your name like a madman when he accused you of belonging to the Resistance. How I would love to detain you. In a few hours you'd be willing to do anything I told you to, but it appears you have a powerful associate. When he's gone, which won't be long now, you'll be completely at my mercy."

I tried to push past him, but he wrapped an arm around me and started squeezing. "I prefer the hunt over the kill. Though it takes me half a lifetime, you'll end up in my clutches," he whispered, his lips grazing my ear. Then he let me go so suddenly I lost my balance.

I fled. Fortunately, I kept my letters at the library, out of his reach. I could not even think what would happen if he found and read them.

It was a chilly morning with heavy rain that bore through my coat with ease. I had forgotten my umbrella in the apartment and was drenched by the time I got to the library door. I feared a relapse of my illness, but either the fury or the hatred I felt for that despicable man gave me strength and forced me along.

In the doorway I ran into the boy, Pierre, who had come a few months before asking about painting.

"Mrs. Ferrec, how nice to see you again."

I was still too upset to form a reply. I just unlocked the door and let him in. I hung my soggy coat over one of the radiators and went to my desk. The boy went directly to the section on painting and it was some time before he reappeared.

"Mrs. Ferrec?"

"You can call me Jocelyn. I'm sorry I didn't answer you before. It's . . . It's been a very difficult morning."

"I understand, it's lousy out. I came on my bike from Saint-Servan."

I finally looked up and noticed that the poor boy was also drenched through and through.

"Hand me your coat and stand here next to the radiator. You could catch pneumonia."

He smiled and handed me his green jacket, then glued himself to the radiator.

"I really hope you don't get sick," I said.

"Don't worry, Mrs.—I mean, Jocelyn. I'm used to the cold and the rain." He shivered as he spoke. "I'm a scout, and I go camping a lot, even in the snow. This week I've got a committee meeting in Paris."

"You're going to Paris?"

"Yes, I go about once a month. I take the train to Rennes and then, in a few more hours, I'm in Paris."

I was intrigued. "But don't the Germans stop you?"

"No, never. I wear my uniform and have permission to travel."

My heart skipped a beat. Could this boy help me send my letters? "Pierre, I wonder if you would do something for me. But it would have to be a secret between us."

Pierre smiled, his angelic face lit up under his matted blond hair. "Whatever you need!"

"It's just delivering some letters. The first is to an author named Marcel Zola and the other is to a friend who's a librarian. Her name is Yvonne Oddon."

Pierre nodded. "It would be my pleasure, Jocelyn."

I asked him to wait just a moment. I put my letters in one envelope and a note to Yvonne in another. After what happened to Denis and after Bauman's threats, my life was in danger. I didn't have time to waste.

Pierre took the two small packets plus a book he wanted to read, hid them under his dried coat, and went out to the street. It was still pouring rain as I watched him disappear behind a curtain of water.

I sat down at my desk and, for the first time since I could recall, felt my lips turn up. I was still enjoying that fleeting moment of peace when the door opened again. Mrs. Remarque, one of my neighbors, stepped inside.

"Marie, how nice to see you here," I said. She was by no means a frequenter of libraries. With a large family and her husband held prisoner like Antoine, she spent most of the day trying to find enough food for her children.

She stood in front of me, and I studied her. I had not seen her for some time. She had aged prematurely in the intervening months, life having beaten her down.

"Mrs. Ferrec, I'm coming to you out of desperation. I don't know where else to turn."

"You can speak freely. Please, sit down. I'll make some tea."

I stood, made some tea, and sat down beside her. The steam rising from our cups played before our faces.

"You already know that the Germans are holding my husband, like yours, as prisoner."

"Yes, our terrible luck."

"My youngest boy is very weak. I haven't been able to get milk for weeks, and he hardly has a bit of bread and butter once a day. He was being fed at school, but he's been sick since yesterday. He's got a high fever, but I don't have any money for medicine, and I'm worried that the rest of the children will catch it. I would never ask you for anything if it weren't for . . ."

"It's so hard to get hold of medicines. There are shortages of so many things, and everyone's afraid of how we'll make it through the winter. The Germans are taking everything, but isn't Lt. Hermann von Choltiz living on your floor, with Mrs. Fave?"

"He was until a few days ago, and we were surviving on the rations he brought to us. But when he got back from Nantes, he started talking about going back to Germany and waiting for a new placement. In the meantime, he's gone back to the barracks the Germans have in the city."

Her words were a bucket of cold water down my back. I knew exactly why the officer had decided to leave. Without realizing it, my argument with von Choltiz had jeopardized the whole Remarque family. On the return from Nantes, he and I had not spoken a word. Now I wondered if I had been too harsh with him. On that day, von Choltiz had been trying to help me.

"What can I do?" I asked.

"Everyone knows you're friends with the lieutenant. Maybe if you spoke with him?"

"We aren't friends," I said, startled. I had not realized until then that rumors about me were circulating.

"Well, I don't know what kind of relationship you have, and I don't judge you, but my children . . ."

I was stupefied. My first reaction was to ask Marie to leave, but her face was so sad and wasted away. I put my hands over hers, dry and bony from scrubbing so many floors, and promised to speak with von Choltiz.

———— • ◆ • ————

That very afternoon I went to the German barracks. I was not at all sure von Choltiz would be willing to see me, but I had to try. One of the guards asked me to wait and then led me to a room with whitewashed walls. Von Choltiz appeared soon thereafter.

"Jocelyn, you're the last person I expected to see," he said coldly. But when I held out my hand, he shook it.

"I've come to ask a favor. I heard you were leaving." His leaving meant one thing for the Remarque family and another for me. Without von Choltiz's protection, Lt. Bauman would have a clear coast to do whatever he wanted to me. Furthermore, I knew he would completely destroy the library.

"I didn't think my leaving would affect you in the slightest. You need not fear for your books. I've written a report stating there's nothing of interest to Germany at your library."

That surprised me. "Thank you," I said in a puzzled voice.

"In the meantime, I've requested a transfer to the Berlin State Library and hope to be leaving soon."

"But you can't go!" I blurted out.

Von Choltiz cocked an eye at me and took a seat. "And why not, may I ask?"

"The Remarque family is defenseless without you on the floor. Marie doesn't even have enough medicine for her sick son."

He seemed let down. "That's what you've come to see me about? Well then, I'll direct the ration officers to increase their allotment and will ask a doctor to see to the child."

I stared into his green eyes, gathering my courage. I felt so alone and helpless. "It's not just that." It came out in a whisper.

"If you're afraid Lt. Bauman will do something to you after I leave, unfortunately there's not much I can do about that. You're better off moving to Paris and keeping a low profile. Bauman will eventually forget about you. I can arrange a pass for you to travel to the city."

I was momentarily tempted to accept because escaping would be easier. But how would Antoine find me if he returned from Germany? What would happen to the library in my absence? Besides, I loved Saint-Malo. My heart was between its walls, the only place I had known happiness.

I teared up. "I can't leave Saint-Malo. The library is my life now. It's all I've got left." It was the first time I had dared say those words aloud. I could feel my heart splintering into pieces, sadness gnawing away at me as the tuberculosis had done the year before. It all felt so confusing. Did I still love Antoine the same way, knowing he very well could be dead? I had so little hope to go on. I momentarily blanched, wondering if I longed for my husband or just for the sensation of loving and being loved. Had I always been alone? Antoine had been the only thing keeping me alive.

Von Choltiz took hold of my shoulders and stared into my eyes, his face close to mine.

"I love you, Jocelyn. I fell in love the first time I saw you in that alleyway. I loved you when you were so brave and even willing to die for your books. When we're all dead and gone, others will take our place. New authors will write new stories; they'll seek their fame and fortune, and still others will come after them. What is there after love?"

I let out a long, slow breath and, trembling, got to my feet. My cheeks burned under my tears. "I still love my husband."

I walked out of the barracks in a daze, letting the raindrops mix with teardrops and salty ocean spray as I went up the wall. The sea, eternal and immune to our fragile existence, crashed and crashed against the ancient manmade barrier.

Regardless of how much I wished it, I could not stay on the wall forever. I slunk home weighed down by fear of what would happen with Bauman once von Choltiz left the city. A world I no longer recognized overwhelmed me.

Then, at the height of my confusion, I received three letters: two from Paris and one from Germany.

19

Three Letters

Saint-Malo
October 6, 1940

I hardly slept after my interview with von Choltiz, nor the following night. Autumn had started dampening the life out of everything, washing the world in dark reds, browns, and grays. I was throbbing with confusion after that afternoon. I did feel something for him but certainly could not call it love. I fell into a depression, and the city along with me seemed to grow sadder. Children no longer played in the streets or ran around on their bicycles while old men and women cursed their audacity. People could not trust each other anymore. Your neighbor might sell you to the enemy for a few marks or to take over your house or land. Fog and gray clouds locked Saint-Malo's inhabitants into their homes for several months, but more than that, the occupation had destroyed our sense of community and our pride in being French. It was better to be a living coward than a dead hero.

I went to the library that morning, always looking over my shoulder. I feared that Bauman would follow me. Nightmares about him had plagued me the night before: He had locked me up and was torturing me. Just before I felt death, von Choltiz appeared to rescue me. I woke with a start, nauseated that, among other things, von Choltiz showed up in my dreams. Meanwhile my own husband's face grew harder to recall.

Pierre was waiting for me at the door of the library with a reassuring smile. I opened the door, and as I hung up my coat, he plopped two letters down on the desk.

"I did what you asked! And they're waiting for your answer. If you want, I can take it next week."

"Oh, thank you so much, Pierre! I'll write back right away."

Pierre placed the painting book he had borrowed on the desk and then went to look for another.

I opened Yvonne's letter first, having recognized her handwriting. We had corresponded for years, starting when I was still in school and she was training in the United States.

Dear Jocelyn,

I'm so glad you've taken this important step to reach out to me. It's time to act. We can't sit around with our arms crossed. The world needs saviors, and though we might not feel like we're cut out for the job, the heroic are flesh-and-blood people like us who decide to take action.

Soon I'll send you some copies of the *La Résistance*, our newspaper. I hope you can share them with the right people, and perhaps you'll contribute an article. You always wanted to write, so here's your chance! Literature is a weapon against evil.

The boy who brought us your letter will be our link. We're still organizing ourselves, but there's no turning back now. It's better to give our lives for freedom than live on our knees.

I hope that, like Marie Durand—the woman who held out in the Tower of Constance for thirty-eight years without denying her faith—we can fight until our last breaths.

Your friend and fellow booklover,
Yvonne

PS: Please destroy this letter. From here on out, we'll need to use false names.

I put the letter on my desk, pushed everything else away, and lit it with a match. I brushed the ashes into the wastebasket and then turned to the second letter.

Dear Jocelyn,

Writers are used to listening to stories. In a way, they are the fire that feeds our souls. Even so, your letters have moved me deeply. I've heard there's a magic paradise for authors where we can rewrite the sad story of the world. In real life, though, our pens hold the life and death of our characters while we are powerless against reality.

I've not come across a love story as delightful and equally heart-wrenching as yours. Do we have anything left to us but love in these difficult days?

I do not feel worthy of writing your story. I'm used to changing the fates of my characters in the blink of an eye, but your life, these years of struggle and suffering, are surely, as the eternal Balzac would say, the power of the human comedy. I think your story portrays our age better than any other I've come across.

It would be an honor to write about you, though my pulse races at the prospect. Whenever an author releases a new book to the world, he risks being loved and hated—though no one thinks at the core that it's a true act of generosity. Authors expose their souls in every line they write; but in this case, you would be the one exposed. Many people would judge you and would not understand the choices you make. Who can enter someone else's heart and understand the reasons behind their actions?

Starting today, I am indebted to you. I can only reflect reality, but you're building it day after day with your own blood.

Warm greetings from your great
admirer,
Marcel Zola

That second letter left me breathless. I was tempted to burn it like the first. Who was I such that someone else would write about my life? Even more, what would the people who read it think? Would they understand the choices I made? Would they know how to interpret my heart?

Pierre returned with another art book under his arm. He set it carefully on the table and asked, "Were the letters what you were hoping to hear?"

"I think so," I said, filling out the book's card.

"It made me feel like a spy!" His eyes gleamed with excitement.

"Please be careful. Life isn't like in the movies. The things that happen are real, and they can't be undone."

"Don't worry, I'll be very careful. Plus, the adults never pay attention to us. They think we live in a parallel universe."

Pierre picked up the thick book and left after bidding farewell. I put Zola's letter away and sat for a while, thinking. I was about to get my coat to go to Céline's house for a bite to eat when the mailman came into the library.

"There's a letter for you, Mrs. Ferrec. It's from Germany. I hope it's good news."

My heart turned over. The address on the envelope was typed, and my hands shook as I received it. Sometimes it is better to not face life, to let uncertainty dampen all our feelings and turn us into machines who simply survive. I took a deep breath and opened the envelope while paper so thin it was nearly transparent floated out. I emptied my mind and let fate take the reins, though I knew deep down that I had never fully let go.

Part Two

In Sickness and in Health

20

The Beloved Invalid

Rennes
November 11, 1940

The letter from Germany informed me that Antoine was scheduled to be released and repatriated for humanitarian and health reasons, but the process was long and slow. A letter from Paris had arrived informing me that my husband would be brought by train early in the morning on November 11. They would take him as far as Rennes, and I was to pick him up there.

Von Choltiz was still in Saint-Malo. Instead of being transferred indefinitely to Berlin, he traveled back and forth to Germany, carting off for Hitler the literary treasures found in the private libraries of Brittany's wealthy. When in Saint-Malo, he stayed at the army barracks. I had avoided him over the past few weeks because of everything that had happened between us. I did not want him to misinterpret my actions. I needed his protection, but I loved my husband.

Things were getting worse. Lt. Bauman harassed me whenever possible and, though most of the time I managed to avoid him, I did not know what would happen when Antoine witnessed the SS officer's insinuations and threats.

I waited impatiently on the platform. The train was delayed since nothing worked as it should in Occupied France. The Germans and their needs and whims took absolute priority, despite the suffering this inflicted on the population. A small group of collaborators prospered at the price of scarcity for the rest of us.

Finally, a train whistled, and the machine chugged into view. A column of smoke rose to the leaden gray sky as the noise of the approach grew deafening.

I studied every window that flew by, not seeing him. I worried that Antoine would have changed irreparably or that he would have been too weak to travel. I bounced up and down on the balls of my feet, anxious but ready. I was growing desperate when an old man got off the last wagon and dragged his way through the light rain that had started to fall. I stared at him a full minute before recognizing him. His hair was graying, and he was very thin. His eyes were sunken into a sad face that took on new life when he saw me. Our ten-month separation had lasted an eternity.

He dropped his suitcase and opened his arms. I ran and flung myself into his embrace. We wept and time stood still as we captured that moment to recover the days the war had stolen from us. I—who had always been so strong and capable of facing anything—had been so afraid. Words were unimportant right then. The flood of love's current drowns out all the rest.

"I have missed you so much," he said, holding my cheeks between his scarred, bony hands. The war had absconded with his health and youth as quickly as it had my peace and happiness. Since the very day of our wedding, everything had been bad news, tragedy, and pain; but none of that mattered now. We were together again.

We walked out of the station with our arms around each other's backs, unwilling to separate further. I had come in Denis's car, and I dreaded having to tell Antoine what had happened to our friend.

Antoine put his suitcase in the back and said he wanted to drive. "It'll do me good. I'll finally feel like I really am free. I was under German guard all the way to the train station in Paris. It was a terrible journey."

I stroked his graying hair. I needed to touch him to believe he was really there and not a phantom of my imagination. We had barely left the station and started back to Saint-Malo when a gendarme patrol stopped us.

"Papers, please," said a policeman with an inexpressive face covered by a black mustache.

"What's going on?" said Antoine. "I'm a policeman in Saint-Malo."

The gendarme seemed friendlier after that. "Some teenagers have raised the tricolor flag at the Nantes Cathedral, and the whole city is singing 'La Marseillaise.' The German authorities have had to step in, and there've been some skirmishes."

"Of course they are. It's November 11," Antoine said, nodding. It was the anniversary of the armistice of 1918, and the people were celebrating the French victory over the Germans.

"Be careful and stay away from any large groups or commotion."

We continued on our way, leaving Rennes behind for the countryside drowsy with the cold and the approach of winter.

"I wish I could've come back in spring," Antoine said. I leaned my head on his shoulder. "In Germany it's always cold," he went on. "We were all but starving and had to work from sunup to sundown. I thought I would never get to come home . . . I was injured, never seeming to improve, and then I got sick."

"Forget all of that, Antoine. You're safe now."

"Safe? I went to war to fight for our freedom, and now the Nazis are controlling France."

"You'll grow used to it. It's better if we don't draw attention to ourselves. The Germans usually don't bother people who stay out of trouble."

Antoine frowned. "I find it very hard to believe that someone like you is content to follow orders blindly. I think you've got a lot more to tell me. Don't leave anything out. I want to know what all has happened."

My husband and I had never kept secrets from each other, but for his own safety I needed to omit certain details, especially the awkwardness with Hermann.

"Let's start with Denis. Where is he? Why didn't he come with you?"

My head dropped. I had wanted to prepare him before explaining what had happened, but life does not let up. I swallowed back tears, and he understood my hesitation. "The Nazis detained him. The SS accused him of selling banned books, and a lieutenant named Bauman had him sent to a concentration camp in Dachau, Germany."

Antoine's gaze flicked away from the road a moment. "Dachau is even worse than where I've been. The Nazis built it to lock up political dissidents, but now they're filling it with Jews."

"Maybe they'll release him soon, like they did with you?"

Antoine started crying then. The tears flowed down his pale skin to the dirty, threadbare collar of his shirt. Antoine and Denis had been friends their whole lives. "When will this nightmare end?" he moaned.

I put my arms around him as best as the car would allow. Sometimes an embrace is the only thing that reaches a broken heart. As we entered Saint-Malo, Antoine's face warmed again. He loved his city, and seeing it once more allowed him the illusion of feeling like things might be like they always had been.

We parked the car nearby, and even though he was weak and tired, Antoine wanted to walk around and see the city before going home. We meandered through town and passed the monument to those who died in the Great War. Typically, people would leave flowers at the monument as a simple way to honor their loved ones. No one had dared leave flowers this year. People quickened their pace near the monument, trying to avoid their own cowardice. A few boys wandered up to it, but two policemen hollered at them to move along. Antoine went up to his former colleagues.

"Antoine, how wonderful to see you!" the older one said.

"What are your orders today?" my husband asked.

"We've been told not to let anybody leave flowers at the monument or commemorate our victory in the Great War. We're not to provoke the Germans."

As Antoine caught up with his fellow police, a girl around ten or eleven years old made her way to the obelisk, holding a bouquet of flowers. The policemen stopped talking to watch her, and the passersby paused and collectively held their breath. She dropped the flowers and started humming "La Marseillaise," reclaiming a bit of our country's dignity.

Within moments a group of German soldiers appeared, shoving and kicking the passersby who had gathered around the monument and joined in the song. Antoine looked at his colleagues. They shook off their momentary paralysis and started helping the Nazis clear the plaza. My husband's face said it all. Now he knew what had happened in his beloved Saint-Malo during his absence. The world was not the same.

21

Encounter

O ver the next several weeks, Antoine kept close to the house. The exhaustion of facing reality left him no outlet but to isolate and lose himself in books. While I was in the library, he whiled away the hours in the sunroom contemplating the ocean battering against the city walls. Mercifully, Lt. Bauman had been sent to Berlin for a time, which allowed us some peace and the chance for Antoine to adapt to our new life. His lungs were not improving or responding to the medicine, though I also blamed his low spirits. He seemed to have little will to live. He did not talk much about what he had experienced on the front or in the prison camp.

Hermann started coming by the library in the mornings

when he was in Saint-Malo. At first, we did not speak. He would ask Céline for help or simply pass me the card of the book he wanted, but eventually we resumed discussing literature and history.

"How is your husband?" he asked a few days before Christmas. The city was muted. Only city hall had dared put up a few decorations. People could not understand why the Germans were still in our country. No one thought they had come to stay. Most of Saint-Malo's inhabitants hated or avoided them, but there were a few acts of resistance even though nearly everything was in short supply and our ration cards came nowhere close to covering the basics.

"He's not well, still very sick in his lungs. Some days he can hardly get out of bed." I was nervous about the conversation drifting into personal territory.

"I'm sorry to hear that. The war is wearing on us all. My colleagues are fatigued. At first, they looked on active duty in France as a privilege, like a long vacation, but everyone wishes to go home, especially this time of year. Plus, with the different attacks, they no longer feel as safe."

If he was trying to earn my sympathy, the well-being of his compatriots was the very last thing I cared about. We had lost so much. Happiness is always more fleeting than tragedy. That Christmas would be the saddest holiday we had ever experienced—and this even after I had forsworn celebrating it when my parents died.

"When will your colleagues be leaving us?" I asked, though I doubted he would know.

"Soon enough, I imagine. Rumor is, Hitler wants to invade the Soviet Union, but first he's got to take care of the Italians in Northern Africa and Greece."

His words did not cheer me. I still held on to the ridiculous hope that the war would end soon and things could go back to how they were before.

"I have something to tell you in private," he said, glancing at Céline, who never let him out of her sight.

I paused, knowing I couldn't refuse him. "Let's go upstairs," I said.

We climbed the spiral staircase and sat in front of the window. My eyes wandered to the locked glass cases with the rarest and most valuable books of our collection, the very ones Hermann had wanted to take away at first.

"Don't worry. I think they're safer here," he said, reading my mind.

"So what is it you want to tell me?"

His gaze met mine, but I looked away.

"I know you're a married woman, and I respect that, but if I do get the transfer I had requested, I don't want to go without you knowing what I feel for you."

"You have already told me. And besides, sometimes we fall in love with the idea of a person more than with the actual person," I answered.

"No, I know you well enough. I adore your courage, your energy, your intelligence. Were it not for this war and if I'd met you under different circumstances, I'm convinced you would've been the love of my life."

"I'm very, very sorry for you, but I already have the love of my life. He may be wrecked inside and out, just a shadow of who he was, but loving is much more than a feeling. It's also a choice."

"I understand that and love you all the more for it." He reached out his hand toward my hair, but I pulled back. I did not want him to touch me. I felt confused and guilty even sitting alone with him. "If only we had more than one life, I would love you to the end," he said, getting to his feet.

He placed an envelope on a glass case. "The commander has invited all the police to a Christmas party tomorrow night." He did not look at me as he spoke. "This envelope contains a special pass."

"I don't think we'll be able to make it," I answered.

"To refuse would be considered an affront. All the local government leaders will be there as well as the police—and you're the librarian and your husband is a police officer."

"We'll see."

"I can only protect you if you work with me."

"I understand."

"You'll always be in my heart," he said, turning to go.

I stayed where I was seated, with the sealed envelope on the glass case. My mind couldn't make sense of anything. I closed my eyes and began to cry, begging God for things to go back to how they used to be. I longed for the happy times, the bright mornings when Antoine and I would walk hand in hand to eat at a restaurant by the port; the afternoons spent reading with the ocean as our backdrop; even his care over me when I was sick. Now everything was confusing and painful. Remembering is easy, but love will not let us forget that we once loved and dreamed about living forever with our beloved.

22

The Little Spy

When I told Antoine that we had to go to a Christmas party thrown by the Nazis, he nearly fainted. Yet he had no choice but to give in. Since his return, he had avoided all society. He had not wanted to see his colleagues or friends, only his elderly mother and his uncle who lived on the outskirts of town. I dusted off his tuxedo and pulled out my nicest evening gown, a lovely green satin dress with matching long gloves and heels. I locked myself in the bathroom and spent a good part of the afternoon getting ready. Then at the dresser, I put on the jewelry Antoine had given me when we first started courting and which I had never gotten to wear. I found him sitting in the living room. The tuxedo still fit him. Though he was much thinner than the last time he had worn it, he always carried himself well.

"You're ravishing," he said with a sparkle in his eye. It was the first time he had looked almost chipper since his return. He wrapped his arms around me, and we held each other for a few moments, dreaming of the end of the war and this long parenthesis in our life. We still could not kiss. Antoine was afraid I would catch whatever he had and that my tuberculosis would flare up again.

"We should go," I said.

As we went down the stairs, we ran into Mrs. Fave.

"How nice to see you again, Mr. Ferrec."

"And you, Mrs. Fave," Antoine said, his hand in mine.

"Looks like you're headed to a party. In these times not everyone can afford such a luxury, but while you were away your wife made the most of it. The Germans must be good company."

I gave her a stony look, which she returned with a cold smile.

"Merry Christmas!" she called, slipping into her apartment.

Antoine gave me a quizzical look but did not say anything as we kept going down the stairs. We got into Denis's car and drove the few miles that separated us from the commander's residence, one of the old mansions outside of Saint-Malo. It was late, but we had special written permission from Hermann.

When we arrived, the white lights decorating the front stairs pulsed in the cold evening air. The entry was flanked by two armed guards in dress uniform, and a soldier was parking the cars. We went up the stairs to the front door, which another soldier opened for us. In the foyer, a soldier dressed as a waiter took our coats and directed us to the main hall. Some fifty people were chatting over wine or dancing to the army band. Only a dozen or so French were in attendance: the mayor, a few city councilors, a count and his wife, two of the wealthiest men in Saint-Malo and their wives, and the leaders of Saint-Malo's Fascist Party. We recognized them all but knew none of them well except the police chief.

"My dear Antoine!" the commissary called when he saw us, waving us over.

"Jean, I'm so glad to see you again."

"Please meet Marcel, Honoré, and William. They work with the German government to get us our food, winter clothes, and other supplies."

My stomach twisted in the presence of such people, but I forced a smile.

A blond woman, the wife of Marcel, the biggest meat distributor around, came to save me. "I'd better whisk you away from these boring charlatans. They'll spend the whole night talking business. The French women are over here by the appetizers." She nodded at someone at another table then went on. "I'm Susan. Delighted to meet you. You do such good work at the library. I heard you even take books to the school. My son is a student there. Perhaps you've seen him?"

I connected the dots between her facial features and the horrible boy who had attacked the Jewish teacher a few months before. I tried not to break my smile.

"This is Anna, and this is Joséphine," Susan went on. The two women were wearing expensive but vulgar dresses, a sign of their distinction as newly monied.

We sat down, and the three women started chatting.

"What a charming party. There's been nothing like this in Saint-Malo for years. And people say the Germans are barbarians. At least they've brought some order to town and have rid us of all the communists and Jews," Susan said.

"Yes," Joséphine chimed in. "Marshal Pétain has saved France from anarchy and communism."

I grimaced and took a sip of champagne to relax. Now was not the time to get entangled in an argument with these women.

"Now, your husband just got back from Germany, isn't that right, Jocelyn?" Susan turned to me with a confidential tone. "I hope all our men will be back soon. We're no longer at war with the Germans, though I for one am in no rush to restore peace in Europe. Our husbands are making a pretty penny on the military," she said, giggling.

"When it's somebody else's son or brother dying on the front, it's easy to like the war," I answered.

She pursed her lips, and the extra wrinkles that formed around her mouth were none too becoming.

I glanced around and was surprised to spot Pierre, the boy who had taken my letters to Paris.

"Excuse me, ladies. I see someone I need to say hello to."

They started whispering about me before I was even out of earshot. I sighed. At least I had given them something to talk about and fill up the next few minutes of their vacuous lives. I waved to Pierre.

"Mrs. Ferrec—I mean, Jocelyn. You're the last person I expected to see here!" he said.

"I could say the same about you."

"My father is the mayor of Saint-Servan. He doesn't much care for fraternizing with the Nazis, but he didn't have a choice today."

"The same thing happened to us," I said, lifting my eyebrows. Just seeing Pierre improved my mood, despite our being surrounded by German uniforms and their lovers.

"I'm working for the Special Operations Executive now,"

Pierre whispered. "Jean Moreau is my code name. My job is to sketch the city's defenses. Did you know the Germans are starting to fortify the entire Atlantic coast? They think that the Brits and Americans might attempt a landing."

What an absurd idea. I had hoped that the Nazis would leave us, that the British would sign a peace agreement, and that France would slowly return to normal. For that dream I was willing to join the Resistance and demand the Vichy government grant legal status to all political parties and immediately reestablish a republic. But all I said was, "Sounds like a dangerous job."

"It is, but like I said before, kids are pretty much invisible to the Germans." He beamed with his angelic smile.

Just then Hermann approached, and Pierre bid me farewell.

"Mrs. Ferrec," Hermann said coldly.

I returned his greeting. "Von Choltiz, I hope you're enjoying the party."

"This lot turns my stomach," he said. "They're a pack of leeches."

"Well, you look like you fit right in," I said, eyeing his dress uniform, his slicked-back hair, and the cigarette he smoked while balancing champagne in his other hand.

"We all have to survive somehow. Things can't be this bad for long."

Antoine came up and eyed Hermann with caution.

"You must be Antoine, Jocelyn's husband," Hermann said courteously.

"Yes, but I didn't catch your name." I could tell Antoine was not pleased.

"Forgive me for not introducing myself. My name is Hermann von Choltiz, head of library and bookstore records, which is how

I know your wife. I also tried to help retrieve your friend Denis from prison, but he had already been sent out of the country."

This got Antoine's attention. "Thank you so much, even if your attempts failed. Do you think there's anything else we can do from here?"

"I'm afraid not. Dachau is under the SS's jurisdiction, and they're the only ones with the authority to release him."

One of the waiters began ushering guests to the dining room. We were seated at a long table presided over by the commander, who put in his monocle and stood to say a few words. "Thank you all for coming. Though we're still at war, this will surely be the last Christmas we'll suffer the unhappy scourge of this conflict. Just a few months ago we were enemies. We've faced each other in two bloody wars, but the Third Reich will bring long-lasting peace and prosperity like the world has never known. Long live the Führer! And Merry Christmas to all!"

The entire table stood and toasted Adolf Hitler. Antoine and I looked at each other before a listless, mute clink of the glasses with the French around us. I had no idea what the new year would bring. If I had learned anything from life and the war, it was that we could make no plans and that everything could change in a matter of seconds.

23

Resist

Every week Pierre buzzed around the port on his bicycle, taking note of the fortifications the Germans were gradually building. He could not take photographs or even pull out his notebook and sketch, but he tried to commit every detail to memory. Then he would come to the library and draw for several hours straight.

The newspaper *La Résistance* had begun to arrive by December. Pierre brought them from Paris and I hand-delivered them to our contacts in Saint-Malo. That morning I prepped ten copies and nestled them into my saddlebag. I asked Céline to close up at noon, then I got on my bike. Outside the ground was crunchy with frost. At night it fell below zero and had snowed a few times, but by noon the roads were safer and I rarely hit ice patches.

I left the walls and headed for the home of Josua Goll, the former teacher. The only time we saw each other now was when I brought him the newspaper. I parked in front of his house and knocked. He was slow to answer, fearful of the fascist hordes that grew by the day and chased down Jews and anyone not lining themselves up with the new France.

"Mrs. Ferrec, how wonderful to see you. Please, come in. I'll make some coffee."

As a rule, I did not tarry when delivering the papers, as it was too dangerous to hold on to them for long. But I had a soft spot for the elderly teacher. I sat at the round table in the small living room, and within minutes he returned with cookies and two steaming mugs of coffee.

"I'm sorry I can't offer you more, as I don't get much these days. My pay as a retired teacher is none too robust, but I can't complain. I'm better off than many others."

I returned his smile, appreciating his humility.

"There are rumors that the Allies are holding out well in Greece and Egypt," he went on. "I tune into the BBC whenever I can."

"Be careful," I warned him.

He shrugged. "What can they take that they haven't already stolen? My life? Teaching was everything to me. Now I'm just a social parasite, an old man waiting to die."

I tsked. "Don't say that."

"But it's true. If only the Americans would enter the war . . . but they're too caught up in getting rich selling weapons to the Brits."

"Well, the Germans will head home soon, and we'll get our lives back," I answered.

He guffawed at that and nibbled a cookie. "I'm from Germany, though I've been in France since '33. As soon as Hitler came to power, I got out of there, though Germany had gone to seed long before. I'm convinced that if it hadn't been Hitler, some other fanatic would have come up with something similar to Nazism. The Germans never got over the trauma of the Great War. They thought they were a mighty power, their Prussian spirit sweeping everything aside. I was born in Nuremberg, the cradle of Nazism. At their annual meeting they would turn the city, together with Munich, into the symbol of the eternal Germany. Little by little, we Jews were excluded from daily life. We were like ghosts, living specters. I thought I'd be safe here in France, so I became a citizen to escape their clutches. I wasn't alone—a lot of Germans did the same. Now I'm stateless. To the Germans, I'm a dirty Jew; to the French, I'm a foreigner. Every single day I expect to hear them banging on the door, come to blow my brains out."

I shuddered. "Surely they wouldn't do that."

"The Jews in Germany, and especially now in Poland, are being wiped out. They've set up new ghettos so that the poor wretches die of hunger and disappear without a trace. The worst of all is that I've never even considered myself a Jew. My family wasn't religious, and I've only been in a synagogue once or twice. Many of us have turned our backs on our culture in order to fit in, to overcome the stigma of being different. But for the Nazis, if you're born a Jew, you're always a Jew."

"You'll be safe here, I'm sure. The French authorities would never be accomplices to crimes like that." I found myself repeating the nonsense of the naïve because I could not bear for Josua to suffer more. I wanted to comfort him though I knew the words rang hollow.

Josua pursed his lips, meditating on his response. "We've been persecuted since the sacking of Jerusalem in AD 70. I don't know how we've managed to survive, but Jocelyn, believe me: There's just as much anti-Semitism in France as there is in Germany. We'll never be safe anywhere."

———————•◆•———————

Josua's words reverberated through my head as I delivered the rest of the newspapers to a farm, the home of a nobleman, the modest apartment of a fisherman, and the small house of a seamstress. I was on my way back to Saint-Malo to deliver the last few when a German truck flew by me and I lost control of my bike, landing flat beyond the road's shoulder.

The front wheel of my bike was bent, and the tire was flat. I lay there on the frozen ground for a few moments, stunned. My right leg and ribs hurt, yet my head jerked up when I heard voices.

"Madame, we're so sorry we drove you off the road. The driver didn't see you," a soldier said with a thick German accent. I started shaking when I realized they had stopped to help me.

"It's fine, don't worry. I'm all right."

"Your leg is bleeding, and your bicycle is wrecked. Let us drive you home."

"Oh, please, there's no need. I can push the bike back. It's not far."

Yet one of the Germans picked my bike up and put it in the back of the truck, while the other helped me to my feet. I glanced at my saddlebag and could see some of the papers sticking out. If the soldiers saw it, I would be ruined.

The soldier helped me climb into the front of the truck, where I sat between them. They drove me to a bicycle shop.

I tried to protest while they pulled the bike out of the truck. "Really, it's fine. I can bring it later . . ." Then the soldier hoisted the bike through the air, and a copy of the newspaper fluttered out as he set it down in front of the mechanic. The German frowned and hastily put the paper away in his pocket.

I held my breath, sure that he would realize what it was.

"So where can we take you now?" he asked, without a hint as to what he had just seen.

"Um, in front of the library will do."

When they pulled up in front of the library entrance, getting out of the truck again was a painful process. Just then Céline showed up at the door.

Seeing me hurt and with two German soldiers, she croaked out, "What happened?"

"We accidentally bumped her off the road," said the one helping me out of the truck. Céline held the door open wide, and the soldiers helped me inside to a chair.

"Again, I'm so sorry about what happened," said the soldier who had been driving.

"Please, don't worry about it," I answered.

I let out my pent-up breath as soon as they drove away. Céline turned to me, her eyes wide. "Please tell me you had already delivered all the papers."

I could hardly form the words, which came out more like a squeak. "No, there were still a few in my saddlebag. The soldier saw them and took one with him."

"No, Jocelyn, no!"

"I don't understand why he didn't arrest me right then."

Céline began tending to my leg, wiping away the blood and

debris. It hurt, but it was only a minor wound. Finally, she spoke. "It's too dangerous. You have to stop."

"I cannot. We have to fight, to stay united, to tell people what's really going on in France and in the rest of the world."

She gave me a look that was a maternal mix of disapproval and tenderness.

"Do you want me to walk you home?"

"No, it's not far. I'd rather stay here to calm down a bit first. My nerves are shot."

Céline left a few minutes later, and I leaned back in my chair. My leg and ribs still hurt quite a bit, but I was more worried about the German. Surely he would denounce me any second. Then the phone rang.

"Jocelyn?" I heard on the other end of the line.

"Yes." It was a frightened whisper.

"It's Yvonne. I'm calling to tell you to be careful. Someone has turned us in, and the Gestapo are after me. I won't tell them anything, even if they kill me. Tell Pierre not to come near here anymore. They're watching the building to trap as many of us as they can."

"Are you sure? Can you get away?"

"I'm in my office, and the concierge just called to tell me they're on their way. Where can I go? Only God can help me now. May he be merciful. I'm just a dreamer who believes in freedom."

I could hear the sound of knocking at the door and then voices in German on the line.

"I'm free, Jocelyn—that's what matters. They'll never be able to lock up my soul. It can never belong to them . . ." Then she hung up.

I sat there stunned with the receiver in my hand. I knew the line was cut, but I could not hang it up. Fear paralyzed me. I closed my eyes and begged for Yvonne's life. I had never known anyone so brave. The grievous fact that the best were always the first to go weighed me down. Life respected the cowards but was implacable with the heroes.

24

An Englishman

Saint-Malo
May 3, 1941

Antoine's condition worsened with the onset of warmer days, and Dr. Aubry came to the house nearly every day to see him. I tried not to worry, but things were not going well. Since the Christmas dinner at the German commander's house, Antoine had grown more distant. I did not know if he harbored some ridiculous jealousy toward Hermann or if he was frustrated that his illness kept him from serving the city he loved. Or was he mentally unable to leave behind the battles at the front? I tried to talk with him and offer affection any way I could, but it only grew harder to connect. I figured he needed time to adjust, so I spent more and more time in the library. Hermann would stop by when he was in town, but I made sure we were never alone.

I was on edge for weeks waiting for the SS or the Gestapo to come get me. In March, several members of the Resistance in Paris were arrested, but the German soldier who had found the newspapers gave no signs of life until one spring morning.

I did not recognize him at first. Enough time had passed that I had nearly forgotten that entire day, but when he dropped the copy of the newspaper onto my desk, fear froze my blood.

"You may not remember me, but you must recognize this clandestine newspaper. My French isn't very good, but I can see from a mile away that it's a paper of the Resistance."

"I don't know what you're talking about," I mumbled.

"You're the woman we ran off the road in February. I've thought about it a lot since then and have finally made a decision."

"Decision about what? I don't understand."

"My name is Klaus, and I'm from Berlin. I come from a working-class family, and my parents were communists, but I joined the Nazi party in '35 when I was only seventeen. It was one way to rebel against my elders. I thought Hitler would build a new, egalitarian society. But he started out by locking up all the communists, then the socialists and any kind of political dissident, priests, and pastors who didn't agree with his policies. Now he's killing hundreds of thousands of Poles, Czechs, and people from other countries. I'm fed up. I've seen too much. I've got to do something."

I gaped at him. Could this be a trap? Maybe this was the Gestapo's way of hunting out the entire group, though after the raid in Paris, the only person I knew who was still formally connected to the Resistance was Pierre.

"I don't know anyone in the Resistance," I said.

"But you've got these subversive newspapers."

"They've arrested the entire group from Paris." My explanation did not seem to deter him.

"If we don't do something, millions of people will die. You must see by now that Hitler won't ever stop. When he conquers Europe, he'll head to America and Asia. You don't know what's going on in Poland and other places. It's terrible."

I was quiet for a moment. I knew he was right, but what could a librarian do to prevent the inevitable? Finally, I said, "Very well. I do have one idea."

I explained something I had been thinking about. One of the few ways to not raise suspicion was to start a book club. At most we could include seven people because the Nazis forbade larger gatherings except for religious services.

"That might be a good idea. And no one will suspect you if you invite a German." Klaus smiled at me. He was missing a few teeth, and the sadness surrounding his smile told of how he had struggled during the year and a half of war.

As soon as he left, I made a list of potential people to invite. Antoine was too ill, and I doubted he would be in favor of putting our lives on the line like this. Céline did not seem resolute enough, plus she was getting up in years. That left Josua Goll and Pierre. I needed to find one or two more.

"Of course!" I said aloud without realizing it, just as Céline came in, giving me a quizzical look.

She came over to my desk and asked. "Of course what?"

"Nothing," I said, covering the list with my hand.

"What's that list for?"

I did not know what to say. For someone trying to be a spy, I was terrible at lying.

"I think you're going to get yourself in trouble. I've heard the Nazis are executing Resistance members all over France. Those who aren't guilty of violent crimes are sent to Germany for terrible sentences of forced labor. You know your health isn't that strong and you could have a relapse. Plus, what will your husband do if you're not around?"

"Your imagination is running away with you, Céline."

"Imagination? I've seen how that Nazi von Choltiz looks at you. If it weren't for him, that SS pig would've burned the building down with us inside. Not to mention Pierre. I know he's taking things back and forth to Paris, including those long letters you write every day."

Céline was much less absentminded than I had thought.

"Don't worry," she went on. "I hate the Nazis and won't turn you in, of course, but I want to be part of whatever it is you're cooking up."

My eyebrows shot up in surprise.

"I may be weak and old, but I'm sharp and not likely to raise suspicion. I can be a connection or hide someone in my house, whatever you need."

Her courage filled me with hope, and I put my arms around her. The occupation had not yet lasted a full year, and it seemed to me like most people did not even care anymore. Some were getting rich on the suffering of the rest, and the town in general just looked the other way. Women were sleeping with the soldiers for better rations, and the children were starting to see the Germans as the heroes.

"Count Thierry le Gonidec is on your list," she observed.

"Yes, I've been delivering a newspaper to him."

I told her more about my idea, and we sat down and started planning out the meetings: their content, the people involved, the time frame, and all the details. I hoped everyone we wanted to contact would be excited to collaborate with us.

At midday we went to eat at a restaurant nearby before heading to Thierry le Gonidec's villa. He was not from Saint-Malo originally. Born in Verrières-le-Buisson, a Parisian suburb, he was from a respected and conservative Catholic family. He had studied in Paris, then joined the navy. The day France signed the armistice with Germany, le Gonidec had been on duty in Egypt. Céline had told me all this over lunch.

We went through the gate that led to a wide lawn, walked up the front steps, and knocked at the door. A few minutes later, the navy officer opened it and stood looking at us in surprise.

"I'm Céline, the librarian. We met years ago, and you recently came by for a few books." We had decided that Céline would do most of the talking, as an elderly woman was likely to be more successful against any reluctance.

"Yes, I'm so sorry. I must not have returned them in time, though I didn't know you made house calls to collect overdue books. Do I owe a fine?"

"No, Mr. le Gonidec, we've come about another matter. May we come in?"

"Yes, of course," he said, stepping aside. "Forgive my manners. I don't have any servants, and the house is rather a shambles."

"We understand, Mr. le Gonidec. Nature hasn't gifted men with orderliness," Céline said generously.

He led us to the library, where I was surprised and delighted by the quantity of books, including some first editions of famous French authors.

"They're not mine," he said as the bookshelves drew me like a magnet.

"That's too bad," I said wistfully.

"I haven't introduced my companion," Céline said. "This is Jocelyn Ferrec, the current director of the library."

"The police sergeant's wife?" he asked, shaking my hand.

"Indeed," I answered with a smile. Though I had delivered many issues of *La Résistance* to the agreed-upon spot on his porch, I had never actually crossed paths with the count.

The velvet couch where we were seated was comfortable despite its old, shabby appearance.

"Would you like some tea?" our host offered.

"No, this will be brief. My friend Jocelyn and I would like to start a book club."

Le Gonidec raised his eyebrows, wondering what this was about. He was very handsome, with a dark complexion, delicate features, and large eyes. He carried himself with the military elegance of years of training and discipline.

"I'm afraid I don't have much time. You may not be aware, but my days are full of travel, importing and exporting, ah, products."

Céline gave me a look asking for permission, and I nodded.

"It's not actually a typical book club, you see . . . Jocelyn has been delivering the clandestine newspaper to you, as you were on the list of people who want to do something for the Republic, to take action."

Le Gonidec's face remained unchanged, as if he had no idea what we were talking about.

Céline went on. "The book club would be part of the underground network, making pamphlets, helping members of the Resistance—that sort of thing."

The man burst out in loud peals of laughter. "Two librarians, for the love of all things good and holy! What can you do against the Germans?"

Céline was incensed. "In these times, all French citizens have a duty. We can't expect anything from the Vichy government."

"The Vichy regime is just a puppet of the Germans, but there's little we can do until de Gaulle comes with his troops."

"So you're going to sit back and do nothing while the Nazis plunder and subjugate our people?" I asked, leaning toward him.

"I'm a professional military man. The German army is the most powerful army in the world. They are creating a defense along the Atlantic coast to prevent a future landing by their enemies. Until then, the best thing is for us not to do anything that makes the situation even worse."

The aristocrat got to his feet. We did the same and left the house in a fury. Before we reached the edge of the lawn, we were startled by the sound of a man's voice calling to us. Had we been followed? We could barely make out the face in the shadows of the bushes where he was half hidden.

"Excuse me, madames. My name is Aitor Riba. I work with Thierry. Don't pay attention to him. I listened to everything from the next room over. Your idea sounds brilliant to me. If you're able, would you be willing to help me hide a British pilot? A fishing boat is coming next week to take him to England."

My eyes met Céline's in silent agreement. We had entered the Resistance without even knowing it.

25

The Book Club

Saint-Malo
July 16, 1941

We met once a week at eight o'clock. Klaus was the only one who could not come to all the meetings. After just two months, we had managed to accomplish a few important things. Céline had housed a British pilot for a week, after which Thierry—who decided to join us after all—and his friend Aitor smuggled him to Mont-Saint-Michel, where a fishing boat took him to England. That had been our first success, and we were well on our way to more. Klaus was leaving anonymous messages in the bathrooms of restaurants frequented by Germans, hoping little by little to get through to a few. Céline and I distributed a rudimentary newsletter every other week to about fifty trusted people, and Josua joined Aitor in transmitting information by radio.

That day we gathered like usual in the library. Antoine and I had gotten into an argument when I told him I would be back later. Totally out of character for him, he had yelled at me and asked if I was going to see my lover. It had been two weeks since I had seen Hermann, but he showed up that night in the library. We were on the upper floor, with the main entrance locked, but all the members of the club knew they could enter the building unobserved by a side door. In case anyone found us, we would explain that we were a book club. We had even requested and been granted permission by the local authorities and the German command.

Pierre and Josua arrived first, and Thierry and Aitor a little later. Céline had prepared some observations on a reading from *The Three Musketeers* in case the Germans sent an inspector.

"Should we wait for Klaus?" Pierre asked.

"No," I said. "If he hasn't arrived by now, he probably can't come."

"Well, let's discuss the immortal work of the great Alexandre Dumas," Céline said in a joking, exaggerated tone.

"The other day they almost found us," Aitor said. "The Germans have a nearly infallible system of detecting radio transmitters. Every week we change our location, but they always end up tracing our signal."

"Then we shouldn't transmit from the same spot twice," Josua said.

The rest of us nodded.

Thierry piped up. "Troops are on the move. Many Germans are being sent to Russia. We have to let the navy office know as soon as possible." He was hoping the British would be willing to try a landing if they saw the Nazis moving on to fight the Soviets.

"But the numbers are still low. Some of the French from the Legion of French Volunteers Against Bolshevism have joined the Germans being sent to Russia," Aitor explained.

Céline grunted. "I hope the Soviets give the Germans a good whipping."

"The German army is far superior." Aitor sighed.

"True," she said, "but they beat Napoleon. The biggest advantage the Russians have is the cold. If they hold out 'til winter, the Germans can never take them."

"That's what we all hope, Céline, but the devil seems to have sided with Hitler."

We heard footsteps coming up the stairwell, sounding like military boots. As one we turned and watched the door with bated breath. It opened slowly to reveal Hermann. He eyed us suspiciously from the doorway, and we tried not to squirm.

I stood and went to him. I closed the door and led him to another room.

"What is this?" he asked. "If this is an illegal meeting, I'll have to report you all," he threatened, though his tone belied confusion.

"It's not what it looks like," I said. "It's just a book club meeting."

He pursed his lips and rolled his eyes. "You take me for a fool."

Just then we heard more steps. I looked down the stairwell and saw Klaus. Hermann scrutinized him.

"Lieutenant!" Klaus said, saluting at attention.

"At ease, soldier. What on earth are you doing here?"

"I've come for book club."

Hermann frowned, and I followed him back into the other room.

"I don't know what you're plotting, but I can't protect you if you get wrapped up in a mess. You're lucky Bauman has been sent to the Russian front, but that doesn't guarantee your safety."

I was delighted to hear that news. It had been quite some time since we had seen him, but the constant threat of his presence still kept me up at night.

"If you'd like, you can join us. You'll see we're not doing anything bad or illegal."

"You don't realize you're playing with fire. We have moles and SS and Gestapo spies in nearly all the clandestine groups. Don't assume yours will be safe."

He left in a huff, slamming the door. The group was staring at me with worried faces when I returned.

"What did he want?" Céline asked.

"Hard to say. But he's gone now."

Sweat beaded on Klaus's red, worried face. He loosened his collar. "He'll denounce me to the commander." His voice trembled.

"No, he won't. Don't worry about him. He's as tired of this war as you are," I said, returning to my seat.

"We should wrap this meeting up," Thierry said.

"Yes, but let's not all leave at the same time," Céline suggested.

Josua and Aitor left first, then Klaus and Thierry, and finally Pierre. "Be careful," he said, gracing us with his youthful smile.

"We're more worried about you," I said.

When everyone had gone, we turned off the lights and went downstairs.

"I have a bad feeling," said Céline.

"It's not worth your worry. I don't think Hermann will denounce us."

"He might not, but every day we hear of more groups that the Nazis are chasing down and neutralizing. We should stop now before it's too late. The Soviets will take care of Hitler and his henchman."

"So now you're a fan of the communists?" I asked wryly.

"Anyone who can take care of the Boche has my favor. I truly don't think anyone could be worse than them."

———◆———

I headed for home. Antoine was sitting at the table waiting for me, his legs covered by a blanket despite the warmth of the day.

"Where have you been?" he asked when I kissed his forehead.

"At book club, like I told you."

"Have you been with him?"

That comment drove me up the wall. I had never loved anyone like I loved my husband, not even when I was scared and all alone and Hermann had helped me.

"You are the only man in my life, Antoine."

"How can you love a residue of humanity? There's nothing left of a man in me."

"You'll get better, my love. The doctor says—"

"Don't lie to me, Jocelyn. There's simply not enough medicine in Saint-Malo, and without it, I'll never get better. I'm coughing up more and more blood, and I grow weaker and weaker every day. I can hardly get from the bed to the table without help."

He spoke the truth, but I refused to acknowledge it. I did not know how to. He had helped me when I was so sick, but it terrified me to be with him and watch him shutting down and becoming a ghost of himself.

I slumped down exhausted beside him and turned up the radio he had been listening to on low volume. The BBC was announcing that the non-French Jews would be sent to camps in France.

"Dear God in heaven!" I exclaimed, thinking of all the Jewish people I knew in the city, including Josua and the Remarques.

For the first time in a long time, Antoine looked up at me with a tender look. He touched my face gently as my tears splashed down on the tablecloth.

"One day this nightmare will be over," he whispered. The station started playing music, and I closed my eyes and tried to remember good times—days of wine and roses when it felt like nothing bad would ever happen and the world was safe and beautiful.

26

The Flowers of the Republic

Saint-Malo
July 17, 1941

We were woken sometime before dawn by noises. I startled awake, and Antoine was sitting up in bed beside me, breathing heavily.

"What was that?" I asked.

"Noises on the stairwell," he said.

I put on my robe, went to the door, and cracked it ever so slightly. I could hear the clomping of boots and knocking at doors. I peered over the stairwell and could tell the commotion was coming from below. My heart pounded, but I decided to go downstairs. The Remarques' door was open, and the children were screaming and crying, but I did not see anyone. I stood outside for a moment, then went in.

A few gendarmes had gathered the whole family in the living room. All but the oldest two children were howling and clinging to their mother, whose face was painted with terror. They looked like animals cornered by wild beasts.

"What are you doing here, madame?" one of the policemen demanded as he shoved me to the door. I tried to resist, but it was useless. He took me out to the landing and yelled, "Keep your nose out of other people's messes! It's not worth it!"

"What have they done? They're a good family," I said, my eyes smarting with tears.

"The government has ordered all the Jews to be sent to camps. It's a provisional measure. Perhaps they think they're all Soviet spies. Most of the Jews are communists anyhow," the gendarme said.

"And the young children? Are they dangerous too?"

"The children are like rats. They seem innocent while they're young, but they grow up to be a plague."

Two other policemen herded the family out and down the hall, the children wailing the whole time. They had changed their clothes and carried small suitcases. Marie gave me a terrified look when she passed me.

"You can't take them!" I started yelling in my horror. "Neighbors, everyone in the building—they're taking an innocent family away!"

Mrs. Fave came out of her apartment. "What's all this racket?"

"They're taking the Remarque family away," I said, grabbing one of the children by the arm.

"Why all the fuss? Let them take the Jews. Everyone knew about them, but the Germans didn't know for sure they were Jews. I'm the one who denounced them," she spat.

"You? You're a witch, a murderous old witch!" I raved as the gendarmes dragged the children away from me and down the stairs.

Suddenly Antoine appeared at the top of the stairs and shouted at the men. "Michel! What's going on here?" Antoine, who was nowhere near strong enough to go back to work and probably never would be, had put on his uniform, though the buttons were misaligned and I could see house shoes on his feet.

"I'm sorry, Antoine, but we're in a hurry. We've got several houses to go."

"But I'm your sergeant!" Antoine was furious, but his voice trembled weakly.

"They're orders from higher up. This family wasn't registered, but the neighbor gave us proof that they are Jews."

"Leave the family! I'll answer for them. Tomorrow I'll go to the commissary and speak with the captain."

"I'm sorry, Antoine," the policeman said, then pushed Marie farther down the stairs.

I tried to pull on another policeman's arm, but he shoved me aside and yanked the child from me. Antoine bounded down the stairs and put his hands on Michel's back. "At least leave the children," he said.

The gendarme shook off Antoine's grasp, and my husband fell down the stairs. His former colleagues did not help him up. They just went on their way with the Remarques. I ran to help Antoine, and from the landing above, Mrs. Fave sneered down at us. "I hope you two will be next. At last someone is cleansing France of all the communists, Jews, and Masons." With that, she turned and slammed her door.

Antoine had fainted. I tried to hoist him on my shoulder and drag him up the stairs, but he was too heavy for me. A few minutes later when everything was quiet, Leo, one of the neighbors who had not come out during the commotion, appeared and helped me move my husband upstairs and into bed.

Leo called Dr. Aubry, who did not hesitate to come despite the late hour. An hour later he arrived and examined Antoine, who was still unconscious and bathed in sweat.

"You have to help me bring his fever down," he said.

We put him in the bathtub and filled it with cold water, but he did not respond. The doctor was worried. We got Antoine back into bed with no blankets covering him and the window open, but it had been a hot, suffocating night. Just as dawn was breaking, Antoine came to long enough to look at me, then fall back to sleep.

———— • ◆ • ————

The telephone woke me a few hours later. I had fallen asleep in a chair with my hand holding Antoine's. I was dazed as I answered.

"Who is it?" I asked nervously.

Céline's tense voice answered, "Jocelyn, they've taken Josua. All the Jews in Saint-Malo have been loaded into buses headed to Rennes, and from there I think they'll be taken to Paris."

"Antoine is in a bad way. I cannot leave him," I said apologetically.

"I'll call Thierry. This is really serious. I never dreamed the French would dare go this far. We have to call an urgent meeting today, but let's do it at my house, not at the library."

All morning I was anxious. I tried to feed Antoine, but he would not eat. His face grew more and more pale as the day dragged on.

The woman who helped around the house came by, and I

asked her to stay with Antoine until I could return. Then I dressed and went out without fixing my hair or putting on makeup.

I was horrified to find how normal everything seemed. People were visiting the beach, children were holding ice cream cones, and summer tourists were enjoying drinks on café patios as if nothing in the world was amiss.

Céline's house was not far, and once there, I knocked and waited. She opened nervously and looked all around before closing the door behind me. "Are you sure no one followed you?"

"Who would follow me?" I asked.

"A collaborationist or one of those fascists with their little mustaches."

I was too worried about Antoine to concern myself with being followed. Klaus, Thierry, and Pierre were already waiting in the living room. Aitor had not arrived yet.

Thierry's voice was muted with concern. "We've got to destroy any evidence. I don't know if the radio is still in Josua's house," he said.

"I was barely able to get here. They're moving all the Jews, and there's a special security unit about. The authorities are worried about reprisals from the Resistance," Klaus said.

"We must calm ourselves. It won't do anyone any good for us to lose our heads. Thierry and Pierre should go look for the radio, as I doubt the Germans will be searching their houses. And Klaus can't ever meet with us again," I said.

We were about to break up the meeting when we heard knocking at the door. Céline went to open it but tried to see who it was first.

"Dear God, it's the Germans," she whispered.

Pierre and the rest of us headed for the back of the house. We did not know if the Nazis had cordoned off the entire area, but it was clear that someone had ratted on us—perhaps even Josua once he was taken prisoner.

"Go out the back," Céline said. "I'll try to stall."

"But they'll arrest you!" I said.

"It doesn't matter. I've had a long, happy life. I haven't let these pigs turn me into a coward, and I'm not going to now. If I don't stall, they'll arrest every one of us."

We went to the back door, but just as Thierry and Klaus slipped out, two Germans grabbed them. Pierre and I ran upstairs. I opened the window, and Pierre gave me a look of sheer terror before stepping out. We scampered across the roof to the next building and went into the first window we saw. Luckily, the apartment seemed empty. My heart pounded in my ears as we ran down the stairs and crept out the front door. We could see the Germans down the street, but we tried to walk calmly as if nothing was wrong to avoid arousing suspicion.

Pierre went home, yet I was so worked up that I went by the library before returning to Antoine. I wanted to destroy any evidence there that could incriminate the group.

I burned our documents in a metal wastebasket and was getting ready to leave when Aitor walked in.

"Aitor! Did you get away?"

He looked at me indifferently, then said, "I didn't tell them anything about you or the boy. Call me sentimental, but Pierre is too young. But with you I've got a personal interest. I know you have several valuable manuscripts here. I'll take them with me, but first you'll have to do me another favor."

He pulled out a gun and aimed it at me.

"Please don't hurt me," I said, not understanding how someone from our inner circle could turn on me so quickly. "Take whatever you want from the library."

"That's exactly what I'm going to do, but first we'll have ourselves a good time."

He jumped at me, and I screamed. I tried to push him off, but he was too strong. My attempts at fighting back glanced off him uselessly.

"Please!" I implored, now almost in tears.

We heard footsteps, and Aitor turned and took aim. Two shots went off, and Aitor fell to the floor. Hermann was still pointing his gun when our eyes met. I was shaking all over with the nauseating sensation that there was no one left I could trust and that my small world was about to disappear forever.

27

Lover and Death

Saint-Malo
July 22, 1941

Céline was locked up in the castle along with Klaus and
Thierry. None of them gave us away. Klaus was executed
by the firing squad a few days later, and the others were sent to
Berlin. Hermann got rid of Aitor's body. I was sure no one would
miss him.

The night of the raid I was weak and trembling when I went
home. Antoine was a little better, but I did not leave his side for
the next several days. I had a feeling that we did not have much
time left together. Life seemed to be laughing at me again, stealing away yet again the beloved man it had almost let me have
back.

"Could you read to me, Jocelyn?" Antoine asked. The sun was setting over a calm sea.

"Of course," I said, swallowing back tears as I picked up a book. I read slowly, haunted by the fear that, if I stopped, my husband would no longer be beside me. My voice plodded on in a dismal litany with no intonation or variety, just a wisp of wind passing through leaves on a tree. I looked up periodically to make sure Antoine was still there. He put forth a big effort and smiled at me. For a moment his eyes were bright like they used to be, and I caught a flash of the young man who had wooed me, the one who had saved me from existing in monotonous, humdrum exile. I had rejected all joy after my parents died, but Antoine had brought me back to life.

"People don't want to die. I don't want to either, but I feel satisfied because I met you, and God, for a brief instant, let us be reunited. I've never been as happy as when I'm in your arms. You're my home, my whole life."

His words cut me to the quick. I sucked my breath in hard as tears welled up in my eyes.

He went on. "I beg God to protect you, Jocelyn. Forgive me for not valuing our love these past few months. I was con-fused and angry, not ready to die. Not because I was scared of death, but because I didn't want to leave you. The world has gone completely mad, and you're the only one worth staying alive for. On the front I saw so many men fall beside me. The bullets flew everywhere, taking my companions down but leaving me unscathed. I wondered a million times a day why some died and others lived. What's the point in all that? Now I know: There's no point at all. It's just part of our existence. But I want to believe you and I are part of something bigger—that all this beauty, the centuries of human knowledge, even all our good deeds, won't all just disappear."

"Don't strain yourself, please," I begged him. I wanted to stretch out each second, steal time back from death.

"All that's left is to say goodbye. I'm grateful to be conscious and lucid here in the end. My body can't go on anymore, but my mind feels sharper than ever, and I've never seen things as clearly as I do now. We work so hard to accumulate things, to achieve, to triumph; but the real victory is always and only love, in giving yourself away and expecting nothing in return, in forgiving and making the world a better place."

I was sobbing by then. "I love you," I eked out. Inside, my heart was tossing violently on a storm of tears.

"I love you too. Please, be happy, and don't forget me. I'll be waiting for you on the other side. I imagine heaven like a huge library, and each of the millions of volumes recounts the life of one of the billions of people who've walked the face of this earth. Nothing will be erased, nothing forgotten."

I held him and let the book slide to the floor. His body eased little by little as his soul ascended to his paradise, the library where each soul held its story until the seals would one day be opened and those souls would be reborn to make a new heaven and a new earth.

28

V

Saint-Malo
August 25, 1941

Antoine died twice. The first time was when I thought I had lost him in the war, drowned in the sea of soldiers marched off toward Germany. The second time was in the bedroom of our apartment with his face turned toward the ocean as evening cast the sea into pure shadow.

The next few days were terrible. I had no one to share my grief with, and sorrow strangled me and emptied me of everything. In those days, I would have been grateful had a bomb or a stray bullet found me.

After months of seemingly nothing, the British began bombing the Atlantic ports held by the Germans. Normandy and Brittany felt the first effects. Many innocent people lost their lives to the bombs of our allies, though the angry parts of me thought it was only fitting that our country should be purged into waking up again.

The Nazis had taken away everything I loved. It was their fault Antoine was dead. Their mistreatment of him and then the shortages of medicine were to blame. Céline was locked up, and Denis had disappeared into some camp in Germany. The only one left was Pierre, who was trying to get me to reopen the library and sometimes managed to drag me out for a bike ride or a picnic in the countryside.

That day Pierre showed up with his bike and a basket packed with food. "My mother put something together for us. I added wine for you and a Coke for me. Let's go to the beach. The weather won't stay warm for much longer."

I frowned. The countryside was one way of escaping the reality of the city, but the beach was something else altogether. The beach had always been a happy place for me and Antoine, and I was by no means ready to feel happiness again.

"Let's go to the woods instead," I said, trying to act interested.

"No, I've already got my swimsuit. The beach is the only place I can really forget about the war." Eventually I gave in, unable to disappoint his sweet little spirit. Youth is much more persuasive than maturity, reminding us of what we have forgotten: that the present is the only thing that actually exists.

We got our bikes and rode for half an hour to Pierre's favorite spot. Few people were there, just a few families with umbrellas and picnic baskets, a group of boys, and a little farther off, a group of German soldiers.

We took off our outer clothes and threw ourselves down on the towels Pierre had brought. My sunglasses partially dimmed the glaring sun, and a big straw hat covered my face.

"Just listen," Pierre said, pointing to the ocean.

The waves whispered their lovely songs while the voices of children playing filled the atmosphere with so much life I could hardly take it. I pulled out a book and started to read.

"No," Pierre said, lowering my book. "No reading today." He pulled me to my feet, knocked off my glasses and hat, and dragged me to the water. We walked in with great strides. It was so cold, and in that moment, I would have detested the feel of anything that reminded me I had a body that was alive. I did not have the right to be happy.

After swimming a bit, we stretched out on the towels again. The breeze gave me goose bumps, and the sun slowly dried up the waterdrops shining on my back.

"Look." Pierre held up a photograph of our book club.

"Don't remind me," I said, grabbing it with my damp fingers. It was hard to believe that just last month we had all been together. "It's just us left. At first, I thought they'd be coming for me any minute, but I suppose they didn't have our names. That traitor didn't give you and me up for some reason." I did not tell Pierre what had happened with Aitor later in the library or that Hermann had done away with him.

Pierre changed the subject. "The Germans are advancing fast through Russia. Nobody can stand up to them."

We had all been hoping the Soviets would whip Hitler, but Stalin seemed as paralyzed as the rest of the world. Meanwhile Great Britain was just trying to survive and halt the Germans in Africa.

Some children from the family to the right of us started running around pretending to fire pretend guns made of sticks. I was horrified to see them playing at war. Generation after generation, we were condemned to repeat the same folly.

"The Special Operations Executive has put me in touch with a new contact named Raymonde. I can take your letters to Paris again."

Pierre's comment was like a punch to the stomach. I had not written in weeks, and I doubted if I had the strength to keep telling my story. Then Antoine's words floated up to me—that his heaven was like a huge library full of the stories of everyone who had gone before us. Would it not be marvelous to bring a bit of that paradise to the inferno we were living in every day?

"Getting back to writing would do you good," Pierre insisted.

"What is Marcel Zola like?" I dared to ask. I had never seen a photograph of him and did not know what he was like in person, though I could intuit his soul from his writings.

"He's really different from anyone else I know. He's about fifty years old, has gray, almost white hair, a receding hairline, wrinkles all over his wide forehead, small sneaky eyes that you can tell have seen a lot. He's got a wide smile that fills his cheeks, which are really wide even though he's skinny. He always dresses well, but not showy. He's really nice and calm, like he's wrapped up in a big world inside himself."

"How do you know him so well?" I asked, taken aback. Pierre's skills of observation were well honed.

"I heard he was giving a talk on literature at the Sorbonne. He's not a full-time professor, but they invite him to give lectures on occasion. I'm guessing the room was full of Nazi spies, but no one could accuse him of anything. We all left encouraged and feeling change might be possible."

I marveled at Pierre. He started unloading the basket his mother had packed. Food always tastes stronger outdoors in nature, as if it somehow returned to its natural element. After eating, we walked for a while along the shore. A group of German soldiers was splashing in the waves, seemingly without a care.

"You see that? They can do that feeling so safe and secure, but we can't."

Pierre glanced around and motioned toward their clothes on the beach. When the men appeared especially distracted, we grabbed their possessions off the beach, ran to the walkway, and threw everything they'd brought into a trash can. That little exploit cheered up our whole day. It is the only day from that summer that I look back on with a smile.

We hurried to pack up and headed back into town on our bikes. But something caught my attention on the way.

"Do you see that?" I asked pointing to a huge letter *V* painted on some walls.

"I haven't seen that before," Pierre answered.

As we continued, we saw dozens of those *V*s everywhere. Surely it was a sign that people were starting to lose their fear of the Germans and rooting for an Allied victory. France's honeymoon with the Third Reich could not last forever. The Nazis would not delay in showing what malicious occupiers they had always been, even though most of our citizens had looked the other way. Our countrymen had fantasized that as long as they were not Jews, communists, or socialists, they had nothing to fear. They failed to understand in time that the simple fact of not belonging to the German "superior race" turned them into beasts in Nazi eyes.

29

The Gendarmes

Paris
December 28, 1941

The Christmas of 1941 was far worse than the one before. Everything, simply everything, was in short supply or impossible to get. The Germans needed endless resources for their war in Russia, which was weighing them down, and France was the fat juicy cow they could squeeze 'til she bled. The Germans took the lion's share of the harvests, the raw materials, the petroleum, the animals . . . Then finally, they started sending our boys to work in their men-vacant industries. Vice Premier Darlan attempted to reign in the Nazis, but the French people were given crumbs to live on.

All summer and fall Pierre traveled back and forth to Paris. I started writing my letters again and formed a new group of resisters. It was small, and we did not do much of import, but we committed ourselves to making life difficult for the Germans.

The Nazi contingent in Saint-Malo was drastically reduced. Fewer soldiers walked the streets, women took care not to be seen in public with the enemy, and anti-German paintings cropped up everywhere.

That year I received a letter from the Ministry of Culture, who wanted to hold a meeting in Paris to promote two propaganda campaigns. One campaign about Jews in France had already been presented at an earlier meeting and was met with great success in the capital. Soon they would launch a new one about Bolsheviks and France, and they wanted us to be aware of how important it was to spread these ideas in every department in the country.

I traveled there with Pierre, a perfect excuse to meet his contact and get instructions on how to be more useful to the Resistance. Yet I also harbored the secret hope of meeting you, Marcel.

After reading your letters for so many months, I valued your correspondence friendship. I was curious to know if you were how I pictured you or just a projection of my hopes.

We took the train to Rennes since there was no longer a direct line to Paris from Saint-Malo. The railway system was at the service of the Third Reich, and the needs of French travelers were far down on the list of priorities. In the third-class car I was shocked to see so many people traveling despite the restrictions, the need for permission, and the high cost of tickets.

We shared a compartment with a Catholic priest, a woman with two daughters, and two students who were going home for break. Pierre dozed off just after we left Rennes. The trip would take nearly all night because passenger trains stopped anytime a German military car needed the rails. Young people seem eternally hungry or sleepy. As we get older, the body breaks down, and neither food nor rest brings relief; I was still somewhere in the middle.

I started walking the hallways to distract myself and noted that we stopped for a very long time at an out-of-the-way station near Laval. Through the dirty glass windows, I could see a large group of gendarmes and dogs climbing into one end of the train.

It did not take much imagination to figure out that those regime sellouts would be coming after Jews and any kind of dissident, especially communists. Communists had become an obsession for the crazed Nazis and their collaborators.

At first I was nervous, then I calmed down remembering our papers were in order. I went back to our compartment, where the mother was staring out the window with a worried expression. The rest of the passengers, including her daughters, were asleep.

"What's happening?" she asked as I entered.

"The gendarmes are doing an inspection."

This news caused her concern to turn into visible shaking. She rummaged for something in her purse but apparently her nerves kept her from finding it.

"Are you all right?" I whispered. I was seated directly in front of her, and she leaned forward to answer.

"I don't have papers. We managed to avoid the raids in July and August and were going to Paris to hide in a friend's house. They say it's easier to go unnoticed in the city, though lots of people told us we should head for Vichy."

"Jews?" I mouthed the word, and she nodded. We could hear the gendarme boots coming down the hall.

"What can I do?" the mother hissed in desperation.

The priest's eyes popped open. He had heard our exchange.

He turned, his great belly straining against his cassock, and said, "Daughter, I can't help you, but I can protect the girls. I can tell the gendarmes they're students at the charity school where I teach. You'll have to flee and then find us later. They'll be safe there with the nuns."

The woman looked at her two children who slept, peaceful and oblivious, and began to cry. My heart broke to watch a mother making the hardest choice of her life.

"Take care of them, I beg you. They're the only thing I have left in this life. We've already lost my parents, my husband, and my sisters. They took our grocery store and our house. These suitcases are all we have. The remains of our unfortunate family are inside."

The woman's words moved even the priest to tears. "'Whoever loses mother or father, possessions or anything else for my sake will receive double in return.' God will reward you, daughter, if not in this life then in the next."

The woman—a complete stranger—stood, and we embraced. Something deeper than friendship united us: Neither of us had lost our humanity. Many people think human beings are what is wrong with the world, but the real problem is dehumanization. Philosophy has relegated us to the condition of rational animals, robbing us of all the virtues that make us special and reducing us to mere beasts whose only purpose is to reproduce and protect our descendants.

"Thank you," she said, turning to the priest.

The priest wiped his tears away and kissed the woman's hands.

She slipped out of the compartment, and in our different ways the priest and I both prayed she would have time to disappear into the night. She managed to exit the train, and from the window we watched as she slunk across the tracks, but the police spotted her and yelled before she made it to the darkness of the forest. She kept running, and we heard shots fired. My heart seized in my throat. Had she made it out?

The gendarmes knocked at our compartment, and a thick, bald, sweaty man demanded our papers. The girls were still asleep, and the policeman pointed to them.

"They're two of my nieces I'm taking back to the school with me. Their family can't look after them anymore," the priest explained evenly.

The gendarme scowled. "Where are their papers?"

"They are minors under my charge. My ID should be sufficient."

"We need some sort of documentation," the gendarme insisted.

A sergeant poked his head in and looked all around. "What's going on?"

"The girls don't have any papers. They're with the priest."

The sergeant saluted the priest, glanced at his ID, and said, "Thank you. May God keep you, Father."

They moved on to the next compartment, and we all sighed with relief. Pierre looked at me, trying to piece together what had happened, and then fell back asleep. I could not stop thinking about what would happen when the girls woke up and their mother was not there.

I finally dozed off right as we were approaching Paris. The girls woke up the same time most of the other passengers did.

The younger, who could not have been older than four, immediately yelled, "Mama!" The other, probably around ten, was looking all around. Her eyes belied her fear, though she was clearly trying to stay calm for her sister's sake.

"Your mother had to go. I'll take you to a school where you'll stay until she comes to get you soon. Don't worry," the priest said with a smooth, soft tone that tried to lessen the blow.

The younger one started bawling, but the older one held her and steadied herself. "Don't cry, Alice. We're going to a school. You remember all the wonderful things I would tell you about school before the Germans came? Before we had to wear the yellow star?" She wiped her sister's tears, and they picked up their suitcases and followed the priest. I watched them go down the platform, wondering if they would ever see their mother again or be on their own forever.

———— • ◆ • ————

First I attended the librarians' meeting in the ministry's office. Pierre went to his scout's group, which was his excuse for traveling to the capital so often, and we agreed to meet back up after lunch.

Paris seemed even sadder than the year before, though I sometimes wonder if we love or hate places based on how happy we have been in them in the past. The beautiful City of Lights had always been dark for me.

What hit me first about the ministry building was how many German soldiers were there, especially SS. The French employees were clearly the assistants; the state was in Nazi hands.

Nearly one thousand librarians were seated and waiting in the large auditorium when I entered. Most rows were already full, and I had to take a seat toward the front. As I settled in, I heard a voice call my name.

"Jocelyn!"

I turned and saw in the row behind me a university classmate,

Isabelle Martel, the librarian of the physics department at the Sorbonne.

"Oh my goodness, what a surprise!" I exclaimed.

"Don't leave without talking with me!" she said just as the program began.

A somewhat round man with glasses sat behind a table draped with red velvet and supporting a carafe of water and three glasses. Two high-ranking SS officers flanked him.

"My dear librarian colleagues!" he began. The audience quieted down, and all eyes turned to the stage. "We are in a great crusade against Bolshevik communism and international Judaism. The only way to defeat these plagues is through propaganda. Our beloved compatriots must be made aware of what is at stake: even more important than our safety is the happiness of our beloved France. At this very minute, our compatriots are facing the terrible Bolshevik killing machine. They are the vanguard and guardians of our Western, Catholic culture, and we librarians have a sacred duty. Until recently, many thought liberty was the paradigm of humanity, but the excess of freedom turned our society into human rubbish, into weak men and women blown about by any Marxist or capitalist idea that came their way. Our German friends"—here he paused to look to his left and then right—"have freed us from a corrupt, weak Republic manipulated by the Jews. Now we can return the favor by supporting their cause. A few months ago, the exposition on Jews in France was a big hit. You can take pamphlets and find a date to bring part of the exposition to your city or town. The Jews are finally starting to show their true nature now that they can no longer hide out like venom among us."

My stomach churned at his words. I had just witnessed a mother forced to abandon her daughters. The German and

French authorities were both oppressing the Jews. What more evidence was needed?

Applause spread throughout the auditorium. I hesitated but eventually imitated everyone else in a halfhearted way, fearful someone would take note of any dissident attitudes in the room.

The speaker went on. "Some libraries are still harboring banned books. Up to now we have been benevolent, but we can no longer allow disobedience or questioning of the new norms. If your collection includes rare, highly valuable editions of banned content, please advise the Einsatzstab Reichsleiter Rosenberg. The ERR will take possession of those editions and store them in Paris. This is what our beloved leader, Marshal Pétain, is asking of us in the war against communism."

Frenetic applause again rang out across the auditorium. Then after viewing part of a documentary against communism, we were dismissed a little before noon.

Isabelle Martel tapped my shoulder. Her warm smile greeted me as I turned. "Want to get lunch?" she asked.

I shrugged, and she took my hand. We found a small restaurant overlooking the river and sat inside by the counter, catching up. It had been years since we had seen each other.

"I'm so sorry about your husband. Life is one surprise after another, and some of them awful."

I leaned forward and lowered my voice. "I presumed you would've gotten out of France by now." Everyone knew Isabelle had a Jewish and Bolshevik background.

"I had to falsify my origin, and I doubt they'll pick up on it. Of course it would be smarter to leave, but I want to fight. You know how I am. For lots of people we're nothing but intellectual parasites, but they have no idea of the power of words. The Nazis have built their entire Reich on words. They've used the radio, propaganda, the press, and even books. We're doing the same," she whispered.

"Not long ago they arrested all the main members of the Resistance in Paris, and in Saint-Malo too. It's getting harder and harder to fight." The conversation was depressing me. Pierre thought in line with Isabelle, but I was no longer convinced. Antoine's death had drained the life from me.

"But we've started another network, and the Brits are helping. Soon there will be thousands of us, and then hundreds of thousands."

"But didn't you hear the applause in the auditorium?"

She tsked. "Most of that was out of fear."

"Could be, Isabelle, but the fearful people are siding with the enemy."

She frowned. "We've got to do our duty. People need to hear another voice; otherwise, we can't ask them to be brave. Most people believe that a world different from this one is possible. Help me show them a better option."

Her words managed to break through and ignite a spark of emotion in me. Could my life be worth something after all? So many times I had felt lost in a world that seemed pointless. Then here came Nazism to give us a mission: to rid ourselves of it. I scribbled my address and phone number down on a piece of paper and handed it to her.

"See you soon," she said, getting to her feet. I stayed seated for a bit longer. Isabelle's words circled around my brain. Antoine and books had been my whole world. Now I had to fight for change. As long as France was occupied, I could not give up.

30

A Pregnant Woman

Paris
December 28, 1941

Pierre waited impatiently for me where we had agreed to meet. We had to be on our way back before curfew, but first, we headed to your house. I was nervous. We knocked and waited, but no one came to the door. I looked at Pierre with my eyebrows raised.

"I don't understand," he said. "I was here just a couple of weeks ago."

My purse held a half-dozen more letters for you, and I had been excited to hand them over in person. Now I would have to take them back home with me. Yet my real concern was that something had happened to you.

"Stop knocking," said an elderly woman one house over. She

poked her head out of the little window on the door and studied us through her thick lenses.

"Do you know Marcel Zola?" I asked.

"Since we were kids," she answered. "His parents lived here. They both died years ago, such wonderful people. So kind, generous, and always willing to help. Their son is just like them."

"Can you tell us where Mr. Zola is?" Pierre asked.

"You look familiar, young man. I've seen you around here before. An old woman like me doesn't have much to keep her busy."

Pierre smiled. He realized he recognized the woman too. "Will he be back soon?" Pierre asked.

"He's gone to Cannes for a few days. He was worn out with Paris, but he asked me to forward him any mail or correspondence that came for him, especially any letters from a lady named Jocelyn Ferrec from Saint-Malo. I went to Saint-Malo once on vacation. The pirate city," she said, opening the door. Over her threadbare floral dress she wore a spotless white apron.

I hesitated. The woman seemed trustworthy. I had written things in my letters that could get you and me both in trouble.

"Could you give us his address?" Pierre asked.

"I'm afraid not. A friend is coming by tomorrow to pick up Marcel's mail. Marcel doesn't have much trust in the mail system," she explained.

At last I pulled the bundle of letters, tied with a red string, from my purse and held them out to her. The old woman reached out her wrinkled, blue-veined hand to receive them, then put them on a table in her foyer.

"Good luck to you both. I lost my husband in the last war and my son in this one. France can't ask me to sacrifice anything else, but you two are young. When all of this is over, you can pick up and carry on with your lives." She gave us a friendly nod and shut the door.

Pierre and I stood there a moment, unsure of what to do next. Then Pierre checked his watch, and we headed for the trolley. We were silent most of the way. We did not see any off-duty soldiers, but Nazi cars patrolled the streets at all hours. We arrived at the station and ran to the platform, just as the train was about to leave.

Our compartment was empty this time, so we stretched out and tried to relax. The trip was needlessly long again. The night "express" stopped in nearly every station along the route to Rennes.

"How did your morning meeting go?" Pierre asked. I summarized the speech I had endured and then my lunch with Isabelle. Pierre seemed nervous.

"What, do you think I shouldn't have talked about all that with my friend?"

"It's dangerous, Jocelyn. The Nazis have informants everywhere. We can't trust anyone. Today I saw Raymonde, my contact, and he warned me about more dangers. In Nantes, there's a new network of the Special Operations Executive. The people are really well trained, but the Gestapo is still capturing Resistance cells. Didn't you hear about what happened a few days ago in La Rochelle?"

I shook my head.

"A group of workers got together to run boycotts against the Germans," Pierre continued. "The first few went well, and they grew more confident. One of the workers got drunk, and a German patrol car pulled him over. The guy got scared and asked to be released. The soldiers thought his attitude was suspicious, so they handed him over to the Gestapo. After a night of interrogation, he ratted on each of his companions. The Nazis arrested them and took them to their bunker. It was fifteen people in total—all factory workers. Their wives were desperate, and one of them, Anna was her name, convinced five friends to help her attack the jail."

I was shocked that the Resistance had dared attack an SS prison.

"They attacked at night, when fewer guards were on duty, and they caught the guards by surprise. I guess the Germans never thought the workers' wives would've been capable of such a thing. They slit the guards' throats, captured two others who were asleep inside, and freed all fifteen members of the Resistance. The next day, the Nazis were furious, of course. No one had ever tried something like that before. They hunted everywhere and finally found them. They took the women, too, including the pregnant one, Anna. She was really close to the end of her term. A German official told the Gestapo chief not to execute her until the baby was born. At first the Gestapo officer agreed. They took her to a clinic and kept watch over her, but a week went by and she still hadn't given birth, so they took her out and shot her just like that."

I stared dumbfounded at my reflection in the window. Though I was not a mother, I could imagine what was going through Anna's head as they shot her, knowing the life of the child within her would also be snuffed out. I let my head drop onto the window. "When will this suffering end?" I moaned.

Pierre was too young to understand everything that was going on inside of me. For him, life was still an exciting adventure, and death was an abstract idea. The people around him were just actors in a tragicomedy that he observed from his adolescent brain. Most people his age were playacting at being adults, but he really was risking his life like the protagonist of a serial spy novel.

"I guess it's just part of war," he said. "Innocent people die, and their executioners don't."

———•◆•———

We got to Saint-Malo near daybreak, after taking another train from Rennes. Pierre and I said goodbye before we got off the train and headed our separate ways.

I headed for home, completely exhausted and overwhelmed with a dreaded loneliness. No one was waiting for me; I had no friends left; I could trust no one. Books were the only thing that got me out of bed each day, and for now, the desperate fight against evil.

I undressed, ran a hot bath, and sank slowly into the nearly boiling water. Another year was about to end—this one, the absolute worst of my life. I had zero hope or excitement about 1942, though a bit of curiosity. I did not realize it at the time, but sometimes curiosity can keep us going—the suspense of wanting to know what is going to happen with our lives and the people we love. Steam filled the bathroom, and eventually I fell into a deep sleep and the same nightmare I had been living for nearly two years now. I wished I could wake up and feel Antoine beside me, hear the soft timbre of his voice as he whispered sweet words in my ear.

31

Applause

Loneliness is the worst companion. People who have never been truly alone might think being lonely is simply the absence of people to love or to share your life with, but that is far from the whole. Loneliness is a relentless presence. There was never a moment I did not feel it: waking up and realizing what was happening to me was real; listlessly eating breakfast with my gaze lost somewhere beyond the empty chair in front of me; working like a robot compelled only by the inertia of life; coming home again, changing clothes, and eating supper in front of the same blank wall. Some days I spoke to no other person. People hardly ever visited the library, despite how cold and harsh the winter was for everyone. There was not enough food, coal, gas . . . not enough of anything. Most people spent their days just trying to survive. Sometimes I ran into Hermann, but we both ducked our heads without speaking, like two strangers. Pierre visited once a week to collect my letters. We would talk a few minutes, and then he would go on his way. Dr. Aubry sometimes stopped by in the afternoon, and we would discuss the war.

The Americans had joined the conflict after the Japanese attack in the Pacific, and the Germans were mired in Russia. The Yugoslavs had rebelled against German occupation thanks to the Partisans; and in France, Prime Minister Laval, back in power, was falling all over himself trying to collaborate with Hitler's war machine.

"Mrs. Ferrec, I'm convinced the Germans will lose this war within a year," Dr. Aubry said. I knew that I could trust him. He was one of the most solid human beings in Saint-Malo.

"I'm not so optimistic. The Nazis have endless willpower and could turn things back around. Until I see them running away with their tails between their legs, I won't believe it."

He placed the book he wanted to check out on my table, and I filled out the card for him.

"I've been looking after a German official, and I believe you know him. He was staying in your neighbor's apartment."

My throat clenched at this. I had not seen Hermann in a some weeks. Though we never spoke, I was always pleased to know he was well.

"Hermann von Choltiz," the doctor continued. "They were going to send him to Berlin, but then he was ordered to Russia." I caught my breath. The Russian front was one of the most brutal. "Yet he's fallen ill, and they've left him here for the time being."

"What's happened to him?" I asked, no longer feigning aloofness.

"He started losing weight and his coloring changed. I ran some tests and learned he has a liver problem. He's on the mend with the right medicine. I saw him this morning at the hospital run by the sisters, and he's looking better."

"Could I visit him?" My mouth spoke before my brain had time to think.

"Of course, it would do him good. We were just talking about you this morning."

This comment both surprised and worried me.

"He's a bookworm like yourself. He had wanted to return to Berlin to join the state library, but now the Nazis need all able-bodied men for fighting. He doesn't seem to be a bad sort."

"No, he isn't the worst of them," I concurred.

The doctor picked up his books and drummed his fingers. "Why don't you take him something to read? Time passes so slowly in the hospital."

As Dr. Aubry left, I fetched a copy of *Nana* by Émile Zola from the shelf, then put on my coat. After fifteen minutes of walking, I was in front of the hospital. It was only four stories tall and could serve around fifty patients. My hands were sweaty and my throat dry. Standing at the door was a nun from Spain named Clara.

"Hello, Sister Clara. I've come to see a German officer named—"

"Oh, there's only one German here right now," she said none too affectionately. Then she told me where to find Hermann. My legs trembled as I walked up the stairs. I kept telling myself I was just going to visit a friend, but as soon as I saw him in one of the beds toward the back of the room, my heart flickered.

Hermann stiffened as I approached. Trying to comb his hair back, he smiled. He looked awful. His cheeks were sunken, his eyes yellowed, and two days of beard growth made him look much older.

"Jocelyn," he said with a mix of surprise and cheer.

"Hermann, Dr. Aubry told me today that you've been ill."

He ducked his head, as if being sick were shameful. "I should have gone to Germany months ago. They were going to send me to Russia, and I actually wanted to go. So few return. The invasion of the Soviet Union has turned into a total massacre, but nothing matters anymore. The weight of the war has hit me. The only way to redeem myself is to die on the front."

His words infuriated me. "And give your life over to this monstrous regime?" Anger increased the volume of my voice. I glanced around, but the other patients were resting.

"You'll never understand it," he said. "I don't fight for Hitler or the Nazis anymore; I do it for my country. What will happen to Germany if we lose? You think our enemies will show any mercy to the women, the old folks, and the innocent children?"

Of course not. The terms of the armistice that ended the Great War were brutal for the Germans, and thousands had died for lack of food and basic provisions.

"But you cannot defeat evil with evil," I said.

He raised an eyebrow. "The Resistance also does evil things. They murder unarmed soldiers and supposed collaborators, and they steal from innocent farms in order to survive."

"You can't make that comparison. We have to fight to free ourselves from you people. We didn't choose this."

Hermann did not reply. He looked exhausted, drained by our brief argument.

"I'm sorry to upset you," I said, sitting in the chair beside him.

"Will we never stop being enemies? I hate this war and its horrible consequences. I don't feel like your enemy."

"How are you feeling?" I asked.

It took him a moment to respond. He studied me with his expressive eyes that were now watery with unshed tears. "Death has circled me several times throughout my life, but this time it has come close. Maybe it would be better to disappear forever. I've often cursed the day I was born. If only that day had never existed. The unborn are much happier than we are; they don't have to experience all this evil and suffering. What is life even for? It ends the same way for the rich and the poor, men and women, wise people and fools. Death waits for every one of us. So what good does the rich man's wealth do him or the famous one's great name? None of it makes sense."

I understood him perfectly, but I had learned to seek peace in the midst of the storm of existence. "Well, life takes on meaning when we dedicate it to others. Love and sacrifice are the only things that can redeem us—not throwing your life away in an absurd conflict. The war will pass, and we can remake ourselves." I heard the words as they came out but did not know if I believed them. What kind of life awaited me, all alone? What would I do when all this was over? If I managed to climb out of bed every day, it was only for the hope of progress and being able to help.

"I'm so sorry for what happened to your husband and to Céline. We've caused so much suffering."

Anger still boiled inside me. I wanted so badly to kill the Nazis myself, but vengeance was not the answer. Hatred rots us from inside and hurries death along.

"Thank you," I said, leaning back from him.

"At least your books are safe. I hope Bauman doesn't come back from Russia. People like him do not deserve to live."

I had pushed Bauman out of my mind completely over the past few months, like a nightmare from years ago.

"Well, when do you think you will be released?"

"The doctor is optimistic. I'm less so. They've said I can be out of here in a couple weeks and then go to the front."

I glanced out the wide window that overlooked the ocean. Freedom was just on the other side of that water. Now that the Americans were in the war, the hope of a landing was growing. But I wanted the fighting to end long before that.

"I'll try to come visit you here. I brought you a book. It's often the best way to face the abyss we're all in right now."

Hermann smiled genuinely as he examined the book I placed in his hands. "Wonderful! I haven't read this one."

"Get some rest," I said, tousling his hair.

Our eyes locked for a second. Looks often say more than words, the universal language that predates speech. Even an infant can say almost anything to its mother through its eyes.

———— •◆• ————

I was less nervous but more confused as I left the hospital. Up to then, Hermann had belonged to a dark chapter of my life that had ended. Yet it seemed like fate might have a different idea. Perhaps the war was changing him.

I walked aimlessly for a while until I stopped at the entrance to the movie theater, which was showing *The Little Princess* with Shirley Temple. I bought a ticket and sat in the back row of the nearly sold-out theater. A film, a true factory of dreams, is an easy way to avoid reality.

The movie opened with the famous British anthem "God Save the Queen." The theater erupted in applause, though a few soldiers and a couple Frenchmen quit the place, muttering curses under their breath. I was heartened to see my countrymen recovering their dignity. Hope was growing ever so slowly, though hope itself could not change things. Freedom would come at a high price.

A reverential silence was kept throughout the rest of the film until the noble British soldiers were all standing in salute at the closing scene. At that, the crowd went wild with cheering and clapping. Then the screen went abruptly black, as if the projectionist had been forced to shut down an act of rebellion. I left the theater feeling bolstered. At least I could be kind to Hermann, and the nightmare of the war would one day be over. And who knew if after death a new resurrection waited for us—some other life that we could not imagine while consumed by our current sadness?

32

Rumors of Invasion

Saint-Malo
June 5, 1942

Hermann stayed in the hospital longer than predicted, recovering very slowly. Visiting him in the afternoons became a habit. We would spend a couple hours talking about books, philosophy, religion, and the war. Sometimes we argued like madmen; other times we laughed 'til we were crying; and still other times we shed real tears over the hard times of our lives. Every afternoon Clara the nun frowned at me when I bid her farewell, as if the act of visiting an enemy were in and of itself a betrayal. I took her frowns to be a lack of Christian love until one night I heard her sobbing in the room next to the reception desk.

"Sister Clara, are you all right?" I asked, stepping gingerly into the small room. A liturgical calendar with the image of Christ was the only adornment in the plain space. Clara was hunched over in a chair.

"I'm fine," she choked out between labored breaths.

"Can I help you? Has something happened?"

She lifted her red eyes and pained expression to me. "A letter from my mother. She lives in Santander, Spain—where I grew up. I haven't had news of my family for a very long time. They've been in hiding until recently, hunted down by Franco's regime. The postwar years have been far worse than the war itself. The repression is just ghastly. Thousands have been executed, imprisoned, exiled . . . and there's so much hunger. A few months ago, my family decided to leave the village where they were in hiding. They thought that after three years they wouldn't come to any harm, but the authorities detained my father. He's an older man, over sixty, and has never hurt a flea. But he was well-known in the coal union. They've condemned him for treason and crimes of war, and he never even held a gun! They've sentenced him to death by the Spanish version of the guillotine—the garrote vil."

I gasped. "And nothing can be done?"

"There's no justice there, Jocelyn. The whole country is an army barracks run by the caudillo. Next to him, Pétain is a novice. They're going to strangle my father in cold blood and leave my poor mother all alone in the world."

Her big dark eyes seemed to throb with pain as she looked at me, and her dark, curly hair threatened to break free from her veil. I embraced her. "I'm so sorry," I said over and over.

"I don't understand how you can come visit a Nazi. Don't you realize what these people are doing in France and all over the world? In this very building . . . I—I shouldn't talk about it," she said, cutting herself off.

"I don't believe that German is like the others."

She pursed her lips in skepticism. "A wolf is always a wolf, and a lamb can only be a lamb."

"Hermann might be one of the lambs," I said. "At least, he is becoming one."

She wiped her tears and looked me directly in the eyes. "Just be careful. They say the war will be over soon, and they could accuse you of colluding with your German lover."

I shook my head. "But he's not my lover. I'm a widow, Sister Clara. Believe it or not, this man has saved my life twice. At the very least I owe it to him to help take care of him while he's in this city. Soon he'll be sent to Russia." I was offended at her words, but I knew she was not the only one who would make such an assumption. In a provincial town, hearsay and rumors were the bread of life.

———— • ◆ • ————

I headed home after that. I was opening the entryway door when I heard a "Pssst!" and turned to see a shadow coming toward me, frightening me half to death.

"It's me, Isabelle. It's best if we're not seen together."

I was both relieved and surprised that she would show up unannounced. We'd had little contact all this time. I had stopped convening the new Resistance group and did little more than give Pierre any relevant information I learned from Hermann, though he was none too well-informed about the state of the war since he was on medical leave.

We went up the stairs without turning on the light in the

hallway, though I knew Mrs. Fave was always watching me. I opened my door as quietly as possible and hung up my jacket. "Have you eaten? Can I fix you something?" I asked.

"Well, I wouldn't turn down a bite to eat. I've come straight from Paris."

We went to the kitchen, and I prepared some vegetable sandwiches. It was nice to set the table and share a meal with someone.

"They figured out my identity, and I had to flee. The Special Operations Executive is preparing a way out of the country for me."

"You can stay here. The Nazis don't get too involved with the inhabitants of Saint-Malo anymore. The mayor finally convinced them to respect us a bit. The problem is that some neighbors will report anyone and anything. We could tell them you've been sent from Paris to help me," I said.

"Won't city hall ask for confirmation or papers?"

"The administration is a complete wreck right now. Most of them don't know whether to call Vichy or Paris for these things. That's the problem with having two bosses." The side of my mouth quirked up.

"Two bosses?" Isabelle looked at me with deadpan eyes. "The only boss is Hilter. Pétain is a stupid, old, well-trained dog."

We ate in silence, both out of hunger and a desire to avoid tensions.

"I'm in contact with Maurice August, the architect, and with Margarite Blot. Both are in the Resistance cell that's forming up here. We're hoping the Allies will try an invasion soon."

"An invasion by sea? Ever since they got here the Germans have been fortifying the defenses along the coast. Pierre has made detailed drawings of several miles all around here. It's practically impregnable."

"The Germans need to send more and more men to Russia and Africa. They couldn't take Malta. The British are bombing their cities and their factories. Soon people will grow tired of Hitler, the military will turn their backs on him, and, if the Allies get a foothold on the continent again, the Germans will run like rabbits back to their holes."

Isabelle's optimism was enticing, but I did not yet see any Germans retreating. They all seemed convinced of their victory. Hermann, who was now fully opposed to the war, was still sure Hitler would conquer Russia, or at least part of it, and that the Allies would sign a treaty with him before 1944.

"The Resistance cell has a few targets in this city. The Germans seem really secure up here," Isabelle said.

"But every time a soldier is killed, there are reprisals against the citizens."

"This is war, and collateral damage is inevitable." Her cynical tone infuriated me.

"But you sound just like them. Every single life is important—"

"Perhaps, but so many people have died to save France, and many more will die still, while the majority is just content to try to survive and another group gets fat off the Nazis. Every time we kill a German, all the other Germans around grow in their fear of us and wish they could go back to their country. We have no choice but to demoralize them before the final battle."

I fixed tea, and we moved to the living room. Isabelle kicked off her shoes.

"Did you bring any clothes?"

She shook her head. "I had to get out with what I had on me at the time."

"Don't worry. We're about the same height, and I have plenty of extra clothes."

She smiled at me, and we put aside political talk to catch up on things that had happened since our university days.

"Life has not been simple, shall we say. I've always felt like a foreigner even though I grew up in France. I'm part Jew, Catholic, Pole, and Russian. The Nazis persecute nearly every one of those identities. I was forever bouncing around from one place to the next, and, when I got the job at the physical geography lab at the Sorbonne, I thought my days of wandering had come to a sweet end. But that hasn't been the case, of course."

I understood. I shared her sense of uprootedness, of not belonging to any one place. Many call this freedom, but it is also lonely and confusing.

She continued, "It's just terrible what all is going on in Paris. They've started requiring Jews to wear a yellow star like in the Middle Ages. The other day, a twelve-year-old threw himself out the window and killed himself because his friends wouldn't talk to him anymore. Veterans are putting their medals from the Great War right next to their yellow stars, but the fascists rip them off and throw them away. The world has gone stark raving mad," she said bitterly. She took another sip of tea and leaned her head back, trying to clear her mind of it all. "So that's why I've taken up arms. Men have thrown them down in cowardice, so now women must take a turn."

"You're very brave, Isabelle."

"There's only bravery or death," she said, looking at me again.

"Honestly, sometimes I think death would be better than all this," I confessed.

"Don't say that, Jocelyn. You'll come through Antoine's death. We never forget the ones who die, but we eventually learn how to live with their memories."

I thought about her words as I prepared for bed. I had not told anyone, but I had never changed the sheets since Antoine's death. I just could not bring myself to do it. It had been our bed, our altar to love. Now it was like a tomb. I clutched the toy bear he had given me when we were young and dating. Sometimes I held it at night as I slept, and it eased the loneliness a little. Many mornings it was soaked with my tears.

33

Catholics and Communists

Saint-Malo
June 20, 1942

War is always fought between young people, practically children, who neither know nor hate each other but who—because of the commanding elders who *do* know and hate each other—must kill or be killed. My routine changed a bit after Isabelle's arrival. She joined me in the library in the mornings and afternoons and thus made the days pass more pleasantly. I did not spend as much time sitting alone thinking and feeling sorry for myself. In the afternoons, I visited Hermann, but I did not mention him to Isabelle as I did not want to give her the wrong idea. I would arrive home in time for dinner, and then we would have tea and talk late into the night. By the time I got in bed, I was so tired I did not fret away the hours thinking about Antoine.

That day I ran into Father Roth. I had not been back to church since Antoine's death. I was not Catholic yet felt only slightly closer to my parents' Protestantism; at best I might have called myself a Christian with very deep doubts.

"My daughter, it's been a while since I've seen you. How are you?"

"Well, thank you," I answered.

"You know you can always come talk to me about anything. Grief is very hard to bear, and by God's grace, I can offer solace to the soul."

"Again, thank you."

"I mention you daily in my prayers. I also petition God hour by hour for an end to this war. Do you know what's happening with the Jews all over France? What happened here last year was nothing. Most of our citizens were sent to French refugee camps, but now there are rumors that they'll be sent to Germany for forced labor. Horrors! Men, women, and children. Our savage overlords hold nothing sacred and respect no one." His face reddened as he grew angrier. He took a deep breath to calm himself, then cleared his throat. "I've heard you're in the habit of visiting a German officer."

"Yes, he's been ill."

"I don't judge you, Jocelyn. We should help all who are in need and love even our enemies, as the Lord said. But I need something from you. Can you keep a secret?" he said, casting a glance around.

"Go ahead, Father Roth."

"In the Hotel Dieu, a dozen Jewish refugees are hidden

among the infirm. Several of them are children. We want to get them to the Pyrenees, where they can then get through Spain and to Portugal. But they have no papers. It is extremely difficult to get documents. Is your German friend trustworthy?"

I was quiet for a moment wondering if Hermann would be willing to go that far. "I can ask in a roundabout way."

"You must act soon, as things are getting worse and worse for the poor Jews. The Nazis are also rounding up Gypsies and homeless people, but at least they're sending most of them to French camps in the south. The Jews, however"—he put his finger to his neck and pulled it fast—"are sent to work."

"I'll ask him soon."

"Thank you, daughter," he said, leaving me with a blessing.

All of this was spinning around in my head as I made my way upstairs to Hermann's room. As soon as he saw me, he asked what was on my mind.

"Just some things at work," I lied.

I had a hard time paying attention to our conversation, thinking all the while how I could ask him for this favor.

"The doctor says I'm getting better and can be released next week, but I'd rather stay in the hospital and see you every day. As soon as I'm out, they'll send me to Russia."

"Oh, let's hope not."

"They're sending everyone, and most return in a box if at all. Sometimes life steals our happiness and we don't mind dying, then it turns around and fills us with hope again right before snuffing out our existence."

"Couldn't you request a transfer to Paris or just stay here?"

"It's out of my hands, Jocelyn. I assure you—if I had any say about the matter, I'd find a way to stay close to you."

He put his hand on my arm, and I flinched. We had talked about countless things these many weeks, but we had never crossed the red line of feelings.

"I'm sorry," he said, seeing my reaction.

"I'm not ready, and I don't think I ever will be. I enjoy your friendship, but my heart still belongs to Antoine."

His face fell, all the hope draining out again.

"I have to ask you for something," I went on. "I don't know if you can or if you'd even want to help, but either way, this request must stay between us."

"I don't think I could deny you anything," he answered.

"Just like in Germany, the Jews are being persecuted here without mercy. A few are hidden here in town, and they need papers to travel through France and reach Spain. Could you get me blank documents to falsify?"

His face hardened into a frown. For the first time he had to pick a side. He could not answer this request by saying he was not like the rest of the Nazis. He had helped me because he loved me, but true love requires relinquishing life for the sake of unknown others.

He considered the matter for a long time and finally answered, "I'll try." Then he smiled. "I mean, what do I have to lose? I won't look the other way anymore. Each person's life matters."

Without even thinking, I put my arms around him, then pulled back away in embarrassment. "I'm so sorry," I gasped.

Hermann smiled. He had crossed the line that separated him from the community of the Nazis. For them, not following orders was to voluntarily withdraw from their group.

A mixture of euphoria and fear pulsed through me as I walked down the hospital stairs. I felt the thrill of being useful again, that things might change and be different. Sister Clara motioned to me when I neared the reception area.

"Father Roth told me what you're trying to do for those poor families. Thank you," she said, giving me an awkward hug as if physical expression did not come naturally to her. I headed home but saw the light on in the library and decided to look in. It surprised me that Isabelle might be there at such an hour. I checked the door and confirmed that it was locked, then unlocked it and opened it quietly, slipped through the dark entryway, and went upstairs. As I opened the door, four people turned to stare at me.

"Don't worry, she's one of us," Isabelle said.

I gave a timid wave and Isabelle motioned for me to have a seat. "Jocelyn, we were setting some goals. Before the summer is over, we want to give the Germans a good fright."

I kept quiet, fearing the consequences of an attack in the city. We heard rumors of vengeance executions for the deaths of German soldiers.

"Maurice suggests doing away with a collaborator and a German official. We have to make it clear to our countrymen that whoever collaborates with the Germans is a traitor and that they'll get what they deserve."

One of the women in the group threw up the *V* for victory, obviously pleased with the suggestion.

Isabelle went on. "The collaborator would be Pierre Travelis. He's practically become a millionaire off supplying the Germans with beef while the population starves to death. Not long ago he bought one of the biggest mansions around Saint-Malo."

"Couldn't we give him a warning instead of murdering him?" I asked. I did not agree with using violence, especially not arbitrarily. Quite a few had gotten rich during the occupation, but randomly picking one collaborator to knock off seemed less than fair.

"We can't give any more warnings. They need to see one of their own taken down. The rest will take it as a lesson and won't be so quick to help the occupiers anymore," said Lucien, another of the group members.

"For a German officer, we've thought of someone easy to pick off, since the Germans are not as out and about as they once were. In the nuns' hospital there's an officer named Hermann von Choltiz who's up for release soon. If we finish him off in the next couple of days, he won't be able to rejoin the ranks of the oppressors."

I sucked in my breath. I could not tell them Hermann had offered to help some of the Jews in hiding or that we were good friends, or they would surely accuse me of collaborating. I paid little attention to the rest of the meeting. I had to warn him as soon as I could of the danger he was in.

———— • ◆ • ————

Isabelle and I returned to my apartment in silence. It was a warm, almost perfect night.

"You didn't seem too enthusiastic about our plans," she said.

"I already told you I don't agree with violent measures."

"Violence is the only language these people understand. It's an eye for an eye, tooth for a tooth," she said through her own gritted teeth.

We climbed the stairs without further words, but just after shutting the apartment door behind us, she said, "Tomorrow you'll help the two who are in charge of taking down the butcher.

All you have to do is drive the car and make sure nobody sees them."

I opened my mouth to answer, but nothing came out. She went to her room, and I was lost in uncertainty. To keep from betraying our principles sometimes we have to fool ourselves.

34

The Lieutenant Returns
to Germany

Saint-Malo
June 21, 1942

I did not sleep a wink that night. I tossed and turned in bed and revisited the meeting in the library in my mind. What could I do? Should I participate in something like that? How could I warn Hermann? Isabelle had not mentioned the timeline for their attack.

I drank my coffee lukewarm, but it was all I could get down. Meanwhile, Isabelle ate vigorously. She sketched out the plans for me, including the escape route and the time and place for debriefing.

"Is it all clear to you?"

"Yes," I said, my head ducked. If she saw my face, she would know how vehemently I opposed being involved.

"I know you don't really like this, and I don't either, but it's a necessary evil."

I nodded and went to the bathroom to finish getting ready. Then we went to the library. I watched the clock all morning, seeing the hands push me closer and closer to the inevitable moment.

"You'd better give yourself plenty of time. That pig will finish his lunch soon then head back to his mansion for a nap. You'll need to intercept him at the door. There are no houses around, and no one will see you. The children will be at school, and his wife is at her mother's house."

I fetched my purse and put on my jacket, though I was sweaty with nerves. I walked to Denis's car and turned it on as quietly as I could. What would he have thought of this? At the train station, I picked up the young man and young woman who would carry out the killing. In under ten minutes we were in front of the luxurious mansion. I parked the car on a dirt road, went into the trees, and stayed there at the crossroads to watch our escape route.

"It won't take us long. As soon as you see us running, turn the car on and drive toward us."

"Okay," I croaked. My mouth was dry as cotton, and my body shook.

"Are you going to make it?" the woman asked. "You can't lose your nerve—our lives are at stake."

"I'll be all right," I answered. The man offered me a cigarette, and I took it even though I did not smoke. Perhaps it would calm me down. He lit it for me, and they walked slowly toward the front door. The gate was closed, and we saw no movement from inside. The two of them hid behind a thick tree and waited for the butcher.

A gold Cadillac appeared on the road, driven slowly by a large man chewing on a cigar. His chin was held high and his face appeared unconcerned, rather blank. He parked at the gate and got out to unlock it, pushing one side open and then the other without noticing the assassins. He drove the car across the boundary line, and as he exited the car again to close the gate behind him, the Resistance members approached from the trees.

"Traitor to the country!" the man yelled, pulling out his pistol and taking aim.

The poor devil hardly knew what hit him. Death caught him so off guard he barely turned around before falling to the ground. His previously spotless white suit was soon covered in dirt and blood.

The front door of the mansion opened, and I saw a woman who must have been his wife. She started screaming and running toward her husband.

At first the two members of the Resistance stood paralyzed. The wife was not supposed to have been home.

"Murderers!" she yelled as she approached.

Then the man raised his pistol again, and two shots pierced the woman before she had time to turn aside. She gave a shocked look then fell beside her husband.

The assassins closed the gate and ran toward me. It took me a moment to respond, but I eventually got into the car, turned it over, and drove us away. My heart raced and thrummed in my ears. As soon as it seemed we were in the clear, my companions started talking.

"When that woman came out, I nearly had a stroke," the man said.

"It's a good thing you took her out. She's as guilty as her husband. Both of them have gotten rich off the people."

My face must have shown my terror because the woman turned to me and said, "Relax. The worst is over now."

Her coldness shocked me. They had probably done this before, but I could not believe that killing two humans, no matter how guilty they were, had not affected their consciences.

"Don't give me that look," she said. "Killing that swine was a patriotic act. Now we're a little closer to the final victory."

I did not answer. I had figured out a long time ago that it was pointless to argue with radicals. For them, nuance did not exist. It was all or nothing. If fate had allowed them to be born in Germany, would they have ended up as committed Nazis, fighting for what they thought was a just cause? I wondered about that.

"And tonight, that filthy German. We can't risk letting him get away alive."

"Tonight?" I asked.

"Don't worry, we won't need a car in Saint-Malo."

I dropped them off at the train station and went back to the library. Isabelle was waiting impatiently. As soon as I was through the door, she peppered me with questions. "How did it go? Are you sure he's dead?"

"Well, it certainly seemed like it."

"Tell me everything," she insisted.

I gave her a brief explanation that seemed to satisfy her. "You know that woman was a fascist like her husband."

"But now their children are orphans." I could not help lamenting what the children would now face.

"They've got grandparents," she said, unconcerned.

I sat down at my desk. My stomach was tight as a rock, and I felt sick.

"I think you've got too many scruples for this kind of work," Isabelle said.

"They're human beings," I spat out in disgust.

"We all are, but some have to die for things to change. Even a child understands that."

"But if the price is selling our souls, what kind of world are we creating? How are we any better than them?"

"I'm going to pretend you didn't just ask that. There's no room for hesitation or doubt. Those two comrades have risked their lives for the rest of us."

I grabbed my things and slammed the door on my way out. I made my way to the hospital to warn Hermann as soon as I could. Fearing that Isabelle or someone would follow me, I changed directions several times. After I was sure no one was watching, I went inside and found Sister Clara.

"The officer isn't here," she said after her customary greeting.

"He's been released?" I asked in surprise.

"Yes, this morning. A man and a woman came by asking for him just now as well. I do hope he can get those papers for the families we're hiding."

"Do you know where the lieutenant has gone?"

"I suppose to the barracks," she said with a shrug.

I ran to the citadel, heedless of the strange looks I got on the street. I was out of breath when I got to the door, where two soldiers trained their guns on me.

"Where do you think you're going?" asked the sergeant in a heavy accent.

"I need to see Lt. Hermann von Choltiz immediately," I gasped out.

The officer went to the guard station to use the phone, and the soldier kept his gun raised. A few minutes later, Hermann came out to meet me.

"What's going on? I'm fine. This is what I was waiting for and—"

"We need to go somewhere," I said in a panic.

As we walked toward the beach, I kept looking all around.

"What's going on?" he asked again.

We stopped a few feet from the water. The ground was damp and the beach empty.

"I thought something had happened to you." I shook with cold and terror. He put his arms around me, and I broke down sobbing.

"You're scaring me," he said in a worried voice.

"I thought you were dead. The Resistance is planning to kill you. I came to warn you."

He looked at me in shock. After a moment, he quipped, "I see any target will do for them."

"This isn't a joke. They just killed the butcher a few hours ago."

At that, his face changed. He covered his face with his hands and mopped his brow with his hat.

"Please get to safety. Don't leave the barracks."

"The commander just told me I'm leaving today for Berlin and then am off to Russia. There's a large-scale operation under-way to get rid of the Bolsheviks before summer is over."

I was as rigid and uncomprehending as stone.

"The war will be decided in Russia. If Hitler can't beat Stalin, Germany is lost. And there is much suffering to come." Hermann put his hand in his pocket and pulled out a thick envelope. "This is all I could find because I didn't have much time. Some passports, visas, and ID and ration cards."

I put them in my purse and tried hard not to cry.

"I'll never forget you, Jocelyn. If God allows, I'll see you again someday." He took my hands, then stepped back to behold me. "This is how I want to remember you—beautiful and brave, trying to save the world with your books and your good words."

We embraced again. The sound of the waves rocked us, trying to make that moment last an eternity. Then everything was loneliness again.

35

A Stranger

Saint-Malo
March 3, 1944

Darkness invaded everything that terrible winter. We listened
to airplanes zooming overhead on their way to bomb factories. Young men went into hiding to keep from being sent to
Germany to work. The shortages grew even more acute, and nearly
everyone was thin and frail. Since we were on the shore, we could
at least buy fish in secret, but most other products were black
market luxuries or impossible to find. Mothers found themselves
with no milk for the babies who had been born amid the horror.
And the Germans daily arrested people we never saw again.

After the murder of the butcher, his wife, and a German soldier the day Hermann left, the German commander gave orders
to take hostages and execute them. Activity on the port was

constant and frenetic, despite two bombing missions by the Allies. The year 1943 was when the tables turned. The Germans started losing on every front. The Nazis were pushed back in the Soviet Union and had surrendered in Tunisia, losing control of North Africa. Their Italian allies attempted to sign a separate peace agreement after arresting Benito Mussolini, and the Allies were advancing through southern Italy toward Milan.

During that long year and a half, I wrote to Hermann. At first his letters arrived every week, then every two weeks, then once a month, and by the beginning of 1944, only once a season. He had managed to get out of Stalingrad before the German army was surrounded, having been wounded and sent to a hospital in Berlin. That was all I knew of his whereabouts and well-being.

Isabelle had escaped after the two attacks. A ship took her to San Sebastián, and another from there to England. I was alone again trying to protect the library's remaining books that were now in danger from the bombings and occasional fires that spread through the city. The only people I ever spoke to were Dr. Aubry, Father Roth, and Pierre. Andreas von Aulock, the German commander in Saint-Malo, had prepared the city to resist any and every invasion. Rumors of a possible Allied landing near Saint-Malo spread like the wind.

From my window I observed the calm sea that sparkled like polished silver under the intense spring sunlight. I had finally come to learn through years of misfortune and hardship how to be content with each day's tasks. Before leaving for work, I would spend a few minutes remembering the people I loved who were no longer beside me. Then I would open up my mind to let fate direct my life as it would. I needed to believe there was a reason for all the pain, that we were more than mere coincidences within infinite meaninglessness.

I glanced at myself in the mirror before heading out. A few gray hairs had started to grow. My features had changed, the girlish face of youth giving way to the surer features of a woman who knew herself and was afraid of nothing.

Sadness cloaked me as I made my way through Saint-Malo's streets. The town felt empty as many inhabitants had left their homes within the walls to take refuge in the country. Some of the buildings were falling down and others were already ruins. The proud corsair city seemed to have given in to the weight of history. I went by Denis's old bookstore. The windows were all shattered, and no more half-burned books littered the floor. Life had lost its shine and become a dingy black-and-white photograph.

Pierre still dropped by every week. He had changed too. No longer the little thirteen-year-old boy I had first met, I feared he would be snatched up at any moment by the authorities and sent to work for Germany's war effort.

"Jocelyn, I have something to tell you."

"And what news do you bring today, Pierre?" I smiled as I spoke. He kept up his contact with the secret agencies and always brought good news. Since there was no one else in the library, we could speak freely.

"The Americans are coming soon. They need to open another front in Europe since it's slow progress through Italy. I've heard they want to be in Berlin by Christmas."

"I'm afraid the Yankees are bigger show-offs than the British. The Germans might be withdrawing in Russia, but they aren't defeated. Those fanatics are capable of shedding their last drops of blood to defend that lunatic Hitler."

"You didn't used to be so pessimistic," Pierre said gravely.

"How long have I been waiting for this war to end? First for Antoine to come back from the front, then to save my friends from the SS and Gestapo beasts. Now the only thing I care about is keeping this old library from becoming kindling for all the fires. We'll all disappear one day. It's just a matter of time. But this"—I took in the whole library with a gesture—"must go on. Books are our legacy, the signal to light the path for future generations. If the Nazis destroy our books, they really will have won the war. We won't know who we are or what we're doing here."

Pierre opened one of the old volumes I was restoring that morning.

"Are they really that valuable?"

"They look just like plain yellowed paper with fading ink and printed letters of little import, but they are much more than that. Herein lies the soul of those who wrote them and the heart of everyone who has pored over their pages. Look at this card: Almost two hundred people have read this book in roughly one hundred years. Most of those people are dead now, but last week a twelve-year-old girl read the book. It keeps living and fulfilling its mission."

Pierre was intrigued. "What is its mission?"

"To make us free. Learning, knowing, and discovering make us free."

I heard the door handle turn and the hinges creak open. A man with long white hair and a gray beard covering sunken cheeks entered with his head ducked. His well-worn clothing hung loosely, and he limped as he walked. I did not recognize him at first, but then he called my name.

"Jocelyn!"

My heart almost stopped. I flew to him and grabbed him up in my arms. "Denis!" I said, in disbelief, incredulous that fate might be restoring a bit of joy to me.

Pierre observed us in surprise, but by the time I could open my eyes again and see through the tears, he had gone.

"What . . . How did you . . . Is it really you? Are you really here?" I finally managed to ask.

Denis slouched into a chair, exhausted, and I brought him some water. He looked so old now, a far cry from the happy, attractive man I had met a few years before, but his eyes were still bright and clear.

"It's been a long nightmare, but I'm home again. I've seen terrible things, hell itself. I never thought I would get out of there alive, and I still wonder if I'm dreaming or if I've actually died."

"You're alive, dear friend, and you're here with me!" I reassured him.

Denis smiled, dried his tears on an old handkerchief, and motioned for me to sit. "Everything was horrible since they arrested me. They interrogated me with torture, especially that horrible German Adolf Bauman."

"I'm afraid that was my fault. He hated me, but since he couldn't come for me, he unleashed his cruelty on you."

Denis let out a long sigh. "That may be, but the fact is, selling banned books was a risk. They sent me on a military train to Germany. In Dachau, they locked me up in a labor camp. It was on the outskirts of town, surrounded by forest. At first I thought it couldn't be that bad, but when I went through the iron gate and saw the faces of the other prisoners, I knew we had lost our humanity. Everyone was wearing striped uniforms and wooden clogs and walking with their heads bowed, as if existing was too heavy a burden to bear. They put me with the political prisoners, which ended up being my salvation. They got the least horrible treatment at camp. Most of them were communists and socialists and had been there since 1933 when Hitler came to power. One of the prisoners, Miller, liked that I was French. He had studied French in Berlin. He was a barracks leader, and I became his assistant. Our barracks never had enough, but at least we did get to eat, and had a blanket and were allowed to shower once a week. Things got worse as time went on. There was less food, more people crammed into each barracks, and so much fighting and killing. When the Jews started pouring in, they were often beaten to death. Some of the prisoners were high-ranking officials from Austria, Czechoslovakia, and France.

"One of the camp officers ordered me to teach his children French. He lived in a big house with his family. Can you imagine? Every day he would leave the camp, walk home, and play with his kids before bedtime."

Denis's description left me breathless. More or less, we all imagined that nothing good could have happened to the Jews hunted down in France and sent north, but we never could have imagined what he was describing.

"Women, old people, and kids were murdered without pity. It was terrible."

"How did you escape?" I managed to ask.

"Sometimes I think it would've been better if I'd died. I don't know if I'll be able to get over it all," he said, breaking down in tears.

"We'll get through it together," I said, wrapping my arms around him. For a flash it felt like time had stood still and it was 1939 again, and we were young, happy friends comforting each other.

He wiped his nose and went on. "The commander of the camp wanted to clean things out and ordered the extermination of several blocks. My friend, the barracks leader, warned me. I was really weak, and he knew they would pick me for extermination. He knew of a transport truck leaving for Munich, so he hid me on a truck, and the driver smuggled me to Munich. I hid out there for several weeks, then they got me false papers."

"I hope no one recognized you," I said, nervous.

Denis ran his hands over his long hair and beard. "My own mother wouldn't know me."

"I'll ask Father Roth to find you a safe place."

We embraced again, and the proximity of another human being was the best gift in the world right then. I called Father Roth, who came shortly thereafter.

"There's an abandoned farm near Saint-Coulomb. You'll be safe there," the priest told him.

Denis nodded. "Thank you. I never thought I'd see Saint-Malo again."

"The ways of the Lord are inscrutable. It won't be long now before the Allies are here and this Nazi plague will be finished," Father Roth said.

We said goodbye, promising to see each other every week. Then I locked up the library and headed home, walking with a smile for the first time in months.

36

The Landing

Saint-Malo
June 6, 1944

All night we had heard the frenetic flight of planes overhead. I could not sleep. I was worried about bombings, not so much fearing my own death as the destruction of the library. I got up early and went to the Café Continental. The news always spread fast there because some neighbors got news from the BBC and would tell the rest of the town. More and more, the people wore their open hostility toward the Germans on their sleeves. For days the soldiers had not left their posts along the wall, the barracks, or the surrounding fortresses.

I went into the café, and the owner greeted me with a big smile that set his black mustache bouncing. "Mrs. Ferrec! Shall I prepare your coffee?"

"Yes, please," I said. The doctor and the priest were seated together with Mr. Chirac, one of the decent businessmen in Saint-Malo who was not profiting from the war.

"They've landed, and not far from here—in Normandy," said Chirac.

I took a seat, mirroring the shock on the priest's and the doctor's faces.

"That's impossible," Father Roth said.

"But it was to come from Calais," Dr. Aubry said.

"The defenses there are stronger," Chirac said.

"What does it mean?" I asked.

"Well, being so close, we'll be among the first to be freed. I can't stand one more day of this occupation. They've taken everything from us, kidnapped our young men, and raped our women. They deserve much worse than what they got in '19." Chirac's face was red with fury.

The chatter in the café swelled. Then we heard noises outside and looked out the window. Two young women had stopped a German who was on a motorcycle. The German must have thought they needed help, but one of the girls pulled out a pistol and shot the soldier in the chest.

The shot reverberated in the street. The soldier fell dead instantly, and we knew the Germans would retaliate.

"Here, girls, now!" the café owner barked at them. He hurried the girls inside, sat them at a table, and served them some coffee. He shoved the pistol behind some barrels of beer, and everyone inside the café tried to act as if nothing had occurred.

I slid into a chair next to one of the girls and asked, "Why did you do that?"

"We're with the Resistance, and we have orders to interrupt German communications. We've cut phone lines, exploded train tracks, and swapped street signs all around. At dawn, parachuters landed in Normandy beyond the defense lines at the beach. The invasion of the continent can't be stopped now."

"But the Nazis already threw them back to sea once," Chirac said, disbelieving.

"It's different this time, sir. There are tens of thousands of them. The Germans can't hold out against so many. Paris will be free within the week, and they'll reach Berlin by Christmas unless the Germans take care of Hitler themselves first. There have already been several attempts on the dictator."

These optimistic young women reminded me of myself before the war began. "But you'll be killed if you get caught," I said.

"We're sisters and only have each other. The Nazis deported our parents to Germany, and nobody comes back from there. At least we've avenged their deaths today," said the one who seemed to be older.

We heard the sound of truck motors. Nazis were the only ones with gas anymore, besides a few of the basic city service trucks. Within moments, nearly thirty soldiers jumped down from their vehicles to search the area. Most people had already abandoned the streets, but the Nazis questioned the few inattentive pedestrians who had not figured out what was happening. Then those poor souls were loaded into a truck and carried off. For each German soldier killed, at least a dozen French were executed in retaliation, though in some parts of France entire villages were massacred and whole farms razed if suspected of harboring anyone connected to the Resistance.

Five soldiers and a sergeant burst into the café, training their guns on us. We all went quiet.

"Sirs, we are peaceful people," the café owner said, raising his arms.

The soldiers barked at us in German to raise our hands, an order we all understood by that time and obeyed without hesitation.

"Did you see the murderers?" the sergeant asked.

"We didn't see anything. We heard the shots, but when we got to the window, the soldier was already on the ground," the owner said.

The sergeant grabbed the front of the café owner's shirt and yanked him up. "You fat pig! You think you can mock us? You can see everything from this bar. How many were there? Could you recognize them? One of the witnesses said it was two women."

"Sergeant," the owner coughed out, "I was serving the tables when it happened. It's just me today, as my boy is sick."

"French swine! We've managed to spoil you, but we should've destroyed this country when we had the chance," he said, spitting as he talked. He jabbed the owner's face with his gun, and blood spurted from his nose. The sergeant looked around and growled at me and the two Resistance girls. "You three, papers!" We were the only women in the café.

He studied us, sticking his greasy, pockmarked face right into each of ours. "Where are you two from?" he spat out.

"We're from Rennes, visiting—"

"They're friends of mine," I interrupted. The man frowned at me.

"You're the librarian—Hermann's friend, yes? But he's not here to protect you anymore. We'll take all three of you then. We can interrogate you easier in the barracks."

"Sergeant, you can't—" Father Roth said, getting to his feet. But a soldier smacked him so hard in the face with the butt of his gun that the priest went sprawling, his face badly cut.

They hurried us into the truck, and within minutes we were in front of the citadel. I had heard some of the terrifying things that went on inside, so I thought this would be the end of me. The Germans were too worked up to be worried about who the responsible parties were. For them, all French were guilty.

They took us to the basement and locked us up together in one of the cells. As soon as they left us, the two sisters began to cry.

"We'll confess. They'll kill us, but you didn't do anything—"

"No," I said. "You will say nothing. If you confess, they'll kill all three of us. The plan is to maintain our innocence. Dr. Aubry and Father Roth will go to the mayor, and he'll intercede on our behalf."

The sisters put their arms around each other on the cement bench, but I paced the cell. We could hear the sea breaking against the wall outside. When the tide was very high, it could enter some of the city streets, and everything would smell of salt and fish.

"They used to lock up Protestants here—those who refused to renounce their faith. Many tried to get to America, but if they were caught, they were put in these very cells. Some spent years without seeing the light of day. I'm sure you two can hold out for a few hours."

I eventually sat down and leaned my head against the cold, rough wall. I closed my eyes and begged God for help. I trusted my friends, but with the Allied landing, the Nazis must have been beside themselves. Nothing is more dangerous than a group of desperate men.

Some five hours passed before the door opened.

"So who do we have here? Mrs. Ferrec, still going by your dead husband's name, I see?"

I recognized the voice, and my blood ran cold.

"Surprised to see me, are you? Surely you thought I'd died in Russia?" Bauman's voice was hoarser than a few years prior. When he flicked on the light, I could see his black uniform. A long scar ran the length of his right cheek up to a dead eye. "Are you scared? I had promised to take care of you, and now Hermann's not here to save you."

With that, the lieutenant dragged me out of the cell and into a nearby room. After tying me to a wooden chair, he waltzed toward a table ladened with instruments.

"I'll have a little fun with you, but first you have to tell me something."

"I don't know what you're talking about," I said falteringly.

"I came across Hermann's report on the library. He never sent it to Berlin, but I notice there are several rare books and valuable letters. The war won't last much longer—oh, the things I could tell you from Russia. The thousand years of the Third Reich is over, and the only thing that matters now is for each man to save his own neck. I was wounded in Sevastopol. I served in Russia for almost two years and was one of the few survivors in my unit. Himmler himself let me choose where I went next. I wanted to come back here, set things straight with you, and then head to Spain with a few of your library's books. I'm sure I can find buyers willing to pay a nice price for them there. If not, I'll head to South America. I'm told that boats sail there every week from Barcelona and A Coruña."

"Everything was destroyed in a fire. The books are hidden somewhere else."

"Oh, come, come, don't pretend I'm a fool. When I've finished with you, you'll tell me everything I want to know."

He picked up a pair of pliers. "I think we'll start with your lovely face." He was so close to me I could see the sadistic gleam in his eyes. I had no doubt he would enjoy every second of the torture session, every moment of my screaming.

37

Close

We wait for death with our eyes closed tight, like children scared of shadows on the wall. Some ancient instinct tells us that the eyelids create an impassible barrier between us and what we fear. But the darkness did not keep me from hearing the voice or smelling the rancid breath of Adolf Bauman. I did not know why he hated me in particular so much, though I figured it was because I was not afraid of him. Nothing terrifies a monster more than not being feared.

"People like you revolt me," he said. "I grew up in a dirty, run-down, working-class neighborhood. We had to slog through mud to get to school, and the other kids laughed at us. Our crime was poverty. I would watch people, dressed in their finery, going to the movies and the opera while I begged among them and my sisters sold flowers. I hated them—their shiny faces, straight beards, and insipid lives full of everything I didn't have. The Party gave me a place to belong, a cause, and the chance to make something of myself. Now I get to burn their fancy books, live in their houses, and have their women. Before, I would've been hanged for it—but now I'm considered a patriot. Isn't it ironic? Wars turn murderers into heroes and rapists into procreators of the Aryan race. Perhaps that paradigm is falling apart, but I'm not going back to the swamp—and now you're going to help me."

He was about to pinch my cheeks with the pinchers when I asked him to stop.

"Have you changed your mind?" he asked.

"This war has taken so much from me, but it has given me other things. I'm not afraid of anything anymore. What can you do to me? Torture me, rape me, kill me, chop me into a million pieces? Perhaps, but this body is fleeting, just like life. I know that I'll rise from this mud one day and live again."

"You're mad. Death sends us into a big expanse of nothingness. Why bother being decent, honorable, and good if that's the end of us all?"

I took a deep breath. "I've learned something from the books. We're immortal. Socrates, Plato, Aristotle, Seneca, Cicero, Descartes, Locke, and even Newton believed it. All the wisdom, all the beauty of the world can't just disappear without a trace. Not even people like you can destroy it. The only thing your darkness does is make the light shine brighter."

He grabbed hard with the pinchers, and pain clouded my mind.

"Stop!" I heard someone shout from the door. Bauman turned, stood at attention, and gave the high-ranking officer an incredulous look.

"We've got enough problems on our hands. This woman is innocent. The other two have confessed. The mayor has requested her immediate release. We don't want a revolt. The French know the Yankees are already in Normandy."

"But, Colonel—"

Two soldiers untied my hands and feet. I lost my balance and fell forward, but a soldier caught me and helped me to my feet. Supported on his shoulder, I fainted.

I do not know how long I was out, but when I opened my eyes, I was in the hospital. Sister Clara was watching over me.

"So you're awake," she said.

"What happened?" I asked.

"Your guardian angel never stops looking out for you, day or night," she said, eyeing the wound on my face. "You'll have a scar, but that's nothing compared to what could have happened. The Nazis don't play around."

"What day is it?"

"June 8. You've been out for nearly two days. Don't think I wasn't just a little jealous."

"Do you know anything about the Allied advance? Did they make it past the beach?"

The nun changed the dressing on my face, which stung a little. Then she brought me some soup.

"Eat a little while we talk. You're very weak."

As I swallowed the first few spoonfuls, I realized how ravenous I was.

"The Nazis are resisting. The Boche seem invincible, I tell you. The Allies are still on the beach and haven't liberated a single city, but they're sticking to it. We hope they make it past the sand."

We heard footsteps in the hall, then Denis stuck his head in. "How are you?" he asked, holding out a bouquet of flowers.

I smiled. "All right, I think. Just tired. I don't think I'm missing any parts."

He leaned against the bed to kiss my forehead, and my arms ached as I took the flowers from him.

"She's bruised, but nothing serious," the nurse said before slipping away.

"So Bauman is back?" Denis asked, terrified.

"News travels fast. Yes, but the worst part is that he's got Hermann's report about the library and is planning to take the best books and desert to Spain or South America."

Denis's eyes shot up in shock. "Could you tell the mayor?" he asked.

"What good would it do? No one's going to believe me. He's a German officer, for heaven's sake."

Denis shrugged. "So what can we do?"

"We'll have to guard the books, but I need to get out of here first." My whole body throbbed as I tried to sit up.

"You can leave tomorrow. Right now you need rest. I'll watch the library in the meantime. There's a rifle out at the farmhouse, and I'll bring it tonight."

His words brought me some comfort. Then I asked Denis to find me paper and a pen. I needed to keep writing what was going on, though I had no way of getting letters to you, Marcel, at the time. I was afraid something would happen to them, that they would be destroyed and that everything I had written would be in vain. I wondered if a paradise existed for letters that had at one time brightened our days and made us happy.

Denis left me, and as I studied my surroundings, I realized I was in the same bed where Hermann had convalesced for so long. I envisioned him stretched out with his frank smile and dimples in his cheeks. He had protected me, and now he was lost somewhere in Germany while the world he knew crumbled like a sandcastle. I recalled our last moments on the beach together, the warmth of his hands, and his hopes for seeing me again one day. Hopes are just wishes we cast into the wind—and the only thing that can bring them back to us are the inscrutable whims of fate.

38

The Attack

Saint-Malo
July 17, 1944

Denis and I set up in the library for what remained of June. We hoped the Allies would break through to Brittany quickly, but Hitler was desperately trying to detain their advance and threw all his fury at them. The Americans were still trying to free Caen, one of the biggest cities in Normandy. The Allies were bombing Germany mercilessly, Italy was practically retaken, and the Soviets were at Warsaw's door.

The Germans did not leave their fortifications. The only troops making rounds in the streets were members of the volunteer militia of French Fascists, whom the citizens feared almost more than the Germans.

The trolleys and communication systems no longer worked. The city grew more and more isolated, turning into the island it had always dreamed of being—it once having centuries ago declared independence for a brief time in history, refusing to accept the coronation of a Protestant king, Henry IV.

Saint-Malo's inhabitants were tough, nearly as invulnerable as their proud rock walls. They were waiting for their imminent liberation; yet they were really awaiting the freedom to return to their ancestral customs, the right to die of boredom and live all year in order to mock the extravagant tourists who packed the beaches during the dog days of summer.

That day we were all watching the sky with fear. Airplanes crisscrossed above us headed to more important destinations, but every now and then a cluster of British planes would drop bombs on the systems at the port, over Saint-Servan, and over the train station. Only a few houses were affected, along with a German ship sunk at the port. A few days before, what remained of the German armada had moved on so as not to end up isolated if the Allies managed to occupy all of Normandy.

"I can't sleep a wink. The sounds of those plane engines play constantly in my head," Denis huffed.

I had not slept well either, barely two or three hours the night before. Every little sound woke me with a start. I was afraid Lt. Bauman would show up in the middle of the night and find us unprepared. Denis, despite his complaints, had actually fallen asleep right away.

"I'll make some coffee," I said. We had already had a bite of black bread as breakfast. The coffee was chicory, a poor substitute for the flavor of a real roasted bean.

I poured the concoction into two cups and sat beside my friend.

"How long do you think it'll take the Allies to get here?" he asked. "It feels like it's taking them forever!"

"They have to get through the first line of defense. Once they cross it, the rest will be easy. The Germans concentrated all their efforts at sea, but they don't have enough men for the rearguard."

"But we're running out of food here, and the bombs are falling closer and closer. Don't they know the French aren't immune to explosions?"

"My mother always said you have to crack a few eggs to make an omelet."

"Your mother was wise," he said, smiling.

We heard the planes overhead again, followed by a knock at the door. I went and asked who it was without opening.

"It's me, Father Roth."

I opened the door just enough for him to slip through, then shut it again quickly. Yet behind him I had glimpsed cobblestones upended and rubble from bombed buildings in the road.

"And to think I used to complain about rain and snow during the winter. Now it's falling bombs," he said, carrying two heavy bags in his hands.

"Here, let me," Denis said, setting the bags on the table.

"I've brought you all I could. There's not much food at the hospital. We don't know whether to evacuate it or not, but many of the wounded can't be moved, and more keep arriving. We're out of empty beds, and the damage to the church is extensive. If this doesn't stop soon, there won't be one stone left on another in Saint-Malo."

The priest rubbed his sore back, then dropped into a chair. "At least we still have water," he said, receiving the glass I held out to him.

"Any other news?" I asked.

"The Allies are closer but still haven't made it to Brittany. Commander Andreas von Aulock has sworn to defend Saint-Malo to the last man."

"Well, there aren't many left," Denis joked.

"I've got to go, but I'll bring you more in a few days. May God bless you both." The priest stood again and made his way to the door, but before I opened it for him, he turned to me and said, "Be careful, both of you. That monster Bauman is wandering around the city."

"We'll be ready," I promised.

I locked the door behind him and went down to the basement where we had hidden some of the rarest books. It was not the ideal hiding place, but it was safer there.

Back on the main floor, we heard engines again, but this time louder than in recent days. The building started to shake, especially the windows, and some of the books fell to the floor.

"What on earth was that?" Denis asked, looking up to see plaster sifting down from the ceiling.

We barely had time to dive beneath a desk. The bombs exploded very close. The upstairs windows shattered, the wooden floor groaned, and some of the shelves were upended, scattering our books. Then sparks flew through the room and reached the books. Before I registered what had truly happened, I looked up to see the library afire on all four sides.

39

The Americans

Saint-Malo
July 17, 1944

At first the sight paralyzed us. The fire spread rapidly along the curtains and to some of the books that had fallen on the floor. Denis crawled out from below the table and frantically looked for water or a blanket but found nothing to help put out the flames. More bombs fell nearby, and the building shook like a tree in the wind. I ran to a set of curtains and yanked hard. My fingers were singed, but the heavy drapery did help to choke the flames. Then I jumped up and down on the fabric until only black smoke and ashes rose. On the other side of the room, books continued to burn. Denis tried to stamp the fire out with his feet, but more sparks flew out and lit on other nearby books.

"Blast it!" I screamed, then ran to help him.

We tried to suffocate the flames with anything we could find. In the fury, I caught sight of a few of the covers. The titles turned black so quickly, and their pages turned inward as if writhing in pain.

"Faster!" I panted, "or else we'll lose it all!"

The sound of the bomber planes was deafening, and the impact from the explosions nearly knocked us off our feet. The smoke grew thick, and it was hard to breathe, but we fought and fought the fire.

"I think we should get out, Jocelyn," Denis cried. The wooden flooring had begun to smoke. If it lit up, too, there would be no hope left.

But we kept at it for another half hour, and the flames finally went out as the bombing of the city started to calm. We threw ourselves down, exhausted and breathless, sooty from the flying ash.

"This is exactly what happens when a civilization goes bankrupt. Everything is fire and ashes," Denis said, dragging himself up beside me.

"Well, at least we've kept disaster at bay for now." I was trying to be optimistic though we had lost at least fifty books, some of them irreplaceable.

"This isn't the first library to burn, and humanity has somehow gone on," Denis said.

I frowned and glared at him. "Every day ten thousand people are dying because of this cursed war, and each one of them is unrepeatable."

Denis shrugged. "Don't hear me wrong. I love these books. I've given my life to literature, but books can be replaced. People can't be."

"Are you sure? Most of the books that were lost in the famous fire at the Library of Alexandria were never recovered or reproduced. Some of the most important works of human history were lost forever."

He sighed. "We cannot stand in fate's way."

"The heroes of antiquity spent their lives challenging the gods and the fates they inflicted on people. Isn't that the story of humanity? We're free beings facing our destiny."

Denis helped me up. We tried to cool down the floor by fanning it, then swept up the ashes and charred books. I looked through some and tried to divine which volumes they were, what their scorched pages had once held. Tears streamed down my cheeks. It was like holding the corpses of the children I had never borne.

Denis put a hand on my shoulder. "I may have sounded insensitive, but I was just trying to ameliorate the situation. I've seen so many horrors in these years that the burning of a few books doesn't seem that serious anymore . . . Yet I know what you're feeling, I really do. We can get over the obstacles life puts in our path. But it's something else to fight against the desolation. The city has been mortally wounded."

"You can go whenever you want. You've lived through hell, and after all of that, I don't want you to die now in an old building trying to save some cheap, replaceable books."

Denis smiled suddenly. "I can't imagine a better way to go!" He hugged me, and his humor cheered me. Loneliness is the soul's worst enemy. To be loved and cherished is often what makes the difference between lunacy and sanity. Denis was one of the few things that kept me tethered to the world.

We finished picking things up and took the half-burned books out to the courtyard and finished burning them. It felt disorienting to light them on fire. Once we had cleaned up the best we could, we were exhausted. We went up to the top floor and took stock of the damage.

Denis pointed at the roof and whistled. "That's a big hole."

"Well, let's hope it doesn't rain much before the Americans put an end to this war."

"Water might be worse for the books than fire."

Denis crawled up to the roof and secured a piece of canvas over the hole. I helped however I could but stayed away from the edge. A growing vertigo kept me from climbing all over the shingles.

Eventually we sat in front of the window that looked out over the rooftop and the entire city. Columns of smoke rose into the blue afternoon sky like cruel offerings to appease the gods of war. Several houses had been crushed, and dust billowed through the streets. On the other side of the wall, the area of the port and the train station seemed to have taken the worst hit.

A volunteer fire truck crawled through the streets toward the parts of the city that were still burning.

"Will there even be a world left to save when the war is over?" Denis's question sounded strange at first to my tired mind, but the sense of it slowly dawned on me. Buildings could be rebuilt, and a new generation would replace the one before; death would not stop requiring inevitable replacements. The deepest wounds were inside our hearts. If people could no longer believe in goodness, hope, and the possibility of a better world, what would be left for them? As a late American bomber nearly scraped the roofs of Saint-Malo, I closed my eyes and wished the war would end before innocence disappeared from the world forever.

Part Three

The Last One Hundred Steps

40

The Long Goodbye

Saint-Malo
July 31, 1944

The Americans made slow progress, but they had just taken the port of Granville, which was too small for heavy-duty ships to dock. According to rumor, they would soon be outside of Rennes, which got our hopes up.

The heat of the past few days had been unbearable. Sudden rain showers were the only things that cut the humidity. The unpleasant weather kept most people off the streets, and Denis and I holed up in the library.

That afternoon someone knocked at the door. Denis went to open it, and I heard Sister Clara's voice.

I ran to the door, worried. "Sister Clara, what is it?" It was not like her to leave the hospital, especially on such a sweltering day.

"More bombs have damaged the hospital. Most of the invalids are in the basement, but we're out of room. There are three wounded Germans we can't put down there with the Jews. You remember there's still one family in hiding."

I was immediately resistant to what she implied. "We can't have the Germans here."

"Then what can I do with them? Put them out of their misery? You know I don't care for the Boche, but they are God's creatures too. On more than one occasion I've been tempted to put pillows over their gasping mouths, but the wrath of men works not the justice of God. They're young devils, most of them hardly twenty years old."

Denis shook his head, knowing I would be too softhearted to deny them entry. "We don't have enough provisions."

"We would supply their food." Sister Clara's response seemed too ready, as if she had done this before.

"It would be for a good cause," I said. "If only to protect those in hiding."

"I need your help," she said, her eyes pleading with Denis.

"You're asking me to carry a German in his sickbed? You're asking too much of me, Sister Clara."

"It's better to give than to receive," she quipped with a wry smile.

Denis finally gave in and went with her. I stayed back, alone for the first time in a few weeks. I tried to busy myself writing my letters, as Pierre would come tomorrow for the next batch. He was not sure if he could get to Paris amid the chaos, but an uncle had promised to drive him to Rennes, and from there buses were still running south and to the capital.

I had been writing for a while when I heard noises from the basement. I thought it might be a rat, so I grabbed the broom and crept down the stairs. I flicked on the light—we still had electricity, though it came and went throughout the day—and caught sight of something scurrying between the sacks and bags of books. I ran after it and found a young man in a German uniform crouching in a corner.

"Please don't hurt me," the boy begged in barely intelligible French.

"What are you doing here? Did Lt. Bauman send you?"

"No, madame, I—"

"Go on, speak!"

"I deserted. The war is lost, and I don't want to die. If my people catch me, they'll shoot me. There are no trials for deserters."

I stood there weighing the situation, unsure of what to do. "What do you want me to do? We hardly have enough food for ourselves, and as we speak, three of your wounded fellow soldiers are being brought from the hospital to stay here."

"Don't worry about me. I'll stay down here, I can eat scraps of bread, just . . . Just please don't turn me in," the boy begged.

"How did you get in?" I asked, looking all around at the brick walls. Out of the corner of my eye I confirmed that the heavy boxes of damaged books still completely covered up the door to the secret tunnel. He had not come in through there.

"Through the coal chute." He pointed at a tiny window. I was shocked, having never considered that anything but a small animal could get through.

"You must be terribly thin."

"We haven't been supplied in weeks, and even though the company steals from the farmers, we only get one meal a day."

I sat down beside him. He seemed so vulnerable, and a wave of heretofore unknown compassion washed over me.

"I didn't volunteer for this war. I was studying medicine in my first year at the university—I just wanted to help people, but I got drafted. I asked to be used as a nurse or medic, but I hadn't even finished my first year, so they didn't let me."

"The war has destroyed all of our lives," I answered.

"I'm an only child, and my mother is a widow, but she had some savings from my grandparents. She cried for days when she learned I had to enlist. I'm the only thing she's got left in the world. I hadn't seen combat until now. I'm lucky I got sent to France. On the eastern front, soldiers are dying by the thousands."

I leaned toward him. "You'll get home to her, just wait."

"Thank you, madame."

"You can call me Jocelyn. Please, just don't make any noise. If you're discovered, I can't help you. You can take care of your needs here in this bucket. I'll bring you food at night while the others are asleep."

"Thank you, madame." He kissed my hand between his tears.

I went back upstairs. Was it a wretched idea to have wounded Germans in the library? We all needed to battle some of the hatred they had sown in our hearts. Then I remembered what my father would always tell my mother when she got angry with one of his competitors in business: "Love your enemies, and perhaps they'll become your friends."

Denis and Clara arrived soon thereafter with the first wounded soldier. We carried him upstairs and laid out several mats on the floor, then they returned to the hospital for the second. By the time they had brought the third, Denis was completely spent.

The three soldiers moaned lowly, as scared and worn-out as we were. Sister Clara returned to the hospital, and that day Denis and I became not only guardians of Saint-Malo's memories but also nurses to three German soldiers.

41

The First of August

Saint-Malo
August 1, 1944

Needing to relax, I went up to the top floor of the library, opened the window that led to the roof, and sat on the sill. The sky was clear with the blinding bright blue of a French summer. No one was allowed on the beach anymore. The ships were anchored at the port, and even the sea seemed depressed at the thought of oncoming battle. For centuries, danger and adventure had been part and parcel of this city's life and heritage, but we all knew that what was coming was a moment darker than any before.

Looking back, the beginning of the war seemed almost childish now—like a rehearsal for what was to come. Hitler grasped power with the tenacity of someone who has no future but fights to the bitter end. This seemed understandable to me for one failure of a man, but it did not make sense for an entire people who were proud and educated. Perhaps that was the problem: Germany had ceased to be civilized long ago.

The waves continued their rhythmic melody, interrupted only by the screams of gulls. Then I looked toward the area where my apartment was and saw smoke rising from the top floor. There had been what we now considered a light bombing raid the night before, but it had been mainly concentrated toward the citadel.

My heart skipped a beat when I saw the smoke. For some ridiculous reason I had believed my home would be indestructible, that nothing could happen to it simply because it was mine. The apartment was not of great monetary value, but it held my memories. Antoine's letters were there, along with some family photos, my school notes, diplomas, and some diaries. I slid back inside the window and went downstairs.

"I have to go home!"

Denis cocked his head at me. I was the only one who had not left the library that whole time. Plus, there were three wounded men to look after, clean, and feed. "Do you want me to go with you?" he asked. "The streets are empty. It could be dangerous."

"Dangerous? Since when has Saint-Malo been dangerous?" I made an attempt at sarcasm to hide my growing anxiety.

"Since a certain Nazi SS officer decided to get rid of you," he said.

I smiled but shrugged him off, grabbing and emptying a khaki-colored backpack. I would need somewhere to put the things I might be able to salvage.

"Dr. Férey came from the hospital just a bit ago and told me the Americans would soon be in Dinan," Denis said. That took me by surprise, as it was only about an hour's drive away. "But don't get excited," he went on. "Commander Aulock has sworn he'll hold out 'til the end. The few ships that were still in the port have been evacuated, and the cranes are aimed out to sea in case the bombs knock them over. We don't know when, but more bombing raids are coming. It might be safer to bring the soldiers down to the basement."

"No, not to the basement!" I said, alarmed.

"Why not? I really don't think those guys are in the position to steal the books," Denis joked.

"This building is solid, with strong walls. It won't fall."

"Jocelyn, there were plenty of buildings in Saint-Malo that were even stronger and more solid, and they're gone now."

"Just don't take the Germans down there," I said, walking out.

I picked my way down the street pocked with holes and mounds of rubble toward my apartment. Not a single store with all its windows intact remained. Some doors, completely charred, had given way, and looters had taken whatever had been left. It was so sad to see the world coming apart before my eyes.

At my building, the entry was open, the paint was peeling, and some of the stairs were cracked in new places—but otherwise, the place seemed normal. Had I imagined the smoke? Or had it been coming from a nearby building instead of mine?

I crept up the stairs, recalling the many times Antoine and I had climbed them, laughing and joking, taking life as a jest.

I unlocked my door and went inside. At first I feared Lt. Bauman had searched it out of pure spite, but everything seemed in order. In my room, I rifled through boxes of photos and letters, picking out what was most important. There was the handkerchief Antoine had given me when I first got sick in Paris, a few train tickets, and some books I could not leave. I glanced around the room with a knot in my stomach. I had never been very materialistic, but I was greedy for the memories of the places where I had once been happy. The room also brought back excruciating moments, reminding me of my illness and Antoine's death. Time after time I had wished for death, to no longer have to suffer the loss of my husband and friends. What had gotten me through lately was Denis's return. I grabbed the stuffed bear from the bed and nestled it into the backpack.

In the living room, I picked out a few things to pack but soon got sidetracked staring out the big window to the sea. The view itself was part of my story of love and suffering. It had been the landscape of so much of my life, and I made the Herculean effort to commit every nuance to memory.

Time stood still until the deafening sound of planes flying over the city broke through. They flew on, and I sighed with relief. I had to get out, though, and find somewhere safer. I grabbed a few more things, then went out to the landing to fetch the hidden books in the attic. Then I heard the engines again, this time lower, and the telltale whistling of bombs.

The building started jiggling like gelatin. I dived under a table and stopped up my ears, then the windows shattered at the impact of a nearby explosion. Screams erupted from my throat.

I knew I could not stay there, so I made a run for the exit. I got to the door just as an explosion took out part of the living room. I dashed downstairs as everything crashed around me, then ran smack into Mrs. Fave. For a flash I wondered why in the world fate had allowed such a despicable creature to live, but the terror on her face erased that thought.

"Follow me!" I yelled, helping her down the stairs.

"Let go of me, you German slut!" she screamed, pulling her arm free and shoving me hard. I tumbled to the landing one flight down. Fearing I had broken something, I managed to get to my feet. She stood on the landing of the flight above, leering over me with a smile that said my misfortune had restored her pride. "Sluts like you deserve what you get!" she said, her fist raised.

Just then, part of the roof and the handrail gave way on top of Mrs. Fave, knocking her down below me to the entryway. With difficulty, I picked my way down through the rubble that had half buried the woman.

"Hold on, I'll get you out," I said as encouragingly as I could.

She was covered in blood and writhing in pain. "You'll soon be joining me," she rasped out. And with that, her eyes went blank.

I dragged myself up and out to the street. Smoke and fire billowed all around, proclaiming the disaster. The Nazis were willing to let the monster of war destroy every last thing before they would surrender. I limped toward the library and came upon Dr. Aubry headed in the opposite direction.

"The bombs have wiped out Wilson Avenue, nearly all of Saint-Servan, and the poorer areas of Saint-Malo," he said.

"I can go with you to help," I said, trying to keep pace with him.

"No, go back to the library and rest that injured leg of yours. The divine comedy has given each of us a role: I save bodies, but you must watch over the soul of Saint-Malo."

42

The Doctor

Saint-Malo
August 2, 1944

D r. Aubry was truly a quiet hero. Though his entire family lived within the wall, he did not hesitate one bit to leave the safety of his home and rush off to wherever injured people remained in the city. More and more people were added daily to the long list of wounded. Patients now overran the hospital and even filled a nearby building, and Dr. Aubry saw to as many as he could. He only slept two or three hours at a time, then returned to making rounds among the sick who remained at home and new victims of the bombing raids.

That afternoon, he came by the library to check on our soldiers. He seemed worn down and depressed.

"How are you?" I asked the good man. We often had long,

meandering talks about any subject under the sun. He was widely educated but rarely spoke of himself.

"Ah, what does it matter? I'm tired, horrified, and disgusted, but right now my duty is to give my body and soul to this city."

"You have to take care of yourself though. If something happens to you, what will we do?"

"This can't last forever. The American line is just a few miles away. The Germans have set up strongholds in Saint-Ideuc, La Fontaine aux Pèlerins, and on La Montagne Saint-Joseph, but resistance is futile. They haven't figured out yet that—similar to what happened in France four years ago—luck is now against them. We can't defeat destiny."

"We never know our demise is upon us until it's too late," I said.

"That's one of the problems of knowing we are immortal; sometimes we confuse the impossible annihilation of the soul with this finite, mortal body."

I was quiet, thinking over his words. I had never given too much thought to my soul. I had been angry with God for so long that I was indifferent to the idea of immortality, even when I had been on the brink of death.

"Every evening before heading home, I go by command headquarters to speak with von Aulock and beg him to lay down his arms and put an end to this massacre, but he always answers the same way: 'Honor forbids me to surrender. I must keep fighting for Germany.'"

"False patriotism is the true scourge of the twentieth century. It's caused more victims than malaria, scurvy, and tuberculosis combined," I said. "Yesterday I saw you running in the direction of the train station."

"Oh, it was terrible. Hundreds wounded and many dead. The people were terrified. Many are hiding out in the gate of Saint-Thomas, the citadel, or the Great Gate. The ones who can't fit in there are taking shelter in the wine cellars, but if the siege lasts much longer, hunger and disease will have their way. We ought to evacuate the city."

"I don't want to leave," I said.

"You're being reckless."

"But just yesterday you told me I had to protect the soul of Saint-Malo."

"On the radio the British are saying Brittany will fall within days. Churchill announced that Mont-Saint-Michel has been liberated."

Denis brought over something like tea. "One of the soldiers has taken a turn for the worse in the last few hours," he said.

Dr. Aubry shrugged and sighed. "There's hardly any medicine left. And that's another of my dilemmas: Who to save and who to let die? Should it be the older ones, our enemies, the weakest ones? I don't like playing God." His face was grave, his cheeks sunken by the weight of the soul burden he carried. "Yesterday more wounded soldiers showed up. A German truck with a few soldiers apparently tried to break through the American line and get into Saint-Malo, but the Americans shot at them. Four of them got through, and two of those are wounded. I was called to headquarters to look at them. The officer leading them was a man I treated a couple years back at the hospital—your friend, whose name I can't recall at the moment."

That jolted me to attention. Perhaps I had misheard. "An officer?" I asked.

"The one who got the documents for the Jews in hiding. You used to visit him every afternoon."

"Hermann von Choltiz?" I was incredulous.

"Yes, that's the one. He arrived yesterday with the injured men."

43

Sleepless

Saint-Malo
August 4, 1944

The Germans set up a hospital for all their wounded men.
They evacuated Combourg, a division of Americans had
occupied Dinard, and others were heading toward Saint-Pierre-
de-Plesguen.

Commander von Aulock called a meeting with Saint-Malo's
authorities. Dr. Aubry had told me about the meeting, and I
decided to go, more as a means to see Hermann than to learn
what the colonel had to say.

At headquarters, the mayor, Auguste Briand, and the prefect
ushered everyone into a large room. Not long after, the German

commander entered with his Prussian arrogance. Yet his raised chin and the monocle over his eye could not dissemble his gaunt weariness.

"Gentlemen, please have a seat. I've called you together regarding our concerning situation. The Americans are very near. They have requested unconditional surrender—which, naturally, I have rejected. Our lives will be purchased at a high price. We may be defeated, but if we delay the Allied advance to Paris, our army might yet reorganize and make Germany impregnable. Then we can work out a separate peace agreement with the British and the Americans, consolidate our efforts, and face our true enemy—the Bolshevik danger."

The mayor spoke up in concern. "But, Commander, the city cannot withstand more bombing."

"The only thing I can do is let the civilians leave," he said, as if offering an overwhelming gesture of goodwill.

"To where? The trains aren't running, and we have no means of escape. We're caught between fire. You must let us take shelter in the citadel and the underground bunkers. The citizens of Saint-Malo have never risen up against you, save a few unfortunate exceptions."

"I can't predict your plans. Your cordiality is admirable, but in Saint-Cast-le-Guildo a group of resisters rose up and had to be contained by cannon fire."

"Then let's allow the people to leave. Whoever wants to go can leave the city," the mayor concluded.

"Do as you please, but the remaining civilians will die. At the slightest hint of rebellion, we will not hesitate to respond with deadly force." The commander removed his monocle as he spoke, by way of dismissal.

We filed out of the room. I felt deflated for not having seen

Hermann, and I wondered if Dr. Aubry had been mistaken. Perhaps he had confused one patient for another.

"Mrs. Ferrec," I heard an unmistakable voice call out. "I must say, this is the last place I would have expected to see you. Just a few days ago you were almost mine in the basement, but you managed to slip away once again. Never fear—people like me move through chaos like fish in water, and I assure you, Saint-Malo will be in complete anarchy within days. Don't think I've forgotten you. Oh, no, indeed . . . You're always on my mind."

Swallowing my fear, I wheeled around and pierced Lt. Bauman with a disgusted look. "I've been waiting for you too. I'm sure a coward like you will try a surprise attack at night, but I'll give you the welcome you deserve."

He let out a sneering laugh. "I know why you came today. You heard that your lover was back. You think he can protect you again? Things have changed. The chain of command is up in the air. Besides, what will one more cadaver matter in a mountain of carnage and rubble? This city is about to become one enormous tomb."

In my heart I knew he was right about the carnage. And I knew he would come after me the first chance he got, but I was not about to become easy prey.

I forced a calm I did not feel into my legs as I went down the stairs toward the main doors. A hand suddenly took hold of me and dragged me into a dark corner. My heart nearly burst in defeat— Bauman seemed determined to do away with me then and there.

"Jocelyn!" said the voice of a shadow in a soldier's uniform.

I blinked, not comprehending what I saw.

"Oh, how good it is to see you! It took me months to get across Europe, and I never thought I'd make it through the American lines, but here I am."

The shadow's face lit up then, and his eyes caught a nearby light. Hermann's face showed the effects of the Russian front's horrors, but then he smiled, and I recognized the man once more.

44

The Last Station

Sometimes life feels like being the lone passenger at the last stop on the train. The wait is interminable, and time seems to stand still; yet the next instant everything speeds up, and we can hardly make sense of the whirlwind that sweeps us away. I could not stop thinking about Hermann after seeing him at headquarters. It was so brief, barely a moment, that I wondered as I walked back to the library if it had actually happened. His sudden appearance had driven all of Bauman's threats out of mind. The only thing that mattered was that Hermann was safe, back in Saint-Malo.

That morning, as people prepared to evacuate, the bomber

planes passed us by headed for other destinations. Yet they returned by noon to drop their deadly freight upon our city. The bombs that had fallen on the citadel and the wall up to them had been an attempt—whether failed or not—to knock out certain concrete sections. Yet now the Allies seemed willing to destroy Saint-Malo down to the very last rock while the Germans holed up safely in the fortress walls.

The bombs paused in the afternoon, and people resumed their attempts to flee the city. Dr. Aubry came to see us before the three German soldiers were transferred to the hospital.

"Why don't you two come to the hospital too? The basement of the building is much safer than here," he said to me and Denis.

I looked around. "You know we can't leave the books."

"Pick out the most valuable ones and come with me. Sometimes we have to sacrifice one thing to save something that is more important."

I threw up my hands in helplessness, encompassing the shelves with a gesture. It was impossible for me to decide which literary works were worth saving. "You remember how recently you were talking about playing God—deciding who should live and who should die? I have that same dilemma with books."

He smiled at me and pointed the German orderlies to the stretchers where the soldiers were lying. "Well, if you change your mind, you know where to find us. The bombings that are coming now won't be like what we've had before. Dr. Yves Lebreton tended to a wounded American yesterday, and he learned that the high commanders have sworn not to leave one stone on top of another until the Germans completely surrender."

"Thank you, Dr. Aubry."

Denis and I were eventually alone again, and I told him about seeing Hermann.

"So he's back here?"

"Apparently he got through the American line."

Denis was quiet. Antoine had been his best friend, and I did not expect Denis to bless my closeness with Hermann. "Nothing has happened between us. I couldn't—"

"I understand, Jocelyn. I think Antoine would want you to be happy. That's actually all he wanted in life." He put his arms around me, and I broke down crying. It was ridiculous to hold out hope for anything. Within days our world would certainly be in ruins, with little chance for life rising up from the ashes. Nor did we have any guarantee of coming through the battle alive— especially not both of us.

"I have to tell you something else," I said to Denis, pulling away. "I didn't want to say anything until the wounded soldiers were gone. I've been hiding a young German soldier, a deserter, in the basement."

Denis twisted his head and stared at me. "Have you lost your mind?"

"You hadn't figured that out yet? We're trying to save a library in the middle of a full-on siege, a Nazi is trying to destroy everything and kill us, I have a heart for one of the enemy, and yes, we have a deserter in the basement."

We called for the young man, who had not seen the light of day in a very long time. His pale face shone with perspiration and a feverish heat.

"We think the city will go down before long, but as soon as the fighting is over, they'll take you prisoner. You understand that, right?" I asked. He nodded at my words.

"What's your name?" I asked our strange guest.

"Bruno. I'm sorry, I thought I had told you," the young man said.

"Well, we weren't too concerned with formalities in our first meeting."

He looked around at the shelves crammed with books. "So this is a library?"

"How sharp for a Boche," Denis quipped.

"I love books."

"You mean you love burning them?" Denis said. "A few of your compatriots have already come by to do that."

The boy hung his head.

"Denis, cut it out. He's just a scared kid," I said.

"Kids his size were torturing Jews in Dachau. I assure you, they aren't what they seem."

The boy raised his head. "I haven't hurt anyone. They stuck me in the Hitler Youth along with everybody else, but that doesn't mean anything to you, I'm sure."

"Mm-hmm. Now that the party's over, you're all denying that you're Nazis. And suddenly a lot of French collaborators are turning out to be Resistance fighters. When the war's over, the politicians will find a way to claim that France freed herself on her own. The world is a stinking cesspool."

Denis and I put some supper together, and we ate in silence. We were all on edge, none of us prepared to die. The inconvenience of death makes it hard to consider it without trembling to the core.

That night, none of Saint-Malo's inhabitants slept. We knew we were living the last days, perhaps the last hours, of our city— and that terrible realization shredded the final strands of peace that fear and war had left us.

45

The Nuns

Sometimes, when we think things cannot get any worse, they
do. The day before, I had attended a burial. After mass in
the chapel of Saint-Servan, everyone dispersed in haste to avoid
both the ruined streets and one another's eyes, wearied with pain
and suffering. Dr. Aubry had told me there that tempers had
been high between the German marines and infantry soldiers.
Everything was breaking down.

The German commander had given the citizens remaining in
Saint-Malo one last chance to get out, but few did. Daily life for
four years had been one long survival game, and by this time we
were convinced we could do nothing to change the inevitable.

"What a rough night," Denis said, rubbing his eyes.

The bombings had been relentless out at Grand Bé that morning, and the hospital was overrun, not only with the wounded but with families seeking refuge. Yet there was simply no more room.

"You could try the hospital. You might be safer there," I said.

Denis smirked. "You think I'm going to let you take all the credit for saving these books?"

I snorted and fixed a light breakfast. Our scant provisions would last a couple more days. Our guest, the German soldier, spent most of the time sleeping in the basement, but when he caught whiffs of food, he crept upstairs.

Denis was annoyed. "Looks like the Boche is hungry again."

"We're all in the same boat, Denis. We're all victims of the insanity that's taken hold."

Our young guest wolfed down his scant food, as hungry as he was terrified.

We heard commotion outside, and I saw the firefighters rushing by. When one saw me standing at the door, he shouted, "Stay inside! Several buildings are in flames. The cathedral's steeple has been blown apart. All night long the Americans bombed the Rocabey barracks, the casino, and other buildings outside the walls."

The firefighter's face was completely black, and the poor man looked exhausted though the day had just begun. "Some of the Germans are looting the houses and buildings," he warned.

"You are heroes," I said, admiring their sacrificial spirit.

He shook his head. "This is all just madness. The Germans are blocking the gate of Saint-Vincent with a tank. Dr. Rival, the hygiene inspector, tried to convince them to let us by, but to no avail."

The firefighter went on, and the bombs started falling again.

"We've only got food for today," Denis said when I came back to the table.

I cocked my head in surprise. "But I thought we had enough for two or three days."

"The German ate too much. I told you we should've just put a bullet in him."

"I'll go to the hospital and see what they can give us."

"Jocelyn, bombs are falling outside!" Denis shouted, as if I could not hear the explosions.

"I'm not deaf," I quipped, grabbing a small bag I hoped to fill with supplies.

I looked all around as I left the building. I had not mentioned anything to Denis, but I wanted to get a letter to the German headquarters. I was worried after not having any news of Hermann since the meeting about the evacuation.

I walked briskly while my eyes took in the destruction of the previous night's bombing, the most aggressive we had experienced yet. Up to then, most bombs had hit the port and the impoverished areas. But now the old city was burning on all four sides before the overworked firefighters and the disdainful Germans.

The German headquarters had also been damaged, but the front arch was intact, the gate still closed, and the guards hidden behind improvised fortifications. They started shooting as soon as they saw me. I waved a white handkerchief furiously, and they stopped.

"What do you want?" they barked.

"To deliver a letter to Lt. Hermann von Choltiz."

"He's not here. He was transferred yesterday to the fort on Cézembre."

That answer petrified me. From the roof windows of the

library we could see the American artillery and planes hammering the small island without mercy.

"Is there any way to communicate with them over there?"

"By radio, but we've had no connection since this morning. We think they're getting bombed with napalm."

I had no idea what napalm was, but I could imagine it was not good. Then I turned toward the hospital, and a blast between the guards and where I stood lifted me up and threw me down in the middle of the plaza. My ears stopped working. Still discombobulated, I managed to drag myself toward a nearby building. I checked myself out as best I could: I was very sore, I was bleeding above my eyes, and my head was clanging.

A firefighter approached me. "Are you okay?" he asked.

I nodded. "I think so. I was headed to the sisters' hospital."

"I'll take you," he said, helping me up.

"What about those two guards?" I asked.

"They didn't make it," he answered, supporting me on his shoulder. I started weeping. I had been talking with them just moments before, and now they were gone—barely men, surely not more than eighteen years old.

It took us twenty minutes to make our way to the hospital. As soon as we entered and went down to the basement, two sisters came to help.

"What happened to her?" Sister Clara asked the fireman. I was still worked up and crying, and for the first time in a very long time, I wanted to give up. They laid me down on a bed, and soon Dr. Aubry came to tend to the cuts all over me.

"It's nothing serious. One of your eardrums burst, you'll have some nasty bruises . . . Your forehead's got a new crease, and I see several contusions on your right arm. But compared with what could have happened, you've been very lucky."

I just stared at him without answering. For certain, luck was something I had not had for years. The firefighter left with the doctor and one of the nuns, then Sister Clara sat down on the edge of my bed.

"I'm so sorry," she said, putting a blanket over me. Despite the summer heat, it was cool inside the hospital.

I started to cry again. All my strength was starting to dissipate. "Sister Clara, my life has been one disappointment after another. I lost my parents when I was a teenager, and I'd already seen my twin sister die when we were kids. I didn't have anyone until I met my dear Antoine. He made me want to live again. Before him, all I ever really loved were books. We got married, and then I got really sick. Then the war started, and he left me to fight, and when he returned, he was so sick. He was never the same, and the worst of all is that—"

Sister Clara wrapped her arms around me and let me weep with abandon. I was shook and sobbed like an inconsolable child.

"Then he died and left me all alone in the world again."

"So that's when you realized it," the nun said.

I looked at her through the tears, her dark face blurry and surreal.

"That's when you realized you cared for the German, the officer who was convalescing here. I have also loved; we rarely choose whom we love. Before the war in Spain, when I was young, a handsome boy came to town. I was just a girl, and I'd never seen anyone like him. This man moved into the house next to ours, renting a room. I saw him every morning, and I would just stare into his brown eyes and at his roguish smile. Something like fiery chills ran up and down me when he was near, and I'd never felt that way before. In the summers the town had outdoor movies in the plaza. Nights were a little cool, and the air smelled like flowers. They would project American and British films on a huge canvas sheet. All the neighbors brought chairs or blankets and picnic suppers. One night I went with my friends, and I saw this stranger. He motioned for me, and I followed him to a park nearby. He gave me a kiss. I was a dizzy mess floating on air. We started seeing each other in secret. He was a barber and wanted to start his own business. We talked about the future and getting married. One night as we walked through the fields, he kissed me, and one thing led to the next. A few months later I was pregnant. My parents forced me to give up the child and shut me up in a convent. My love left town, and I never saw him again. Forbidden love can feel like the most desirable kind, but it doesn't usually end well."

I could see well enough now to notice the tears in Sister Clara's eyes, still dimmed with the sadness of her father's execution in Spain and all the suffering she had witnessed.

"My feelings are complicated. Antoine was the love of my life, and I always thought my heart could never belong to any other man. I didn't think I could ever love anyone like I loved him. Hermann, though, is a kindred soul, and I've seen him change. We have so much in common, and he's respected me and protected me. I don't want to marry him, but I also don't want harm to come to him. He was sent to Cézembre, and that's basically a death sentence. I think they're getting bombed with something called napalm."

"It's a gas," the nun explained. "It burns everything, like boiling oil."

That worried me even more.

"If God has protected him 'til now, maybe he'll do so for a long time," Sister Clara offered by way of consolation.

"Sometimes I think we're all going to die in this," I said.

"Well, that much is true. The one absolutely certain and un-changeable fact is that we are all going to die. We don't like to think about it much, but the awful thing is when you face death every day by watching others falling at your side—children, pregnant women, old people who were trying to enjoy the time they had left. They're all suffering and disappearing day after day. Meanwhile, you're still standing, immune to the bombs, the bullets, and the suffering. Sometimes the worst punishment in the world is to survive while the world you know disappears. That's what happened to me in Spain, in Santander. Every day I would walk down the elegant city streets, watch the people on the beach, smell the churros and roasted chestnuts in the winter and the fried fish and leche merengada in the summer. But all of that disappeared. Now France is going through this. We may survive, but nothing will be the same."

Her words were too bitter to swallow. I was aware then that I had always held on to some kind of hope that life would end up winning over the horror around me. That day after the bomb, lying there in the hospital bed, I stopped hoping. I allowed myself to do nothing more than resist, to survive, and to not think about what the coming days might hold.

46

Refuge or Escape

Now that the end was near, I pushed myself to keep writing. People were all around me, but I felt alone. Dr. Aubry had made me stay in the hospital bed for two days. Sister Clara had sent a message and provisions to Denis so he would not worry. When I was not writing, I spent most of that time sleeping, overcome by the accumulated exhaustion of the last few months. At night I found the murmurs of the invalids around me soothing. During the day children raced around despite their parents' reprimands, and this, too, soothed me. They could not keep from playing because, for them, that was what it meant to be alive.

One blond girl with huge eyes had walked up to me the day before. Her name was Judith, and she was from Kraków. I had no idea how she had come from so far away. She spoke broken Polish, had spent most of her short life in France, and struggled with French pronunciation.

"Are you bad sick?" she asked.

"No, I'll be out of here soon," I answered with a smile, moved to tenderness.

"I want to go back to Paris when the bombings stop. I went to a wonderful school there and had so many friends. We would play in the playground and have so much fun. Mom would give me a snack in the afternoon while I did my chores. Now I'm stuck inside all day. We've been in hiding for a really long time. We're Jews, but don't tell anybody. A lot of people hate us for that." She seemed scared she had said too much.

"Don't worry," I said. "I won't tell anyone."

"Do you know what it means to be a Jew?"

"No," I said. "I don't. Would you tell me?" I was curious to hear how a child would explain this to me.

"Don't you know the story of Esther in the Bible?"

"I read it when I was a little girl," I said. My parents had read the Holy Scriptures to me since I was young, and the church we had gone to every Sunday valued studying the Bible.

"Being a Jew means always being afraid, looking behind you to make sure no one's following, keeping your bag packed near the door in case you have to run away, praying in silence on Fridays, and crying for a land you've never seen."

I thought on this for a moment. "Well then, perhaps I'm a Jew too," I answered.

"No you aren't," Judith said gravely.

I scrunched up my face. "How do you know?"

She crossed her arms and gave me an exasperated look. "Your clothes aren't old, your face isn't covered in tears every day, and you haven't lost everything you've got yet," she pronounced with a maturity that sent a chill up my spine. Then she ran off.

The nuns returned from their morning prayers, and Sister Clara came up to me. "If you want, I can walk you to the library." I sat up in the bed and put on my shoes. "Do you want to see the ocean first?"

I nodded, and we went up to the top floor. The building was very close to the Bastion de la Hollande. The Germans had outfitted it with several cannons. A corporal dozed beside one, seemingly soaking up the sun, though out at sea a dense fog made it hard to make out the island of Cézembre.

"He's there," I said, pointing.

"Dr. Aubry told me the British armada should get there any moment now. If they surrender, there might be a chance . . ."

I sighed, and we went back down. Out on the street, we passed by one of the plazas, and I noticed the farmers' market was still intact. We walked through Rue de Toulouse, which was practically untouched, but Rue des Cordiers and Grand Rue—buried under rocks from the buildings that lined them—had not had such luck. The cathedral's silhouette was eerily foreign without the steeple. We passed the school, where several families had taken refuge. The nuns would prepare huge pots of stew for everyone there, and volunteers would serve it.

We ran into Father Roth, who told us more about the lost steeple.

"How unfortunate," he said with sad eyes.

"It was so beautiful, though the life of any person is more important," Sister Clara said.

"How is the chapel inside?" I asked.

Father Roth shrugged, searching for words. "One of the bells fell, broke the cupola, and damaged the floor and some of the pews. Fortunately, nothing as important as the Virgin was destroyed," he explained with something like relief.

"God tries us but not too far," Sister Clara answered.

We made our way to the library. I tried not to look around too much, not wanting the desolation all around to tear away the shreds of energy I still clung to.

I knocked, and Denis opened the door for me. He did not look well—his cheeks sunken, rings around his eyes, and his beard in knots. But he beamed at me and said, "You look terrible!"

"Well, have you looked in the mirror lately?" I said.

"It's the food from the nuns. I think it'll end up killing us all." He winked at Sister Clara as she deposited a bag beside the door.

She glared at Denis as she spoke. "I've brought you some ham, a few canned goods, and some bread. There are still a few bakers working. This is from Dolé on Rue de la Vieille Boucherie."

"Thank you for everything," I said.

She put her hand on my shoulder before turning to go and said, "Have faith. Faith is a small seed, but it can grow into a tree."

I smiled after her as she walked away. Denis took the bread and ham and made sandwiches. "It's one thing after another with you. I cannot fathom what you were doing in front of the German headquarters. Well actually, yes—perhaps I can. You've gone completely mad."

"Hermann is on the island," I said over the lump in my throat.

"On Cézembre? Well, he's done for." Denis did not mince words.

Again, the young German was drawn to the smell of food. "Are you talking about Lt. von Choltiz?" he asked.

I looked at him with surprise. I had not known they knew

each other, though the garrison in Saint-Malo was small enough for any soldier to be able to recognize the officers.

"I've never served under him, but he was well-known at the barracks. He was part of the ERR. It's a good post. I knew he went to Russia but didn't know he was back."

"Do you know anything about the fortress on the island?" Denis asked him.

"There are about three hundred soldiers there. There are over a thousand in Fort National, besides about 290 prisoners."

Denis's shoulders slumped. "I didn't know there were so many soldiers left in Saint-Malo." That meant it would be harder to free the city.

I thought this information would be very useful to Dr. Aubry. The Allies would be grateful to know how many soldiers were in each fort.

"Jocelyn, maybe this ruffian will be good for something more than stealing our food." I frowned, displeased that Denis would speak of Bruno in such a way. The boy crossed his arms but kept chewing the ham. Denis went on. "There are a few boats toward the west. He could get on one and reach the island, give your note to the lieutenant, and maybe even get him off there."

Bruno's eyes nearly popped out of his head. "Are you out of your mind?" he asked.

"Don't worry, kid," Denis said. "I'd steer the boat. We could go at night, and no one would see us."

That mad idea was a ray of hope in the overwhelming darkness that swallowed the city after every sunset, announcing the end of the day and perhaps the world.

47

Mont-Saint-Michel

We had been without gas, electricity, or potable water for two days. We had to bring water from the hospital's cistern since it was one of the only places in the city with a drinkable supply. The wells had been drained in the attempts to put out the fires, as the Germans refused to let the firefighters near the sea to refill their tanks. A bomb over Fort National had killed at least twelve people and left many more wounded, but all I could think about was Denis and Bruno reaching Cézembre and getting in touch with Hermann—or better yet, getting him off the island alive. I would have gone myself if I had known how to sail.

We waited for night to fall. Then, for the first time in weeks, we locked up the library and left it unguarded. I wanted to accompany them up to the secret exit from the wall. The Germans did not allow us to enter or exit through the one gate still open, but Denis knew of a house of smugglers from Saint-Malo's privateer days. From there, a tunnel led to an area near the beach housing several fishing boats.

We walked carefully through the darkness hoping to go unnoticed by the soldiers on the wall.

"This is the house," Denis whispered, pointing to an old, run-down shack.

Bruno was entirely unconvinced about this plan, but he did not have much of a choice. If he were caught, he would certainly be killed.

Denis opened the door easily enough. The rotten wood gave way to a foyer with cracked pavers. The smell of mold and rotten fish was overwhelming. We felt our way blindly for the wall, opened a door hidden below the stairs, and went down to the lower floor with care. The stairs creaked under our weight. Bruno tripped on a caved-in step and nearly fell sprawling.

In the basement, the smell of the sea was so intense it nauseated me. I covered my mouth with a handkerchief. At the far wall of the basement was a window covered by a little wooden door, but it actually led to a small tunnel. The tunnel was low and very long, and we had to crawl on hands and knees for nearly two hundred yards before coming up to the surface on the other side.

"You'd better not follow us any farther," Denis said.

"I want to go with you until you reach the sea."

"Go back!" he hissed. He did not want to put me in danger, but really I was the one putting them in danger.

"I'm going with you to the other side," I insisted. Denis knew it was pointless to argue with me.

I had worn pants as a precaution. Bits of shells dug into our knees and the palms of our hands as we made our way through on all fours. We were bleeding and sweaty but alive when we got to the tunnel's end.

The fresh sea air whipped our faces. Denis pushed a rusted iron grate out of the way, and we went out onto the rocks. The breeze cleared our heads and blew away the claustrophobia of the tunnel. The ships were not far off.

I hugged Denis and begged him to be careful.

He nodded and smiled. "I hope to come back with your friend." The moon on the water was bright enough to light up his face.

"It's much too light," Bruno complained. "We should try tomorrow."

"Tomorrow? The British will be here any minute by sea. It's now or never."

We pushed one of the boats toward the sea, and its weight grew light as soon as it hit the water. The two men pushed it out against the waves until they were wet up to their waists, the boat rising and falling above them. They jumped in and started to row. After a few minutes of nearly standing still, they picked up speed and grew smaller on the horizon.

I sat on a rock for a while, staring at the stars reflected in the water and listening to the placid beating of the waves. For those moments I was free of war and fear. An image flitted through my mind of Mont-Saint-Michel, one of the most beautiful places in France. One day, well before this accursed war had begun, Denis, Antoine, and I had taken a day-trip to see the island. Denis had driven down the country roads, where crop fields and cow-dotted pastures rolled on and on. We came to a boggy area where mosquitoes smacked against the hood of the car while we sang songs we remembered from childhood. We passed the last few trees, and there before our eyes appeared the famous abbey. The mountainous island rose up sovereign over the swamp, the morning light sparkling off the sand-colored rocks. The water rushed at it, unable to bear such beauty. We stood mesmerized. That small abbey in the middle of nowhere proclaimed that beauty, like love, springs up in unexpected places.

48

Shots

The bombs razed the city with no sign of stopping. Dr. Aubry came by in the morning to ask me to go with him and the rest of the citizens remaining in the city to the cathedral's basements. The hospital was practically in ruins. Being so close to the Bastion de la Hollande, it had been hit directly several times. I told the doctor what Bruno had told me about the German forces in the city, on the island, and at Fort National. Dr. Aubry noted everything down gratefully and went to get in touch with his contact.

Alone again, I went up to the library roof and looked out over the city. Denis and Bruno were not back yet. I could see

Cézembre far in the distance, though all I could make out was a beach and some buildings, a few tall rocks, and some trees. I turned to look back at what remained of my apartment building, where just days before I had rescued the few important belongings I had left. The walls still smoldered, and soon not a trace of the building would be left. The pile of letters I was writing whenever my tasks and the bombs allowed had been growing, though I often wondered if anyone would ever read them. Perhaps it was all pointless, even childish, an act of upmost vanity. Why should people know my story? Was I any better than any of the other millions of people suffering through this terrible war? No, a thousand times no, I told myself over and over. My life was not more important than anyone else's. I was just one more blade of dry grass bent over by the relentless winds of war.

Tears smudged the ink as I wrote. The library was a wreck, and I often wondered what I was even doing there. What point existed in trying to save the few remains of this shipwreck? The most valuable books were safe in the basement, but many others had been destroyed by fire, water, or the violent impact from the bombs, when the dust ate into them like blazing summer consuming the spring.

I was worried about Denis. Then I looked and saw some of the few people left in the city coming out of their hiding spots and starting to clean the streets. They cleared away the rubble and swept the dust off their doorways. In the midst of the chaos, I could sense an incredible strength, a desire to live that burst up from the ruins like flowers growing between the sidewalks and cobblestones.

Then I saw two men in American uniforms crossing the street. Some Germans were on their heels.

How did they get here? I wondered, wishing I could warn

them about the Nazis right behind them. They slipped out of my view, and I prayed they could get away.

I was so engrossed that I barely heard the knocking at the door. When it finally got through to me, I rushed down to answer. It was Father Roth.

"Thank God you're still alive, Mrs. Ferrec. Allow me to introduce Robert Lefebvre."

A boy of some fifteen years smiled up at me. He reminded me of Pierre, whom I had not seen in quite some time.

"Every day Robert takes food to the prisoners held by the Germans at Fort National. He's told me something . . ." Father Roth patted the boy's shoulder to prompt him to speak. Robert hesitated, perhaps shy to speak to a stranger.

He cleared his throat and began. "Father Roth told me you know a German who helped us get a few people out of Saint-Malo with false papers. I think his name is Hermann von Choltiz?"

My breath caught. Had Denis and Bruno gone to look for Hermann at the wrong place? Had he been at Fort National the whole time?

"You mean he's at the . . . Are you sure?" I asked in disbelief. I did not want to believe Denis's efforts had been in vain, that he had risked his life for nothing.

The boy nodded his head with certainty.

"Could you give him a note for me?" I barely dared to hope. I scribbled something down, and Robert put it in his pocket.

Father Roth held out his hand to me. "Daughter, leave all this and come to the crypt. It's the last safe place left in the city. We've had word that massive bombings are on the way tomorrow. The Americans are running out of patience. The Allies are already at the gate of Saint-Vincent; it's only a matter of time."

My eyes grew wide at his words. How many more bombs

could the Allies possibly drop? There was hardly anything left standing in the city.

Robert, meanwhile, smiled at me and said, "I hope to bring you news of the lieutenant soon. I'll be going to the fort today."

"Thank you so much. You're so brave to risk your life."

Robert took off his cap and nodded a farewell, while Father Roth blessed me and closed the door in disappointment. I was shaking. The priest was right, of course. Staying in the library was suicide.

I went back up to the roof. I knew it was dangerous, but it all felt surreal, and nothing mattered anymore. I could hear shrapnel flying by and bombs falling just a few hundred yards away. I saw city hall and the prefecture in flames. Papers floated everywhere—the records of Saint-Malo's life and history. The memory of my city was disappearing. Then I wondered how long it would take for the library to burn to the ground. I stayed on the roof until the sun went down. The cool of the evening had a slight calming effect on my sadness. I looked helplessly toward the island and toward Fort National. People I loved with my whole heart were in both places, but I was impotent to reach or save them.

49

The Last Ones

Saint-Malo
August 13, 1944

The rain of fire meant that night never came. Nowhere was safe. The city's very innards burned as the clock slowly ticked. At five o'clock I could not take it anymore, and I got up in a fit of worry over what had happened to Denis and Bruno, sure they had been captured.

Dr. Aubry knocked at the library door at first light.

"Mrs. Ferrec, forgive the intrusion . . ." The poor doctor was spent, weakened by hunger and a lack of rest.

"Come in, come in," I said, stepping aside. We sat at one of the tables, and he dissolved into tears. His last vestiges of strength dissipated. Eventually he took a great breath and spoke. "I have to ask you a favor, but I've no right to ask you to risk your life."

"Do go on," I said, impatient to know what he could possibly need from me. I could not imagine how I could be of help to anyone in the straits we were in.

"The situation is desperate. Nowhere is safe anymore. The wounded are dying without medicine or even the means to ease their pain. In a few moments I'm going to headquarters to beg for a cease-fire for a few hours to evacuate the people who remain in the city. I doubt the commander will agree, but I'd like you to go with me. I fear that if the soldiers see a man approach, they'll shoot without asking questions. But it might be different if they see both of us. They'll hesitate to shoot an unarmed woman."

"I can't leave the city—" I started to say. I needed to keep watch for Denis. "But I can go with you to headquarters. The books are less important than the lives of hundreds of people."

Before locking up, I gave the place one last glance, heavy with foreboding that I would not see it standing upright again. I also feared that Lt. Bauman would take advantage of my absence to steal the valuable volumes, then set the place on fire. But the lives of Saint-Malo's citizens were more important than a half-ruined building.

"Sgt. Castel will join us too. He's over the artillery at the Bastion de la Hollande. We've tended to several of his men, and he recognizes how dire the situation is."

The three of us walked through the empty, desolate streets. I barely recognized my city. Most of the buildings had been toppled or burned. Others were heaps of rubble.

The tension grew the closer we came to the hardly recognizable Great Gate. We ran into two men near headquarters.

"Where are you going?" the older one asked.

"To the citadel," Dr. Aubry answered.

"Are you mad? They'll shoot you as soon as they see you. It

doesn't matter that you've got a German soldier with you. These people are desperate."

We all knew it was lunacy, but we kept walking. Then a soldier came running toward us before we arrived.

"Sergeant! We already got word. Commander von Aulock has granted a cease-fire of two-and-a-half hours to evacuate all civilians and wounded from the city."

We looked at each other in surprise. The sergeant had contacted von Aulock an hour ago but to no avail.

"It'll be through the Dinan Gate. However, after the cease-fire, any civilian found in the city will be treated as a prisoner of war and will be executed," the soldier explained.

We went to the cathedral. Dr. Aubry had to organize the evacuation of the wounded and the civilians still housed in the church as soon as possible. There were not enough stretchers for everyone, and several trips would have to be made. Dr. Aubry would take thirty at a time, then return with the stretcher-bearers for another group.

"What are you going to do? Will you come with us?" he asked before leaving.

"I have to wait for Denis. And I can't leave the books."

The doctor looked at me with a mixture of compassion, admiration, and exasperation. Then, with a parting embrace, he said, "You're a brave one."

"And a mad one. But I can't fight my conscience because it's all I've got left. Life only makes sense if we can be faithful to our principles."

I walked slowly back to the library. A thick knot in my throat gave me the feeling that time was running out. I opened the door, and a handwritten note fell to the floor.

50

The March of the Desperate

Saint-Malo
August 13, 1944

Forever burned into my memory is the column of Saint-Malo's wounded and civilians abandoning the city. Sadness and satisfaction welled up in me, and I felt proud of my compatriots. The last inhabitants of the city left with their heads held high, small bags in their hands, their clothing dirty and torn—and yet with a dignity that moved even the Germans. The American cannons were still firing, and the Nazis responded by opening fire again. The Dinan Gate was still closed. The mayor approached the officer to force him to open up, but though I could not hear the response from where I was, it seemed to be in the negative.

An hour later, all the wounded and civilians had returned.

Hell would be harder to leave than many thought. While the straggling wounded and civilians were installed in the cathedral again, a commission that had gone to speak with the Americans returned with good news, and the evacuation recommenced at six thirty that evening through the Dinan Gate.

I watched the wounded go by first in every kind of means of transportation: makeshift strollers, stretchers, carts, and wagons. Some walked, slumping on their caregivers. The civilians followed with a slow step, just wanting to get out. By seven o'clock, they were nearly all gone. Watching the procession was like watching the blood drain out of my dying city as it turned into a cold, hard cadaver.

Saint-Malo was in complete ruins—the customs house destroyed, the port a graveyard for half-sunken ships, the trees of the walkways and parks twisted and splintered, the bus station vaporized, and the houses of Place Chauteaubriand burned to the ground. The procession of the wounded and civilians advanced with white flags waving. Some of the prisoners from Fort National saluted them as they passed, while the Germans kept their guns trained on them at all times. A few yards beyond the casino, they crossed the line and came into the territory of the Americans, which I could already see from the library roof. The military medics began tending to the people and loading them into Red Cross vehicles. Even from my distance, the citizens' relief was palpable: They were free. The fear and the fatigue were over, and the war could eventually become a distant nightmare we had all finally woken up from.

I could not keep from crying. But I dried my eyes and saw people coming out of Fort National. The Germans had freed the prisoners who were now joining the ranks of refugees. From far off I could hear voices shouting, "Liberty!"

The word sounded so strange, and I groped at its meaning. Now I was completely alone to face my fate, the last French woman in Saint-Malo.

I wrote another letter for you in the dim light of the waning day. If everything had not been so abysmally real, I would have thought that none of this could actually be happening. Then I went back down to the library and by candlelight beheld the books still standing on their shelves. Then, for the first time in my life, I sensed the purpose of my life, the thing that had brought me to that point and had held me fast despite the adversity. At that moment I understood I did not exist randomly: I had been born for this strange mission, and only I could bear this weight.

51

The Pyre

I woke very early from a nightmare about Hermann and Denis.
They were dying before my eyes while bombs fell over the
city. I searched the basement for something to eat and thought
about the desolate vision of Saint-Malo I had witnessed the night
before. Our little jewel polished by the sea, proud and immovable
in the face of time—now just a pile of rocks along the beach like
a sandcastle destroyed by the waves. I was convinced this city,
which had shown forth France's glory, was destined to rise from
the ashes one day. The heroism of its inhabitants deserved to
write history again.

I returned sadly to my desk and gobbled up the last bit of

ham despite the fuzz of mold starting to grow. Then I checked the clock, impatient. I had read the note as soon as I had gotten inside the library the day of the evacuation. Hermann's writing looked nervous and insecure.

Dear Jocelyn,

Life is God's gift to mortals, but so often suffering makes us forget the happy days. When I saw you in the citadel, my heart nearly burst out of my chest, but then I lost you again. It was almost worse to have you so near and not be able to reach you.

A boy brought me your note, and I hope he gets this one to you.

The commander sent me to help at Fort National. Things are rather dire here. My superior is nearly out of his mind, and most of my work has been trying to calm him down. That is why I haven't walked away and come to look for you. A couple days ago two of the prisoners we took were Frenchmen wearing American uniforms. When my superior found out, he took them out to the courtyard to execute them, even though one was badly wounded. I intervened and asked him to desist, as too many people have already died in vain. For a moment I thought he would turn and shoot me instead. When everything comes unraveled, most people lose their heads and become capable of terrible deeds.

Tonight, since most of the prisoners have been freed, I'm going to try to escape. I don't think our side will hold out much longer, and soon I'll be a prisoner of the Allied army. But I've got to see you first, even if it costs me my life.

I wept over his note, but knowing Hermann was still alive filled me with renewed joy.

I went up to the roof one more time. The city looked calm but emptier than ever before, and I felt like the last person on earth. The streets, plazas, and landmark buildings were hardly recognizable. Then my eyes picked out a figure making its way through the rubble. My imagination insisted that it was Denis, and my heart jumped. He had been gone for almost a week. I ran downstairs and out to the street. The man turned a corner and went to the plaza next to the citadel. It was one of the most dangerous areas. The Germans would shoot as soon as they saw any movement, and the Americans were pummeling that epicenter of resistance.

I went down the alley, and just as I was about to call out to him, the man entered a building. I went up to the door and pushed. It opened easily, and I entered with caution.

The house was almost all dark, but my eyes adjusted quickly. At a noise from the basement, I hesitated but eventually crept down. Candles lit up the large room, and I was stunned to see an enormous supply of food, drink, and every kind of delicacy.

There was a noise behind me, and I jumped in more surprise as a voice said, "What are you doing here? Have you come to steal?"

The whole scene and the questions befuddled me, but I stammered out, "I'm Mrs. Ferrec, the wife of Antoine, the policeman."

The man adjusted the rifle in his hands. His eyes were uneven, his bushy beard gray, and his hair long and disheveled.

"What are you doing here?" he repeated.

"You didn't evacuate with the rest?" I asked stupidly.

"Evacuate? I can't leave all this," he said, waving his left hand at the countless boxes of food.

"Why didn't you let the mayor know? People have nearly starved to death during the siege."

"This is all mine." The expression on his face hardened. I was in shock that he would be concerned over perishable goods while our city was being bombed off the face of the map.

The bombs started up again. The floor trembled and fragments from the roof fell down on us.

"We have to get out of here. This place is going to collapse."

"I can't leave all this. This is what I've managed to store up from a lifetime of work and hard effort."

"They're just things, and you can get others to replace them. But you can't get another life," I pleaded with him.

"This is everything I have, and I won't survive just to become a beggar." His face was twisted with fear and rage.

I turned to go, but he shouted for me to stay where I was. I ignored him and heard a shot just to the left of me.

"Are you out of your mind?" I demanded.

His eyes were wide and inscrutable, but just then a new explosion shook us, and he fell down. I seized the moment to run upstairs as fragments rained down on the boxes of stored-up food. When I got to the top, I looked back and saw the man trying to steady the stacks of crates that were falling in every direction. His eyes met mine just before a section of roof collapsed on him.

I fled the house, but the inferno inside the building was nothing compared to the shower of projectiles and explosions happening everywhere out on the street. As I ran back toward the library, walls were falling down, and I barely managed to dodge the rocks and fire flying all around. I was making my way between immense columns of flames. Now that I was out, I presumed there would be no place to return to, but the Hotel Désilles was still upright.

The door was open when I arrived. Perhaps the explosions

had forced it open. I went in and looked all around, but the hotel was empty. Then I heard a moan from the basement.

The flashlight I held shook with my fear as I made my way down the stairs. I shone it at the back of the room and was surprised to see Denis's face.

"Jocelyn," he said with a smile forced through obvious pain. He looked even thinner than a few days before. His beard was bushier, and he was so weak I wondered if he would pass out as I poured some water into his mouth and gave him bits of ham.

"It tastes like garbage, but I was nearly starved," he said. I helped him to his feet and noticed his hand was damp with blood.

"You're hurt," I said.

He turned to me, and with a strength I had not anticipated, he yelled, "Your friend wasn't on the island!"

I bit my lip and nodded. "I received word from him. They had sent him to Fort National. The German who told me he was on Cézembre was wrong."

"Well, it's a bit late now. We got to Cézembre at night and hid the boat among some rocks. By some miracle we weren't discovered. Bruno went to the fort, but I guess they didn't buy his story because they came after me pretty quick. The wretch had told them I was hiding on the beach, and I barely managed to slip out among the reefs. The Nazis gave up the search in the afternoon. Probably figured the sea would take care of me. I found a little cave that was safe at low tide and ate crabs, but I couldn't stay there forever. One night I went out to look for the boat, but the Nazis had found it and sunk it. I cursed my fate but didn't give up. There was a boat at the small port on the island. I watched it for four hours, and upon a guard change, I went for it and headed out to sea."

"Unbelievable!"

"You have no idea. It wasn't easy rowing to the coast for the last stretch against a current that kept pushing me out to sea, meanwhile dodging the bullets flying over my head. After ten hours I managed to get to the Beach of the Môle. I left the boat and looked for the spot that leads to the smugglers' house, but of course rubble from a bomb had blocked up the tunnel. I had to get across the wall somehow, so I waited for night to fall, but it was pointless. The Germans were watching everywhere. Then this morning I found a dead German and took his uniform. I found a spot where the wall had sunk in and crept through the crack. It took me a long time to find my way in these ruins. I went by the citadel. The Americans were really close to the gate, and they shot at me. A bullet got me. I dragged myself here but didn't see anyone. At least I still had my key!" he concluded with a snort.

I embraced Denis, and he winced in pain.

"I'm so, so sorry," I said, marveling that he was still alive.

I cleaned his wound as best I could, helped him stretch out on a mattress, and left him to rest. Then I came upstairs to write this last letter and put it in the pile that had been growing over the past few weeks, which I now kept in a leather satchel in the basement as a modicum of protection against rubble and sparks. Denis knew to get them to you if anything happened to me.

By the time I made it to the roof, the bombing had stopped. At the citadel, I saw the Americans at the gate and a parade of Germans walking out with their hands raised. If they had surrendered, was it all over? Would I be able to see Hermann before the Allies took him? Had we actually saved the books?

One of the German prisoners managed to get away. He ran down an alley and got lost among the smoke and fire. I tried to follow him with my gaze, but it was useless. The city was a giant pyre where the god of war was receiving his offering of expiatory destruction. I thought of how sometimes the price of our sins can only be paid by great sacrifice. For those four years, France had sold its soul to the devil, and he always requires full repayment of a debt.

52

Words

E verything is made of words. We would not understand a thing
without them. They define our feelings, fuel our ideas, and
inspire our faith. Without them, the world would be in silence.
The book of John begins, "In the beginning was the Word."
Through words the world was built, because something does not
actually exist until it has a name. Human beings have been naming things for thousands of years. In naming things, we possess
them in a way, make them more human, turn them into exten-
sions of ourselves. We have humanized the gods and animals and
have domesticated the world, but these same words can incite
the most visceral hatred and unleash desperate passion.

I waited and waited, but no one knocked on the door. Hermann did not come to find me, and, when I saw Fort National had surrendered, I was distraught. Had he been captured then?

After writing a new letter, I always felt it would be the last one—that everything would soon be over—but our agony only lingered. I went down to see Denis, who rested on a mattress in the basement. Then I went to the books and started flipping through them. I grabbed them at random, trying to understand what made the volumes so special. We housed immortal works, cheap westerns, detective novels, and tomes of history, science, and theology. I wondered what would become of the world without them. Large swaths of the classical world had disappeared in fires, and yet humans had built one of history's most organized cultures from almost nothing. Would not the same thing happen again even if all the books in Europe were burned?

A noise at the door startled me, and I went to see what it was. Someone was trying to force the lock. A chill ran up my spine, and I ran to find something with which to defend myself. We had no weapons, as the shotgun Denis had found at the farm turned out to be a dud, and all I could get my hands on was our sharp kitchen knife. The lock gave way, and the door creaked open slowly. Boots slapped the hardwood floor toward the stairs. I slid between the shelves and watched. The only light at that hour—around one o'clock—came from the sputtering candles on the desks and shelves.

The shadow wore a German uniform. I could not see the face, but I recognized the man's manner and the black pistol he held. Lt. Bauman lit a cigarette and leaned casually on a desk.

"Mrs. Ferrec, let's not play cat and mouse. The Americans are crawling all over the city, and I don't have much time. My compatriots at the fort and the citadel have surrendered, and the rest won't hold out much longer. It's very awkward to fight knowing our defeat is sure. The commander just wanted to buy Hitler enough time to get reorganized and launch a counter-offensive to squash all these gum chewers, but it's pointless. There's too many of them, and they make weapons hellishly fast. We would've wiped out the communist Russians a long time ago if they hadn't had American weapons."

Why was he telling me all of this? Bauman took several drags on his cigarette before continuing.

"The savage Bolsheviks had more guts than we gave them credit for. Turned out to be a bad idea to invade the Soviet Union. You know, greed breaks the coffers—which is why I want to reach an agreement with you. Like I said, I don't have much time. I need to escape by sea before even the rats can't get out of Saint-Malo."

He started walking again. I could feel him getting closer, and my heart raced.

"So you're going to give me three or four of your most valuable books and letters. I'll store them in a leather case, and I'll go out the way I came in. I won't do anything to you, and I won't burn this pigsty to ashes. There's no point in that anyhow. It'll all come down soon enough."

He started looking for me among the shelves, and I scrunched into a corner hoping the darkness would hide me.

"Where have you put them? I hope they haven't been destroyed. They're my ticket to safe passage from Spain to South America. Nobody will care to look for people like me there. I admit that I've done a few things that in the prudish mentality of the Allies can be construed as crimes, but they aren't. We're just animals; the strongest survive, and the day everyone understands that, the world will stop putting up with all the sick, the weak, the invalids, and those who can't keep up. You've survived because you're strong, and I admire that."

His words chafed at me, but I did not want to get within his reach. I spoke from the darkness. "And you're better than everyone else who's died? Maybe the world is unfair. Good people have lost their lives, and yet a scoundrel like you has survived. The first ones to die aren't the weakest ones; they're the best ones. The idealists, the altruists, the compassionate—those who can't stop loving."

"Love?" he scoffed. "Love is a weakness. It deceives us and makes us vulnerable. I was a son and a brother; I've been in love and dreamed about being happy. It's all a lie. Happiness doesn't exist. All that's left for us is to cheat fate. What's the point in doing good? All those others are dead, and I'm alive."

Bauman walked toward where I had spoken. He was hunting me, but I was not going to make it easy for him. I tiptoed to the other end of the room toward the stairs.

"Where are you going, Jocelyn? You can't get away this time. Your dear Hermann isn't here to help you. He always thought he was better than me—so refined and polite, a true gentleman, or so it seems. You think he hasn't killed innocent people? Nobody gets out of Russia with clean hands. There it's all-out war, while here in France it's just child's play. The commander let all the wounded and the civilians evacuate the city. In the USSR, he wouldn't have blinked an eye at cramming them all into a church and setting it on fire."

I wanted him to come up the stairs. There was a little alcove where I could wait for him and jump out when he passed by. So I spoke again. "Your people have lost. Your barbarianism did no good. You all said you wanted to create a new world, but that was a lie. Nazis like you are the worst kind of barbarian.

The barbarians destroyed the classical world, but it had already destroyed itself first. We're the reason you were able to win. When we see people like you playing with politics, we keep quiet and presume you'll never come into power. A lot of rich and powerful people supported the Nazis out of fear of communism, and the common people felt like you Nazis understood them, that you spoke their language. Then you seized democracy to destroy it from the inside, even though we had already allowed corrupt, incapable people to govern us. You persecuted the communists, the socialists, the Jews, then the Gypsies, the religious, and anyone who didn't fit into your demonic idea of society. We're the ones to blame for keeping quiet while you destroyed the world."

Bauman reached the top stair, and I went silent. I crept forward, and when I could see his back clearly, I jumped and drove in the knife. Bauman screamed and turned and shot, but the bullet lodged into the wooden beams above us. We struggled, and he shoved me down the stairs. At the bottom, I realized something was wrong with my leg. I tried to stand, but terrible pain paralyzed me. Bauman walked down the stairs slowly, stopped just above me, and with a malicious smile, said, "I've been waiting for this moment for a long time."

And with one blow from the butt of his gun, I was out.

53

Fire

Saint-Malo
August 18, 1944

It was still dark when I came to. I had been unconscious for perhaps an hour, and in the meantime, Bauman had ransacked the place. In fact, the sound of books smacking the wooden floor is what woke me.

"Awake so soon?" he said when he heard me stir.

For a few moments I struggled to recognize what was real and what was a dream, but the deformed face of Lt. Bauman snapped me to immediately. "I can't find the books I need, and I'm getting fed up. If you don't tell me where they are, I'll burn the whole place down with you inside."

Somehow he had not found the entrance to the basement,

which meant Denis and the books might still be safe. Bauman must have spent his time searching upstairs.

"I don't believe you. Why would you let me go free after I give you the books? What guarantee do I have that the building won't burn down anyway?"

"None. The only thing I care about is getting out of this cemetery town."

"Well, maybe I'm ready to die," I answered.

"You're insane. I always knew you were. All these books, their adventures and feats, the thoughts and ideas of thousands of authors—they've twisted your mind."

"Perhaps, but it's a blessed lunacy. If sanity means being a brutal murderer, I'd rather be insane a thousand times over."

Bauman grabbed me and hoisted me in the air, then let me fall to the floor. I screamed in pain from my leg.

"Words are pointless, don't you see? Now tell me what I want to know, or I'll force it out of you."

I was writhing in pain when we heard a voice from behind.

"Bauman, what do you think you're doing?"

I did not have to see the face to know who it was.

"So Lt. von Choltiz has come to save little Miss Jocelyn, his damsel in distress, once again," Bauman said, pressing his pistol to my temple. "One step and I'll blow her away," he warned.

"We can't harm civilians. It's all over—"

Bauman let out a shriek of laughter and jammed the pistol harder against my head. "I follow no more orders. As you said, it's all over."

"She's an unarmed woman."

"And I'm a desperate man."

Hermann took a step, and Bauman shot at the floor.

"I'm not going to warn you again. You know I despise people

like you. You think you're better? You've robbed, murdered, tortured, and terrorized innocent people. Don't give me lessons on humanity."

"You're right about that," Hermann said. "We've all done despicable things, but anyone can change. Put your weapon down and get out."

"I'm not leaving without the books, the ones you should've turned over to the office in Paris. But then you went and fell in love with the little librarian. How pathetic."

Rage flashed on Hermann's face, and he looked ready to spring. I knew there was no alternative. "Wait," I said. "Please, don't shoot."

I could not see Bauman's face, but I could sense his smile.

"Did you hear that?" he barked at Hermann. "Put your hands up, and don't do anything stupid."

"I can't go get the books because of my leg," I said. "But Hermann can get to them. They're in the iron chest in the basement. It's very heavy. I'm the only one with the key."

"I'll get it," Hermann said, glaring at Bauman.

"Well, go on. I don't have all day," Bauman spat.

Hermann disappeared into the shadows, and we heard his footsteps on the stairway. A few minutes later he reemerged lugging a huge, heavy metal chest. He dragged it toward us in a cloud of dust.

Bauman bent and began to examine it. "Where's the key?" he demanded.

I hesitated, knowing he was entirely untrustworthy. "How do we know you'll go away and leave us in peace?"

"You *don't* know, but I don't want to waste any more time. I'll leave as soon as you give me what I want." He held out his hand for the key.

"I don't have it on me."

"What? Quit toying with me."

"The key is upstairs in the mahogany desk drawer."

"You'll have to come with me," he said. "If I send your little boyfriend, we'll probably never see him again."

"But I can't walk."

"Then you'll limp. You think I'm that stupid?"

He scooped me up, then supported me, and we began making our way slowly up the stairs. I was surprised that he seemed entirely unaffected by my stabbing attempt from just an hour before. It took us a few minutes to reach the top part of the stairs. Meanwhile, Hermann watched helplessly from below. Suddenly I lurched forward, grabbed the handrail, and shoved Bauman down the stairs. Then I stood and tried to hide in one of the upper rooms while Hermann ran to take Bauman's gun. They wrestled, and I heard a shot.

I peeked out and saw Bauman standing over Hermann. He saw me and charged up the stairs. "My patience has run out, you whore!"

I was momentarily paralyzed at the sight of Hermann on the floor, but I shook myself and started climbing the stairs to the roof. Bauman caught me halfway up, and I fought him, kicking his face with my good leg. Pain racked me, but I crawled to the roof. Bauman shot at me, but it missed, and I kept climbing.

Without meaning to, I bumped into a candle, which spiraled down to the second floor, lighting the books that were scattered on the landing. The flames spread quickly, and Bauman looked behind him. In a few minutes he would be unable to make it back down. He could kill me or try to carry away the metal chest with the books.

He started retreating, and I sat on the top stair, panting. After I caught my breath, I made my way down, scooting on my behind one stair at a time.

Bauman was already on the ground floor when I got to the fire at the second floor. I tried to stamp it out with my hands and then with a towel, but the flames were already climbing the walls and consuming everything in their path.

At last my nightmare was coming true. Hermann was sprawled out on the bottom floor, Denis was asleep in some corner of the basement, and I was watching the fire destroy everything without pity.

Desperate, I forced my way down the stairs to the ground floor. Bauman was struggling to get the metal chest up, but he winced in pain—apparently the wound I had inflicted before had actually done some damage. He finally managed to balance the chest on his shoulders and take a few steps forward. Then Hermann's hand shot out and grabbed Bauman's leg. The Nazi tripped and lost his balance, sending the chest smashing into the floor and splintering some of the planks.

"Blast it all!" Bauman roared, trying to get up, but Hermann held on. Bauman's face and back were bloody, but he had enough strength to kick Hermann with his hard boots. I kept moving down the stairs. I had to stop the fight.

The heat behind me grew by the second, and soon I would be kindling for the flames. All those words carefully stored for so long were turning to ash. As I struggled downward, Bauman pulled his pistol from the holster and pointed again at Hermann. I held my breath to prepare myself for the sound of shots and death.

54

The Last Second

Let go of me, you rat!" I heard a second before Bauman pulled the trigger.

Hermann let go of Bauman's leg and screamed in pain when the bullet shattered his arm. Bauman took aim again at his head, but I reached them just in time and threw myself over Hermann. The bullet hit my chest. At first there was a burning, then a sharp pinch, then pain so intense I forgot all about my leg. I collapsed and Bauman turned away from Hermann and tried to pick the chest up. But it was too heavy for him now.

"Give me the key," he said, aiming at me again.

I was sprawled on the floor next to Hermann, bleeding from the chest and fighting to breathe. The fire moved down the wooden stairs, and the smoke made breathing even harder. The upstairs framing would soon cave in on us if the flames did not get us first.

I made a last effort to smile. I was dying surrounded by my books, with Hermann at my side. What did the rest matter? After all those years of suffering and loss, life had ceased to interest me, and death never seemed far away. It had come sniffing around me so many times that to finally die actually felt like liberation. I had the sense that I had been walking blindly, feeling around in the dark for years—and now I could see things clearly.

Bauman came up and started searching me. I could not move. He found the key around my neck, yanked it off, and then opened the chest as quickly as possible. Inside he found the pile of rocks.

"Where are they?" he screamed in desperate rage.

The flames were already on the ground floor and were spreading through the shelves. Books shuddered and curled as the fire advanced.

I smiled at him, and he shook me violently. "French pig, where are they?" he demanded.

I gasped over the pain and managed to say, "I put them somewhere safe a few days ago," I said.

"Where? Tell me and I swear I'll get you out of here."

"It doesn't matter anymore," I mouthed.

The flames reached the front door. Bauman left me and tried to get out, but it was too late for all of us.

He ran to the door that led to the basement and opened it but came up short at the sight of Denis. Denis gave him a great shove, and Bauman fell beside the empty chest. His pistol flew out of his hand, into the flames. When he tried to snatch it, the metal seared his hands, and he instinctively threw it down. It slid within Denis's reach. Denis carefully grabbed it with his sleeve to protect his hand, then pointed it at Bauman.

"No!" the lieutenant yelled as Denis emptied the pistol's remaining bullets into his chest. Bauman looked stunned, shocked that death could actually come for him.

I grabbed Hermann's hand. It was still warm, and I dragged myself closer to him.

"My friend, my love . . ." I whispered.

He opened his eyes and squeezed my hand.

The fire was all around us, the smoke consuming the last bits of breathable air as the heat roasted us. Saint-Malo's destruction was finally complete. The war had destroyed the last bastion of freedom. The war had taken it all—my life, my health, and the people I loved. I did not expect any dawn to follow this darkness.

55

The City at My Feet

Saint-Malo
August 18, 1944

The whole world thinks dying is simple, but sometimes death laughs in our faces. Every person has an appointed day and hour, and no one manages to skirt destiny.

Denis dragged me to the basement, opened the tunnel that led to the far end of the alley, and pushed and pulled as gently as he could until he got me out. I was delirious, with barely any oxygen left in the one lung that still worked, but the fresh night air brought me around somewhat. I had wept as I teetered between life and death and had felt my hand being separated from Hermann's lifeless fingers.

Denis lifted my head onto his legs and tried to revive me. With no strength left to breathe, my mouth gaped open like a fish drowning outside the water.

"Are you alive?" Denis asked, wrapping his arms around me. I would have preferred to disappear, though I did not believe we were ever fully extinguished. Something immortal survived our bodies—that indescribable thing that makes us unique and special.

I looked up, and my eyes studied the library lit up against the darkness. Burning pages fluttered all around, and ash covered everything.

"We did all we could, Jocelyn," Denis said, tears dripping down his blackened face.

The silence around us was so pleasant that for a moment I forgot the suffering and watched the stars. The fire and bombs had destroyed the noble city and its beautiful church, the home of Jacques Cartier, Duguay-Trouin, Broussais, Surcouf, Chateaubriand, and Lamennais. With the citadel half ruined and the gates burned to a char, the wall was the only thing left to bear witness to a world that had disappeared forever.

Epilogue

Saint-Malo
September 2, 1944

Marcel Zola managed to find a ticket to Rennes and spent all day on the train. Paris had just been liberated, and the country, little by little, had started to feel like France again. The brilliant sunshine on the day that General Leclerc marched into the city chased away the gray days of the Vichy regime and the collaborators who had tried to turn the nation into a slave to Nazi power.

The writer got off the train and looked for some sort of transportation to Saint-Malo. News had spread about the city's destruction, but he was not prepared for the magnitude of the catastrophe. A farmer with a worn-down truck agreed to take him to the outskirts and recommended he look for lodging outside the city, as nothing was left inside the walls.

Zola had been in the city once, fifteen years before, on a trip with friends to the Brittany coast. He had been moved by the imposing walls, the cathedral steeple, and the luxurious slate-roofed stone houses. He picked his way through the gate, and as he looked up, the weight of preliberation grief washed over him again. It would be years, decades, before this city could return to life—and not just because of the material loss, as the wounds on the soul would take a long time to heal.

Many French opportunists had switched sides right before the old regime sank, but reprisals against collaborators had spread throughout the country. After years of fear and suffering, the pent-up rage burst forth with such a vengeance that even the most extreme seemed taken aback by the violence of the victims.

Zola asked a passerby where the library was, and the man pointed to a street on the west side of the city. It was hard to find his way in that wasteland of rubble and charred wood. The citizens had cleaned the streets as best they could, piled up the shells of artillery, buried their dead, and rescued the few who had managed to survive the massacre. Some Germans had held out until August 30.

Marcel stood stunned at the doorway of the library. Part of the façade remained, but the windows were burned out, the roof had collapsed into the first floor, and beyond what was left of the door was pure desolation and ruin. Marcel saw one book intact among the rubble, but most were charred at best or mere piles of ashes.

He walked around the area and imagined the space Jocelyn had described so often in her letters. With effort he managed to control his emotions. Returning to the city gate, he asked someone about a Mrs. Ferrec. The man answered that, the last he knew, she was at the hospital in Saint-Servan. Marcel noted the directions and started walking. It was night when he arrived.

He asked after Jocelyn, but the nun at the door said she was no longer there and that he should talk with her friend, Denis Villeneuve.

Marcel went up to the second floor and searched among the tags on the beds, Then, by a window in the back, he found a man reading a decrepit book with a worn-out cover.

"Mr. Villeneuve, forgive the interruption. My name is Marcel Zola."

Denis sat up straighter and dropped the book. "Good heavens, is it really you?"

"Yes. Mrs. Ferrec has been writing to me for years. I wanted to meet her now that all this is over."

Denis's face clouded over for a moment. He rummaged in the drawer beside him and pulled out a leather sheath full of letters tied with a red string.

"This is for you. I was to mail them to you, but I haven't been able to leave the clinic."

Marcel took the letters and glanced at them.

"What happened?" he asked, already imagining the answer.

"It'll be better if you read the letters. Jocelyn wrote until the very end." Denis's eyes filled with tears. His breath caught, and he held a handkerchief over his face.

"I'm so sorry. I—I didn't know . . ." The author trailed off.

"Life is capricious. It let her survive the siege of the city but not long enough to see the end of the war and beyond."

"We've lost many of the best along the way," Marcel answered.

"Jocelyn believed in the power of words. This war has destroyed millions of lives and a good part of our culture, but words can save us."

"You really think so?"

"Isn't that your profession? Write and tell the world the story of Saint-Malo and its library, so that everyone knows that here lived a woman and a city that never gave up. If you immortalize this human tragicomedy, it won't have all been in vain."

The author bowed his head in grief. He had come to love Jocelyn as a friend, though they had never met. As he bid farewell to Denis, he mused on how very real was the power of words to build up or destroy, to love or to hate.

"Jocelyn is in the cemetery beside the Rance River," Denis called out after him. "Pierre marked the spot."

Marcel returned to his hotel, dragging his feet. The package of letters was heavier than any luggage he had carried. He placed it on the bed's clean sheets, then set himself down and wept.

When he was calm, he picked out one at random.

Dear Marcel,

The darkest night is looming over my soul. Everything I loved was fuel for the flames. I managed to save some of the books by hiding them in a tunnel under the library, but most have disappeared forever.

I'm very sick. A bullet destroyed my left lung. The effects of my tuberculosis make it nearly impossible for me to breathe, and I can feel my life slipping away little by little. Life is nothing more than an amount of time, and each of us has a limited allotment. The last grains of sand are about to fall for me, and then I'll cross over into eternity.

What waits for us beyond death? You may think nothing— just a great silent void that swallows everything—but I've seen all the people I love on the other side. I didn't believe it before; I found it unimaginable that a God—some cruel, severe being— could allow such suffering and pain. But I don't think that way anymore. Otherwise, all the deeds and works of humanity would succumb to the passage of time, and the universe would become a lonely, desolate scene. More than anything, I want to think that all those who died unfairly will at least find some sort of peace and justice.

Marcel spent the whole night reading Jocelyn's letters, then stored them in his case. The next morning, without even pausing for coffee, he made his way to the cemetery.

He asked the grave digger for the tomb of the Ferrecs. The pale, thin man showed him a grave near a weeping willow, just beside the fence that separated the cemetery from the river. It was a lovely spot to rest eternally. In lieu of a large granite gravestone, a simple piece of wood roughly carved by hand, as if by pocketknife, marked the spot with the names *Antoine* and *Jocelyn*. Even so, the names shone in the soft September sun. Marcel left a flower on the grave and opened the last letter. He had saved it to read there at Jocelyn's tomb.

Dear Marcel,

I have no idea how the future will judge me. Perhaps my existence will be one more blurry page in the book of life, only mattering to my Creator. But if you ever tell the world what happened with the Saint-Malo library, I hope your readers will forgive me.

I'm an ordinary person. I loved, I struggled, I searched for happiness however torpidly, as one groping in the dark. I gave myself to my books and my husband, I loved my friends, and I tried to preserve my city's memory. I didn't succeed.

After regaining consciousness at the hospital, Denis told me that Hermann had died in the building. I felt guilty. I had somehow drawn him to that fatal destiny. The doctor told me

I couldn't live with the one lung I had left, that I would slowly dwindle until one morning I just wouldn't wake up.

I have spent my remaining strength writing, to the point of exhaustion. My life is nothing special, Marcel—hardly a drop of rain in a storm. But I hope that all those who have loved and dared to live find themselves reflected in it.

Dear Marcel, I'm begging you to steal back from the abyss, from the ashes of Saint-Malo, the words the fire burned away, so that one day people will know that the only power strong enough to change the world is love.

Marcel knelt at the grave and traced his fingers over the name, caressing the memory of Jocelyn. Then he stood, tucked her last letter into his jacket, and walked to the river. He sat and watched the current, letting life flow by, before gathering his strength to return home.

Clarifications from History

Jocelyn and Antoine Ferrec are not real people, but they are based on the story of love and suffering that a reader told me when I visited Zaragoza, Spain, on St. George's Day in 2017. In our brief encounter, that young woman told me how she and her husband, both booklovers, fell ill right after their marriage. A very aggressive cancer attacked her first, and then her husband grew sick. Standing beside her mother and with tears in her eyes, she recounted the beautiful love story that I honor through this book today.

Many of the characters are fictional yet inspired by real people, including the author Marcel Zola, whom I always pictured as Albert Camus, the famous French playwright and author of the same time period. Denis, Céline, Hermann, and Lt. Bauman are also fictional, as are other characters.

Most of the descriptions of the French Resistance are real, and many fictional characters are based on real historical figures. Yvonne Oddon really existed, as did the clandestine newspaper *La Résistance* and the group at the Musée de l'Homme. Isabelle

Martel is based on Hélène Mordkovitch, Thierry le Gonidec on Honoré d'Éstienne, and Aitor Riba on Alfred Gaessler.

Pierre, the adolescent who fed the Allies information about the German defenses in the area, was a real person.

The Nazis created different organizations to destroy and burn banned literary works and made several lists of forbidden books as described in the novel.

The pillaging of France's cultural heritage was tremendous, and highly valuable books were robbed alongside works of art.

The library of Saint-Malo currently exists in the building described in the novel, but there was no library there in the time period of the novel's events. Some details about the building's architecture have been adapted to fit this story.

Historical figures like the mayor and Commander von Aulock are real.

The destruction of the city during the first half of the month of August 1944 is also real. Saint-Malo was completely decimated.

Timeline

1939

September 1: Germany invades Poland, initiating
World War II.

September 3: Great Britain, France, Australia, and New
Zealand declare war on Germany.

September 17: The Soviet Union invades Poland.

September 27: Warsaw surrenders.

1940

June 10: Italy declares war on Great Britain and
France.

June 14: The Wehrmacht enters Paris.

June 22: France signs an armistice with Germany.

July 10: Complete governmental powers are given to
Marshal Philippe Pétain in the new constitution for
Vichy France.

1941

June 22–December 6: Germany and the Axis
partners invade the Soviet Union, taking control
of many cities. A Soviet counteroffensive pushes
the Germans out of Moscow.

December 7: Japan drops bombs on the US military base in
Pearl Harbor.

December 11: Germany declares war on the United States
of America.

1943

January 14: The Casablanca Conference begins.

January 31: Germany surrenders in Stalingrad.

May 12: Axis powers surrender in Northern Africa.

July 25: Benito Mussolini's fascist government in Italy falls.

1944

January 22: The Allies land in Anzio.

January 27: The siege of Leningrad ends.

June 6: The Allied landing on Normandy begins.

July 25: Allied offense against German defenses in
Normandy begins.

August 17: Commander Andreas von Aulock surrenders to
Allied forces in Saint-Malo.

August 26: General Leclerc's troops march through Paris,
proclaiming the liberation of France from Nazi
occupation.

Discussion Questions

1. When we first meet Jocelyn Ferrec, she is writing to an author she admires. Why do you believe she wants to correspond with Marcel Zola? Have you ever reached out to someone whose creative work you loved?

2. From the beginning of the story, Jocelyn's life is marred by illness and frailty. How does her condition inform her views of the world around her? What does it make her appreciate? Does it ever make her stronger?

3. Describe how Saint-Malo changes throughout the story and how the residents respond differently to their home's occupation. Do the changes happen quickly or slowly? Do you imagine yourself resisting the occupation or simply doing whatever it would take to survive it?

4. Why does Jocelyn have such faith in the books in her library? What do they represent to her, and why are they of such importance to her homeland?

5. Consider how Jocelyn and Denis see the world

differently. Do you relate to one more than the other? If so, how and why?

6. What is the purpose of hope in this story? How does someone like Jocelyn maintain hope when all seems lost, when no day seems better than the one before?

7. When we are introduced to Hermann von Choltiz, he is a Nazi through and through. By the end of the story, his view of the world has changed. Describe this evolution in him and discuss whether or not you would have been able to trust such a man.

8. Would you consider Jocelyn a heroine, or would you— like she does—consider her ordinary? How might her actions and her demeanor defy the typical definitions of what it means to be heroic?

9. What does this story tell you about the power of love? About the power of mercy and sacrifice?

10. Of all her many losses, what do you consider Jocelyn's greatest loss in this story?

Enjoy this excerpt from international bestselling author Mario Escobar's novel of escape, sacrifice, and hope amid the perils of the Second World War.

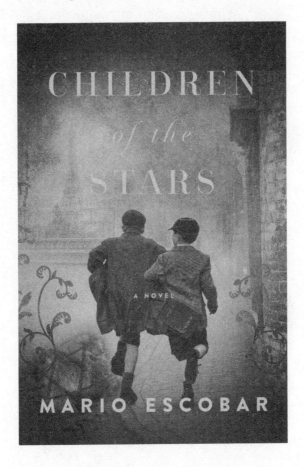

Available in print, e-book, and audio

Prologue

Paris
May 23, 1941

"Every generation nurses the hope that the world will begin anew." Those were the last words his father had said in the train station. The man had crouched down on his haunches in his ironed gray suit to be on Moses's level. The child looked out with his big black eyes and sighed, not understanding what his father meant. The station filled with strangely sugary-smelling white smoke. His mother watched with tear-swollen eyes, and her cheeks were so red she looked as if she had just scaled a mountain. Moses could still remember her delicate white gloves, the damp, cold feel of that spring, and the sensation that his little world was ripping apart. His father attempted a smile beneath his thin brown mustache, but it ended up a tortured grimace. Moses clung to his mother's legs. Jana smoothed the boy's blond hair and bent down. She took her son's chubby, rosy cheeks in her hands and kissed him with her dark lips, her tears mixing with the child's.

Jacob pulled at his brother. A light steam emanated from the engine's wheels, and the train gave a final whistle as if the huge frame of metal and wood were sighing in grief over the souls it had to separate. Aunt Judith hugged Jacob's chest, both protective and worried. All around, German soldiers moved like moths attracted by the light. They had neglected to pin the yellow stars to their chest that morning. Judith feared the Nazis could detect them with a single stony blue glance.

Eleazar and Jana turned away. Their coats swirled among the crowd of people with hands waving goodbye to other loved ones. In the midst of that boundless ocean of raised arms, Jacob and Moses saw their parents melt away until they disappeared completely. Moses clung to his aunt's hand with a ferocity intent on keeping her beside him. Judith turned her head and looked at her nephew's short bowl cut, the blond hair gleaming in the sun that filtered through the station's skylights. Then she looked at the other child, Jacob, with his dark brown curly hair. His big black eyes were set in a serious, angry expression, nearly rageful. The night before he had begged their parents to take them away from Paris, vowing that they would be good and behave, but Eleazar and Jana could not bring the children with them until they had a safe place to hide. Nothing bad would happen to the children in Paris, and Aunt Judith was too old to flee. She had taken them in six years before when the family could no longer endure the pressure in Berlin. Aunt Judith was more French than German; nobody would bother her.

They left the station as the sky began to turn leaden blue and the first cold drops spilled over the stone pavement. Judith opened her green umbrella and the three huddled together silently in the futile effort to avoid the downpour. They arrived soaked at Judith's tiny apartment on the other side of Paris, just where the city's beauty faded into a scabby, gray scene that made the glamour of cafés and fine restaurants seem like a distant mirage. They had taken the metro and then the noisy, rusty tram. The two boys had sat in the wooden seat at the front while their aunt sat just behind and allowed her eyes to relax their efforts against tears.

Moses studied his brother, whose brow was still furrowed. Jacob's freckles blurred together with raindrops and his frowning red lips were tensed to bursting. Moses did not understand the world. Jacob always called him "clueless," but the younger boy did understand that whatever had happened was bad enough to make their parents leave them. They had never been alone before. Moses still believed his mother was an extension of himself. At night, despite his father's grumbling, he slept pressed up against her, as the mere proximity of her skin calmed him. Her smell was the only perfume Moses could stand, and he knew he would always be safe as long as her lovely green eyes watched him.

As the boy had looked out through the dirty windows of the tram, the ghostly figures of the pedestrians jumbled together with the delivery trucks and old wagons that left the streets littered and rank with the droppings of their workhorses. This was his world. He had been born in Germany, but he recalled nothing of his home country. His mother still spoke to him in their native tongue, though he always answered in French, thus somehow making a statement against the place they had been forced to flee. Where would they go now? He felt like the world was closing at his feet, like when schoolmates avoided him at recess, apparently struck with fear or nausea at the sight of the yellow star on his chest. "Children of the yellow star" is what people called them. To Moses, stars were the lights God had created so that night would not swallow everything up. Yet the world now seemed orphaned of stars, dark and cold like the wardrobe where he would hide to trick his parents and from which he always jumped out as soon as possible so the immense blackness did not devour him completely.

1

Paris
July 16, 1942

Jacob helped his brother get ready. He had been doing it for so long he went through the motions mechanically. They hardly talked as Jacob pulled off Moses's pajamas and helped him into his pants, shirt, and shoes. Moses was quiet with a lost, indifferent expression that sometimes broke Jacob's heart. Jacob knew Moses was old enough to get dressed on his own, but this was one way he could show his younger brother he was not alone, that they would stay together until the end and would be back with their parents as soon as possible.

Spring had gone by quickly enough, but the hot summer promised to drag on. Today was the first day of summer vacation. Aunt Judith left very early in the morning for work, and they were to fix breakfast, straighten up the apartment, buy food at the market, and go to the synagogue for bar mitzvah preparation. Their aunt insisted on it since Jacob was almost old enough to assume the bar mitzvah responsibilities of Jewish laws. He, however, thought it was all nonsense. Their parents had never taken them to the synagogue, and Eleazar and Jana themselves had known practically nothing about Judaism until they got to Paris. But Aunt Judith had always been devout and became even more so after her husband died in the Great War.

Jacob got his brother dressed and helped him wash his face. Then they both went to the kitchen, whose blue tiles were now dull from decades of scrubbing. The table, painted sky blue, had seen better days, but it held a basket with a few slices of black bread and cheese. Jacob poured some milk, heated it over the sputtering gas stove, and served it in two steaming bowls.

Moses ate as if safeguarding his breakfast from bread robbers all around. At eight years old, hardly a moment went by when he did not feel rapaciously hungry. Jacob was just as capable of eating everything in sight, which forced Judith to keep the pantry locked. Each day she set out their humble rations for breakfast and lunch and at night prepared a frugal supper of soup light on noodles or vegetables in a cream sauce. It was scant fare for two boys in their prime growing years, but the German occupation was exhausting the country's reserves.

In the summer of 1940, the French, especially Parisians, had fled en masse to the southern parts of the country, but most had returned home months later as they saw that the German occupation was not as barbaric as they had imagined. Jacob's family had not left the city then, despite being German exiles, but his father had taken the precaution of seeking refuge in his sister's house, hoping they would not easily raise Nazi suspicion.

Jacob knew that his family was doubly cursed: his father had been active in the Socialist Party and had written satirical tracts against the Nazis for years, not to mention that both Eleazar and Jana were Jewish—a damnable race according to the National Socialists.

Paris was under the direct control of the Germans, represented by Field Marshal Wilhelm Keitel, and the Nazis had exploited and exhausted the populace. By the spring of 1942, it was nearly impossible to find coffee, sugar, soap, bread, oil, or butter. Fortunately, Aunt Judith worked for an aristocratic family that, compliments of the black market, was always well stocked and gave her some of the basic supplies that would have been impossible to acquire with her ration card.

After their meager breakfast, the brothers headed out. The previous night had been muggy, and the morning foretold an infernal heat. The boys ran down the stairs. The intense yellow of the Star of David shone brightly against their worn-out shirts, endlessly mended by their aunt.

The four sections of the apartment building, lined with windows, walled in the interior courtyard. From there they would pass through an archway and an outer gate leading to the street. Each side of the square building had its own staircase. As soon as Moses and Jacob stepped into the courtyard, they sensed something was wrong. They ran to the street. More than twenty dark buses with white roofs stood parked up and down the sidewalks. People swirled around as French police officers with white gloves and nightsticks herded them into the buses.

A chill ran all the way up Jacob's spine, and he grabbed hold of Moses's hand so tightly the younger child made a noise and tried to pull away.

"Don't let go of my hand!" Jacob growled, yanking his brother back toward the building. He knit his eyebrows together.

They were reentering the building when the doorwoman, leaning on her broom, sneered down at them and hollered to the gendarmes, "Aren't you going to take these Jewish rats?"

The boys looked at each other and took off running toward their stairway. Three of the policemen heard the doorwoman's raucous calling and saw the boys dashing toward the other side of the courtyard. The corporal gestured with his hand, and the other two ran after the boys, blowing their whistles and waving their nightsticks all the while.

The boys raced along the unvarnished wooden floor and the worn-down steps with broken boards, unable to keep their feet from pounding with terrible volume. The police looked up when they got to the stairwell. The corporal took the elevator and the other two agents started up the stairs.

Jacob and Moses panted as they approached the apartment door. Moses reached for the doorknob, but Jacob pulled him, and they ran toward the roof. They had spent countless hours there among the clotheslines, hiding among the hanging sheets, shooting doves with their slingshot, and staring at the city on the other side of the Seine.

When they reached the wooden door that led to the roof, they paused past the threshold, hands on their knees as they gasped for air. Then Jacob led them to the edge of the building. The roofs stretched out in an interminable succession of flat black spaces, terra-cotta tiles, and spacious terraces some Parisians utilized for growing vegetables. The brothers climbed up a rusted ladder attached to an adjacent wall and walked tentatively among the roof tiles of a neighboring building.

The police watched them from the roof of Judith's apartment building. The corporal, winded despite having taken the elevator, blew his whistle again.

Jacob turned for a moment to judge the distance between the men dressed in black and themselves—instinctively, like a deer wondering how close the hounds are.

The younger two gendarmes awkwardly climbed up the ladder and resumed the chase, breaking half a dozen roof tiles as they closed the gap second by second.

Jacob stepped between two tiles and felt something crack. His leg fell through a hole, and searing pain shot up his shin. When he managed to pull his leg out, blood poured down into his dingy white socks. Moses helped him get to his feet again, and they kept running to the last building on the block. A chasm of more than seven feet separated the last rooftop from the next building.

Moses glanced at their pursuers and then at the abyss shining with the intense light of summer. Despite the light of day, a cavernous darkness below seemed eager to swallow anything that dared fall into it. Moses turned his bewildered look to Jacob, at a loss for what to do.

His brother reacted quickly. Just below them there was a small terrace. From there, a ledge circled the building toward the main road. Perhaps they could reach a house, then the street, then try to get lost in the crowd. Without a second thought, Joseph jumped and turned to help Moses, arms outstretched. Just as the younger child began to leap, a pair of hands grabbed his legs. He twisted and hit the rooftop hard.

"Jacob!" Moses screamed, trapped.

For a moment, Jacob did not know what to do. He could not abandon his brother, but if he went back up on the rooftop, they would both fall into the police's hands. He did not understand why, but his parents had warned him about the Nazis sending Jews to concentration camps in Germany and Poland.

The corporal leaned out over the rooftop and saw Moses from the ledge.

"Stop it, you brat!" he bellowed as he grabbed the younger boy from the other policeman, held him by an ankle, and dangled him over the roof.

"No!" Jacob yelled.

His brother's face was purple with terror, and he flailed like a fish yanked out of water.

"Come back up here. You don't want your brother to fall, do you?" the corporal called with mocking as he held Moses a little farther over the edge.

Jacob's heart beat harder and faster than ever in his life. He could feel it in his temples and in the tips of his fingers through his clenched fists. His breath abandoned him. He raised his hands and tried to scream, but nothing came out.

"Get up here now! You and your people have wasted enough of our time today!"

In the sunken eyes of the corporal the boy could see a hatred he could not understand, but he had seen it often over the past few months. He climbed back up the wall toward the roof and stood before the corporal.

The corporal was a tall, heavy-set man whose stomach threatened to burst from his uniform jacket with every breath. His hat sagged to the side, and the knot of his tie was half undone. In his red face, his brown mustache quivered as his lips frowned and spat out words.

Once Jacob came up from the terrace, the corporal let Moses fall with a thud onto the rooftop. The other two gendarmes grabbed both boys by the arms and carried them between them back to the first building. They descended in the elevator and returned to the courtyard.

The doorwoman smiled as they passed, as if the capture of the two brothers had brightened her day. The old woman spat at them and shrieked, "Foreign communist scum! I won't have another Jew in my building!"

Jacob gave her a hard, defiant stare. He knew her well. She was a lying busybody. A few months prior, Aunt Judith had helped the doorwoman acquire ration cards. The woman could neither read nor write and had a disabled son who rarely left their apartment. Occasionally on a nice afternoon, she would labor to get him out to the courtyard and sit him down while the boy, crippled and blind, shook all the while.

Moses had not yet recovered from the terror of dangling over the roof, and he turned his eyes toward the woman. Though she always yelled at them when they ran in and out of the building or bothered the neighbors with their shouts or the noise of pounding up and down the stairs, they had never done anything to her.

The street still teemed with people, and the buses were already half full. The gendarmes shoved the women, hit the children, and brusquely hurried the older people along. There were very few young men. Most had been in hiding for months. The helpless throng, compelled by fear and uncertainty, moved like a flock of silent sheep about to be sacrificed, unable to imagine that the police of the freest country on earth were sending them off to the slaughterhouse before the impassive gaze of friends and neighbors.

The buses roared to life as Moses stared mesmerized out the window. He felt the odd sensation of going on a field trip. Beside him, Jacob studied the terrified faces of the other passengers, all of whom avoided one another's eyes, as if they felt invisible under the scorn of a world to which they no longer belonged.

About the Author

Photo by Elisabeth Monje

Mario Escobar has a master's degree in modern history and has written numerous books and articles that delve into the depths of church history, the struggle of sectarian groups, and the discovery and colonization of the Americas. Escobar, who makes his home in Madrid, Spain, is passionate about history and its mysteries.

———— •◆• ————

Find him online at marioescobar.es
Instagram: @escobar7788
Facebook: @MarioEscobarGolderos
Twitter: @EscobarGolderos

About the Translator

Photo by Sally Chambers

Gretchen Abernathy worked full-time in the Spanish Christian publishing world for several years until her oldest son was born. Since then, she has worked as a freelance editor and translator. Her main focus includes translating/editing for the *Journal of Latin American Theology* and supporting the production of Bible products with the Nueva Versión Internacional. Chilean ecological poetry, the occasional thriller novel, and audio proofs spice up her work routines. She and her husband make their home in Nashville, Tennessee, with their two sons.